Readers are obsessed with the DI Eve Hunter series

*****

'One of the best books I've ever read!'

'I loved DI Eve Hunter and her team'

'Without a doubt the best police procedural
I have read in a long time'

'I cannot wait to see what else is to come in
the DI Eve Hunter series'

'You won't want to stop reading this addictive
crime novel'

'Fantastic characters that you'll fall in love with –
I really couldn't put this book down!'

'Can't wait for the next one . . . and the next one . . .
and the next one!'

*****

www.penguin.co.uk

Deborah Masson was born and bred in Aberdeen, Scotland. Always restless and fighting against being a responsible adult, she worked in several jobs, including secretarial, marketing, reporting for the city's freebie newspaper and a stint as a postie – to name but a few.

Through it all, she always read crime fiction and, when motherhood finally settled her into being an adult (maybe even a responsible one), she turned her hand to writing what she loved. Deborah started with short stories and flash fiction whilst her daughter napped and, when she later welcomed her son into the world, she decided to challenge her writing further through online courses with the Professional Writing Academy and the Faber Academy. Her debut novel, *Hold Your Tongue*, was the result of those courses. *Out for Blood* is her second novel.

out
for
blood

DEBORAH MASSON

CORGI BOOKS

TRANSWORLD PUBLISHERS
Penguin Random House, One Embassy Gardens,
8 Viaduct Gardens, London SW11 7BW
www.penguin.co.uk

Transworld is part of the Penguin Random House group of companies
whose addresses can be found at global.penguinrandomhouse.com

Penguin
Random House
UK

First published in Great Britain in 2020 by Corgi Books
an imprint of Transworld Publishers

A CIP catalogue record for this book is available from the British Library.

ISBN
9780552176514

Typeset in 11/14pt ITC Giovanni
by Integra Software Services Pvt. Ltd, Pondicherry

Printed and bound in Great Britain by Clays Ltd, Elcograf S.p.A.

Penguin Random House is committed to a sustainable
future for our business, our readers and our planet. This book is made
from Forest Stewardship Council® certified paper.

MIX
Paper from
responsible sources
FSC® C018179

For my mini monsters, Holly and Ellis.
I love you.

Chapter 1

Monday

GEORGE CHRISTIE STEERED, TURNING the tractor around. His gloved hands gripped at the vibrating wheel, backside bouncing as the tractor made its way along the fairway. He surveyed the multi-coloured foliage either side of him, clouds of breath being pulled away by the strong breeze, low sunrise spreading across the course. He sighed with contentment. This was why he loved the job. Practically his own boss and, at times like these, he was the only person in the world, in a part of the world that he'd happily live and die on. Hazlehead Golf Club's MacKenzie Championship Course.

Mid-October was a time he especially loved. Late in the golf season, the greens only needed mowing once or twice a week, so his priorities were the maintenance work and repairs to prepare for winter. The course was quieter, later sunrise meaning delayed tee-off times. His job this morning: raking the bunkers.

George looked ahead, saw a spattering of beer cans lying on the green, right in the direction he was going.

He tutted, stopped the tractor and jumped down. He walked towards the cans, shaking his head and muttering under his breath. Sometimes he despaired of the local kids. Surely there were better places to be hanging around after dark, but, judging by the litter and incidents of vandalism or pure thoughtlessness he often found on the course in the early mornings, it seemed they didn't think so.

He carried the cans back to the tractor and put them behind his seat. As he pulled himself up into the cabin and sat, he spotted Tom Bradshaw ahead, teeing up on the fifth. He chuckled to himself. No disputing the old guy's dedication to the game.

Tom was a Yorkshireman who'd moved to Aberdeen twenty years ago as part of his retirement plans. George had seen him nearly every day for the last two decades. In his eighties and a likeable guy, Tom was always the first golfer on the course, no matter the weather.

George sat with the tractor idling; he watched Tom tee off before he got moving again. He followed the gentle downhill dogleg to the left, stopped the vehicle, jumped down and grabbed his rake. Once happy with the state of the bunker, he climbed back on to the tractor, whistling low as he went.

When he arrived in front of the fifth tee, he could see Tom's trolley and clubs over the brow of the fairway. No sign of Tom. George checked again before deciding to wait in his tractor for Tom to return, taking the opportunity to take his mobile phone out of his pocket to try for the umpteenth time to crack the Candy Crush level he was stuck on. After a few minutes of getting nowhere with the game, and with still no sign of Tom, George got down from the tractor and walked the fairway to the trolley, his eyes scanning the grass's condition, his mind on the two Scotch pies he'd packed for lunch, hungry already.

He raised his head as he neared the trolley, doing a double take before gasping, all thoughts of lunch gone. Tom was lying on his side on the ground by the clubs. 'What the . . .' George broke into a run. Had the old guy suffered a heart attack?

He reached Tom in seconds and crouched, bending his head towards the man's chalk-white face to check if he was breathing. Tom mumbled and lifted his hand inches off the ground, trying to point with a quivering finger inside a white and black golf glove. George bent closer, trying to make out what he was saying, hearing nothing but a jumble of nonsense. Instead, he followed the direction of Tom's pointed finger, looking across to his left, eyes widening.

'Jesus . . . Jesus Christ.' George fell back on to the grass from his crouch, his mind struggling to process what he was seeing. Not taking his eyes from the scene, he pulled himself into a seated position, legs out-stretched, the morning dew seeping quickly through his work trousers. There, in the trees by the fairway, a woman stared out at them. Long, lank dark hair fram-ing her pale face. George knew the scrawny, dirt-covered woman couldn't see them looking back at her. Knew she couldn't see a thing. Not as she swung by her neck on the end of a rope that hung from the tree.

Chapter 2

DI Eve Hunter saw the feet first. Beige, grubby-socked soles sticking out from brown chinos that covered splayed legs. A creased sky-blue shirt, the blood at its collar looking like lipstick until you saw it spread all the way down the upper back.

She stood in the white gloss kitchen of the open-plan executive apartment, DS Mark Cooper by her side, and rocked on her paper-covered shoes. As she moved, she was aware, not for the first time, how far her injured leg had come. The limp she'd had was all but gone, thanks to gruelling daily exercises and sheer bloody-mindedness. The only time it caused her any grief now was if she let herself get too tired or tried anything excessively physical. She looked over to the forensics team, keen to distract herself from further thoughts about her leg and where those thoughts might lead her back to.

She was irritable, wanting to get started, the team's main focus – the victim strewn on the floor – briefly visible to her amongst them as they moved about the space methodically.

'Bloody place is stifling.' Eve spoke to herself more than anyone else, but Cooper mumbled in agreement.

Eve was willing to bet underfloor heating was partly to blame. No expense spared in this place. Beige wall tiles and marbled worktops surrounded her, a stainless-steel cooker hood dominating the space. The breakfast bar matched the units; a square glass dining table stood in front of it. Room for four diners on the plush white leather chairs around it. Then there was the lounge area.

A harsh contrast to the recent case they'd been working: Laura Robertson and her two young children, residing in a council flat in Torry, her husband the reason for the domestic abuse case they'd been building; finally getting Laura and the kids to safety as they awaited the trial, only to watch it all fall apart when she decided not to testify and to drop all charges. Charges that were dropped on Friday, a mere three days ago, but, after a weekend full of frustration that she hadn't been able to do more, and mild regret that she hadn't handled the news better, Eve felt a week had passed. She closed her eyes. Laura was probably being beaten around the house already.

She opened her eyes, back in the obscenely expensive kitchen where they were standing. 'You reckon anyone ever cooked in here?'

Cooper turned to the stove. 'If they did, they had an isolated case of OCD, because it didn't extend to the rest of the place.'

Real oak floors ran throughout the two areas. Everything expensive, but far from immaculate. The apartment was probably once more a showroom than a home – although it seemed if there'd been a cleaner they'd handed in their notice. But it wasn't a trail of dust on top of the dining table with the rolled note lying haphazardly beside it.

Eve and Cooper moved further into the apartment. The body lay sprawled on its front in the centre of a cream rectangular rug that took up all of the floor space between two black leather sofas. One upturned hand of the victim visible on the bloodstained rug.

A south-facing window covered the entire wall, three additional windows running up the right-hand side and into the kitchen. No one had made a move to open any of the heavy-lined grey satin curtains, leaving everything as it was while they processed the scene. On the left-hand wall hung a large canvas, beige and brown intertwining circles reminding Eve of the nondescript art to be found on most hotel room walls.

Eve spotted a rectangular piece of plastic lying face down on the breakfast bar. She stretched over, lifted and turned it, coming face to face with a picture of the man she assumed was their victim. She passed it to Cooper. 'A work pass. Dean Johnstone. IT Consultant. Company called In-Serv.' Eve, tight with impatience, not one for hanging around, wanted to be doing something, anything.

Cooper laid the pass back down for it to be bagged and tagged. Eve sought out the victim again. The pathologist, Brian MacLean, sat closer to the body than Eve would ever want to be, obscuring their view. Cooper stood on his tiptoes by her side, leather shoes creaking. He craned his neck, trying to see more, but the victim's face wasn't visible. The head was turned away, towards one of the sofas. The brown hair at the back of his head was matted with what appeared to be a wound at the crown. Something lay on the floor by the sofa, brown-coloured, metallic, with crusted matter on it. Blood, most likely.

Cooper confirmed Eve's thoughts. 'Looks like a blow to the head with some kind of poncey brass ornament.'

The 'poncey' was probably for her benefit, Cooper aware she had a unique taste in ornaments and furniture. Upcycling was her hobby; not much room for expensive ornaments there.

'Poor bugger.'

Poor. The last thing this guy had been, Eve thought to herself. The rent alone for this place would be over a thousand a month. The block was a twenty-minute walk from Aberdeen's city centre, a walk that would take you past a string of luxury hotels and restaurants on the way there.

MacLean and one of the suits gently turned the body. Eve now had a clear view, the victim's face visible, matching the image on the work pass. After what seemed like for ever, MacLean stood and made his way over to them.

Eve stopped the rocking she'd resumed, ready to pounce. 'What you got for us?'

MacLean sighed. 'Expecting miracles again, I see. Initial examination shows blunt-force trauma to the back of the head. The blood-spattered solid bronze statue found by the sofa supports that, for sure.'

'Killed with a single, or multiple blows?' Eve wanted answers; miracles would be better.

MacLean's bag banged off his leg as he stood clear of two of the suits. 'I don't think it was the blow to the head that killed him.'

'Another wound?' Eve looked over to the body again.

'Not exactly,' MacLean answered.

Eve, confused as well as impatient, waited for MacLean to spit out what he was trying to say.

'I'll need to confirm this back at the lab, but from what I can see the head wound wasn't fatal. Maybe a little concussion, the need for a few stitches. It would have rendered him unconscious, I've no doubt about that, but he would've come around without too much damage. If someone hadn't suffocated him before he got the chance.'

Chapter 3

Eve sat ramrod straight next to Cooper on the sofa, where they'd been offered a seat, neither of them wanting to make a dent in the perfectly fluffed cushions. The place could've been lifted straight out of an interior design catalogue. Even the tropical fish in the tank that had been set into the wall appeared to have been selected to colour-match the room's furnishings.

'I can't believe he's dead.'

The cushion's owner, the fish-colour expert, a Miss Lisa Taylor, stood across the room from them in navy satin pyjamas, the wrap-over top plunging dangerously low.

Eve was unsure how bothered the woman was at her neighbour's death. There'd been no emotion when she'd answered the door and they'd broken the news. Maybe she was relieved the music had stopped.

Cooper went to lay his notebook on the arm of the sofa but seemed to think better of it, and clasped it in his hand instead. Wouldn't do to ruffle the suede. 'It must be a shock.'

Lisa stood there, giving no confirmation or denial to Cooper's statement. 'Are you sure you don't want a cup of tea or coffee? Glass of iced water?'

Eve took in the woman's blonde hair, pulled into a chignon at the base of her neck, not a strand out of place above the smooth collar of her pyjamas. Eve didn't *ever* look that groomed, let alone at 7 a.m. Perfume hung in the air, classy not cloying. She was glad it was Cooper with her. DC Scott Ferguson, with his perfectly quiffed hair and bulging biceps, would've been reduced to a fawning teenager in this woman's company. Who knew, someone like Lisa might've been impressed by an arrogant poser. Truth be known, Ferguson had grown on Eve of late, the two of them having found a mutual respect. Most of the time.

Eve refused the offer of a drink. Their host wouldn't be offering builders' tea. It would be ginseng with a twist of unpronounceable, or something equally fancy. 'Honestly, we're fine.'

Lisa lowered herself on to the minimalist designer slate-grey suede sofa opposite, steam rising from the espresso she'd drained from the coffee machine.

'Well, I need my morning pick-me-up.' Lisa seemed put out, perhaps because she wasn't getting to play hostess or able to roll out the china.

Eve watched her hold the cup mid-air, too hot for her lap and definitely too hot to put on the sofa or cushions. 'You phoned in about the loud music?'

Lisa nodded. 'Nothing new. Used to be on weekends, which I didn't mind much, but lately it's been creeping into weeknights too. All hours. Last night it never stopped.' She paused, perhaps realizing it sounded a little insensitive. 'I have an important client meeting today.'

Eve was more inclined to think she was relieved Dean Johnstone wouldn't be around to interrupt her beauty sleep. 'What is it you do, Miss Taylor?'

The woman looked around the apartment as if it were obvious. 'I run an interior design business. Not long broken out on my own.'

It figured. 'Congratulations. Did you know Mr Johnstone well?'

Lisa curled her lip, as if something sour-tasting had landed there. 'To say hello in passing. I found him a bit . . . over familiar.'

'Over familiar?'

'Yeah, you know, touch of the elbow as he spoke, standing too close if we happened to be in the lift together. A twinkle in his eye.'

'You think he fancied you?'

Lisa exhaled sharply through her nose as she smirked. 'I think Dean fancied himself.'

Eve thought of the photo she'd seen on his work pass. He'd been an attractive young man. 'Did you hear anything else last night, apart from the music? Did it sound like he had company?'

'Dean always had company.' Her tone spoke volumes.

'Friends? Girlfriend?'

Lisa burrowed into the corner of the sofa, curled her legs under her, the swish of satin audible. Cooper shifted next to Eve. Even he was affected by her presence. She was assured. Confident. Stunning.

'As I said, I usually saw him in passing, but I heard a hell of a lot more from him than I needed to.'

Cooper placed the notebook on his lap. 'Yeah. The music.'

'If only. Sometimes I questioned whether it was a good idea to complain about it. Perhaps better listening to that than the alternative.'

Eve was getting the picture. 'Did you ever speak to him about the music or the other stuff you heard?'

'I tried to hint at it once, but he seemed to enjoy that I could hear him fucking. I sometimes wondered if it got him off knowing I could.'

She was to the point, Eve had to give her that. She understood why Lisa described him as over familiar, if she was telling the truth. 'Did you ever meet his partner?'

'I don't expect he was a one-woman kind of guy.'

Eve waited.

'Not that I ever saw the women, but I definitely heard them. Put it this way, they either liked a bit of role play and to pretend they were someone else, or it was different women.'

Cooper cleared his throat. 'Many different women? Often?'

Lisa faced Cooper, blue eyes flashing. Eve imagined she was enjoying making Cooper uncomfortable as much as she'd lamented Dean having done so to her. 'If it was one woman, they had buckets of stamina and drive. The music was on when I got home last night. Blaring. I assumed he was alone.'

'Did you hear any doors? Shouting? Banging?'

The smirk on Lisa's face made Eve wish she'd used another word.

'Nothing. Impossible over the music. The wall pulsed with it. My fish might as well have been in a bloody Jacuzzi. I've no idea how long it had been going on. I was away on business from Friday morning, didn't get back until last night. Someone had to have been there. Unless you're telling me he killed himself?'

Eve said nothing.

Lisa straightened. 'Do you think it could've been one of the women?'

'We can't rule anything out. Did he ever have family round? Friends?'

Lisa took a sip of coffee. 'Hard to tell. I guess things would've been a lot quieter if they were. I never heard him, other than the music and the shagging.'

'Didn't other neighbours complain?'

'Not that I know of. I saw Dean because he tended to come and go the same kind of hours as me. Saying that, I haven't seen him for a while. '

All three of them turned at the knock on the door. Lisa seemed surprised, before seeing one of the police team who had been working next door.

Eve stepped out into the corridor and pulled the door almost closed behind her. 'Yeah?'

'Sorry to interrupt. The body's being moved. Forensics are still working on the room. They've seized the laptop and other personals. Interesting pastimes, I'd say, judging by the bedroom.'

After what Lisa had divulged, Eve didn't need any clarification. The company name on the work pass in the kitchen was the only real lead they had to go on. 'OK. Thanks for letting me know.' She turned and went back into the flat.

'Right, Lisa. We better let you get ready for work. Thanks for taking the time to talk to us.' Eve fumbled inside her jacket pocket and passed her card to the woman. 'If there's anything else you can remember, or you hear of anything, please don't hesitate to call.'

'Thanks. I will do.' She went to show them to the door, stopped. 'There was one thing.'

Eve waited.

'You asked about friends and family.'

'Yes.'

'I'm not sure I should say. Out of respect?'

Not an ounce of doubt on Lisa's face. If anything, it appeared she might burst if she didn't part with whatever titbit she had. 'Anything you have that may help us, we'd be grateful.'

'There was a guy.'

'A guy?'

'Yeah, seemed to be here quite often.'

'You'd see him?' Eve's interest was piqued but it was short-lived as Lisa answered.

'No, I'd hear him.'

'I thought you said unless it was music or sex, you didn't—' Eve stopped herself, the penny dropping.

'Not always, but there were definitely two of them with a woman at times.'

Eve looked at Cooper. Interesting pastimes indeed.

Chapter 4

DEAN JOHNSTONE'S WORKPLACE, THE oil and gas company In-Serv, was a lot grander than Eve had been expecting. She stepped forward and knocked again on the locked revolving glass door. Eight-thirty on a Monday morning, and no sign of life. She dropped her hands to her side and stepped back, ready to try something else, when she saw movement from behind the dimly lit reception desk.

A stooped figure kitted out in uniform shuffled towards the glass, stifling a yawn and looking severely put out. He made a slow show of unlocking the doors.

'Office isn't open to general public until nine a.m.' His large nostrils flared in the early-morning chill.

Eve reached inside her pocket and showed her ID. The guard peered at her photo through the thick glasses he wore.

'I'm DI Eve Hunter and this is my colleague, DS Mark Cooper.'

The guard flattened his greasy salt-and-pepper hair into the side parting he wore, not moving from where he blocked the door. Enjoying the small show of power. A jobsworth. 'How can I help?'

'We were hoping to talk to someone who knows Dean Johnstone.'

The guard's eyebrows shot above the black rim of his glasses. 'Everyone here knows Mr Johnstone. He's the boss's son.'

Eve tried not to show her surprise. 'Do you know where we might reach his father? Or his mother?'

'Can I ask what it's in connection with?'

'I'm afraid not. We need to speak with his parents first.'

The guard paused before stepping to the side and ushering them in like some top-secret operation.

'Are you here on your own?'

'Skeleton staff overnight until nine a.m. When we open.'

Eve ignored the second mention of the official office hours. 'Mr Johnstone, does he have a first name?'

'Robert.' The guard checked his watch. 'He'll be on his way to the airport.'

Eve followed his wristwatch as he dropped his arm to his side. 'What time's his flight?'

'Nine twenty-five.'

'Do you have a mobile number for him? What about Dean's mother?'

The guard checked the main glass door as if someone would be watching what was going on. 'Can't help you with the mother. She died years ago in an accident. But I can try and get Mr Johnstone on the phone for you.'

Eve could think of better ways to announce the news to Dean's father than having his work security guard hanging over her shoulder and listening to every word. 'Thank you for the offer, but it would be preferable if we had the number to try and contact him on our way to the airport. Time is short.'

The guard hesitated, looking between Eve and Cooper as if he might ask for their ID again. He sighed. 'I guess.'

As he shuffled off behind the reception desk to fetch the number, Eve was already wondering how the news of his son's death would impact the widowed Mr Johnstone.

Eve and Cooper stood at the entrance to departures, letting the ground-handling agent locate Dean's father without causing a scene. They'd been unable to reach him on his mobile on the way out here, the line constantly engaged.

Eve craned her neck. 'Here he comes.'

Cooper stepped back. Robert Johnstone walked towards them, the agent by his side trying his best to keep up with the long, confident strides of the man whose expensive hand luggage he dragged behind him.

Mr Johnstone's face was flushed, his high-coloured cheeks and nose most likely a nod to good living. Quite the contrast to his obviously dyed black hair. A grey raincoat was draped over his arm; the tailored black suit, crisp white shirt and yellow patterned tie complemented his enviable posture and height. Mr Johnstone gave off the air of someone who had been inconvenienced but, as he came face to face with Eve, there was no mistaking the hint of worry in his eyes. She wondered whether he'd be wearing the same suit to his son's funeral.

'Mr Johnstone, I'm DI Eve Hunter.' She held out her hand. The man looked at it, paused for the briefest of moments as if he might refuse it, before he clasped it and shook briskly, the gold sovereign ring on his pinkie digging into her skin.

'What's this all about?' His glare darted from her to Cooper.

Eve wasn't sure what to make of him, surprised at the instant dislike she felt even though she knew what she had to tell him. 'Mr Johnstone, if you'd follow me and my colleague, please. We've arranged for a little privacy.'

Mr Johnstone didn't move. 'Privacy for what? I have a flight to catch.'

Eve hesitated. She didn't want to tell him here, not with other passengers milling around. 'I think it would be better to talk away from here.'

'But my flight . . . I have an important meeting to get to.'

'Mr Johnst—'

'Tell me.'

His voice was loud, abrupt. Passengers making their way through to departures were looking over, wondering what was going on. Eve was at a loss as to why he was being difficult, flight or not. Surely he knew this

19

had to be serious, being intercepted by detectives. He stood defiant, sighing impatiently. Her patience and sympathy with the man were dwindling.

Mr Johnstone's hand trembled as he placed his mobile phone on the table separating him from Eve and Cooper. Important meeting cancelled.

Apart from the telltale tremor, there wasn't a lot else to give away how he was coping with the news. Nothing when they'd finally got him to move away from departures. Not a word, nor the usual outpouring of grief she would've expected. Instead he'd walked, Eve taking it as a sign he wanted the privacy after all. But it seemed a little too late for that. Heads turned their way as whispers rippled throughout the crowd from those closest to them who would've heard.

'How did you know I'd be here at the airport?'

Eve studied him. 'We went to Dean's workplace. Your security guard told us.'

Mr Johnstone's eyes blazed. 'Sam? Jesus, everyone will know now. You might as well have taken out an ad in the *Aberdeen Enquirer*.'

'Dean's work pass was the only thing we had to go on. As it turned out, it led us to you and that's a good thing, right?'

Mr Johnstone shifted in his chair, said nothing.

Eve glanced at Cooper before speaking. 'Sam told us about your wife. I'm sorry. This must be difficult for you.'

Mr Johnstone said nothing.

'When did you last talk to Dean?'

20

They were sitting in an interview room of the police station at Viscount House, based in the airport itself. Not the ideal layout, more formal than Eve would've liked, but it was what had been made available to them. Air conditioning whirred above them, the musky scent of Mr Johnstone's aftershave overpowering in the room, catching the back of Eve's throat.

'Friday evening.'

It was his tone; how abrupt he was. That's what irked her. The arrogance Eve recognized in many people like Mr Johnstone. Those with money and the belief they were special, better than those around them or, rather, beneath them. The attitude still there regardless, and out of place with what he'd been told.

She pushed. 'How did he seem?'

'Fine.'

It was like pulling teeth. 'Did he mention any plans for the weekend? Who he might be meeting?'

'No.' Johnstone was clearly getting impatient.

'Do you know who might have visited him? His next-door neighbour said he often had guests round.'

'I don't know anything about that.'

Eve didn't try to keep the sigh from her voice. 'Mr Johnstone, you're not here under any suspicion.'

'I'm aware of that.'

'You seem a little obstructive in your answers. We're trying to get a better picture of your son's movements, in the hope it may help find the person responsible.'

He sat silent.

'Did Dean have a girlfriend?'

'No.'

21

'Definitely not? The neighbour made mention of women being at his flat regularly.'

'This neighbour appears to have too much time on her hands.' Mr Johnstone pulled at the cuffs of the shirt beneath his suit jacket.

'Perhaps, but it's all the insight we have.'

'Dean was single. I'm sure that doesn't equate to celibate.'

Eve shifted as the mobile in her pocket vibrated. She pulled it out. *DC Jo Mearns.*

'Excuse me a second. I need to take this.' She looked at Cooper as she rose from the table and made her way to the door. Both of them aware they were unlikely to be getting anything useful from Dean's father, interruption or not. She closed the door behind her as she stepped into the corridor.

'Hunter.'

'Hey, boss.' Eve still got caught off guard at Mearns's willingness to call her that. Their relationship was vastly different from when they'd first laid eyes on each other less than a year ago.

'What's up?'

'Suicide's been called in.'

'Where?'

'Hazlehead Golf Club. A hanging. Heard it over the radio. Ferguson and I are in the car, closest. First officer responded. Checking if you want us to head to it.'

'Sure. See if you can talk to whoever called it in. Check the details recorded by the first attending officer. Make sure everything's covered. We're finishing up here. Update me back at the station.'

Eve pocketed her phone and turned to the interview room where Dean's father sat behind the door. She sighed, under no illusion her colleagues probably had more chance of getting something out of the suicide victim than she and Cooper had of unearthing any information from Mr Johnstone.

Chapter 5

THE BEDROOM REEKED OF stale sweat. Andreea lay on her back amongst the twisted and crumpled sheets in the bottom bunk. She balled her fists and rubbed at her eyes, which stung from a sleepless night. Vague outlines of other beds, other bodies, seemingly piled high, were emerging in the grey hue of the early-morning light creeping in around the frayed edges of the blackout blind. Andreea knew she wasn't going to see the body she wanted to.

Elena.

There had been no squeak of bare feet on the narrow metal ladder rungs during the night as Elena climbed to the bunk above her. No groan of broken mattress springs as she lay down. No shared whispers between them trying to pretend this was normal. The interaction familiar. Comforting.

Not last night, because Elena hadn't come back.

Andreea's eye caught on the hairy giant house spider above her, scuttling between the warped wooden slats and the dirty mattress. Every so often it would stop, as if exhausted by its efforts, before resuming its journey – getting nowhere fast, regardless of its pace. She was repulsed by its dark body and grotesquely long legs, but no longer scared. In the year since she'd first spotted one in this room, she'd learned there were worse things to be afraid of.

Elena had told her all about the giant house spider, said it was common in the UK. Elena was clever like that. She knew things. She knew the male spiders left their webs every autumn in search of females. And when they found one, they would mate for several weeks before he'd eventually die, and the female wouldn't hesitate to eat him.

If only it were that simple.

Andreea squinted at the sleeping shadows surrounding her. Girls who were too tired to wash when they returned in the early hours, no longer caring whether the smell lingered on their skin or inside them. But none of them were Elena.

True, Elena knew things. But this time she'd known too much.

Andreea wiped a tear from her cheek, returned her gaze to the spider. It had stopped, nestled into the corner of the bunk's metal frame, perhaps listening for a potential mate. Hunting for its female. Always hunting.

It wasn't so different for the girls here. Except no hunting was necessary. These girls were brought to the men and, once they were, they didn't spend weeks together either. The short time it took the men was long enough.

If only they died too when they were done. Instead, it was the girls who felt they were dying, ebbing away a little more each time, slowly being devoured from the inside out, each and every male they encountered consuming who and what they'd once been.

Elena was different. She refused to be swallowed, promising Andreea again and again in their snatched night-time ramblings that they'd find a way out. And Andreea had believed her.

But as the girls returned one by one, her hope had turned to dread. Minutes ticked into hours and, with the break of dawn, and no sight or sound from Elena, pure terror had wrapped its icy grip around her. The grim realization her friend hadn't even made her way back here, let alone to who they once were. She was missing. And soon they'd find out.

Andreea clamped a hand over her mouth to silence her sobs, feeling the raised birthmark that spilled across her cheek.

Elena was right. It wasn't the men who mated with them they had to fear. Elena had *always* known; in the way she *knew* things. Like about the spider and its ways.

But she hadn't known Andreea's secret. Andreea placed a hand on the small round of her stomach, as if she might protect what was growing inside.

She'd planned to tell Elena once they were free, that more than two of them had escaped.

Andreea now worried what would become of them without Elena and her promises. Especially now she understood they were also caught in a web.

Except the venomous predator at the centre of her web didn't die and couldn't be eaten.

Chapter 6

DC JO MEARNS STOOD back from the bare branches of the tree where the woman swayed in the cool breeze. Sunlight glinted off her long, dark, matted hair, the beauty of nature looking out of place in a scene so ugly. The sheer material of the black Lycra tube dress clung to bare thighs caked in dirt. Thin arms hung by her sides, slender hands gently knocking against the tight length of material as she appeared to dance in the wind.

Mearns looked once at her face; she knew she wouldn't have to again to remember every detail. But she couldn't take her eyes off the woman's feet. They were tiny. Black dirt visible beneath her toenails in the open-toed strappy heels she wore, even from the distance at which Mearns stood. She wondered what the woman's last steps might have been, what might have led her to do this. A thought pricked at the back of her mind. Something off about the scene.

Mearns's mind whirred. Trying to figure out what was wrong, imagining what kind of life this woman had lived. Another one lost. That's how she viewed any woman's death since the case they'd worked a year ago. Six women brutally murdered, Mearns the planned seventh, which she would have been if her colleagues hadn't got to her in time. The aftermath had hit them all hard. Mearns had wanted, needed, to do something to help others. People for whom it wasn't too late. People who had managed to survive their own version of hell. She'd been helping out at a local women's shelter ever since. Granted, her long hours didn't allow much free time, but she did what she was able to, whether dropping off much-needed toiletries and supplies, or simply having a cup of tea and a chat with the women who wanted the distraction. Eve had accompanied her on occasion, Mearns never asking Eve's motivation, assuming it was the same as hers.

Mearns refocused as her colleague, DC Scott Ferguson, appeared by her side, unusually silent. The creak of rope against bark echoed around them as one of the team balanced a stepladder against the wide trunk, before edging upwards towards where the rope wrapped around the thick branch, to cut her down.

A stepladder they'd had to fetch and borrow from the golf club. Mearns studied the branches spaced out and upwards from the trunk. *That was it.*

Her thought was abandoned as a loud collective gasp escaped the mouths of the officers standing beneath the body as it came free of the rope, faster than they'd been expecting. Mearns lunged forward instinctively, catching the woman as she fell – a frozen cheek squashed against hers in a macabre hug.

'Shit.' Mearns's Boltonian accent was still strong, eighteen months after being transferred from down south. She stumbled back beneath the weight, wide-eyed, as officers crowded her, their arms stretched out, helping and guiding her towards the sheet on the ground that had been prepared for the body.

Mearns wiped herself down, seeing a young officer approach. The officer, relatively new to the job, had been first to respond to the call.

'I've tracked down the guy who found her.' He sounded nervous, perhaps needing confirmation he'd done all he should have, that he'd remembered procedure. 'I told him to stay put rather than have to see all this again – hope that's OK. You'll find him at the shed by the clubhouse.'

Mearns dipped her chin. 'Come on, Ferguson, let's go find out what this guy has to say.'

Mearns thought George Christie was probably in his early fifties but he might have aged a couple of years after what he'd been through this morning. He sat on a foldable canvas chair outside a large shed that appeared to double as tool storage and shelter for tea and lunch breaks. The shed was a stone's throw from the clubhouse and the car park. His hands were wrapped around a silver flask lid that served as a cup, thin wisps of steam rising into his stricken face as she approached with Ferguson.

'George Christie?'

He stood, putting his cup on the grass by the chair, before smoothing his trousers. He tensed as he stepped forward to greet them, his handshake firm, his face weather-beaten and kind. He smelled of oil, cut grass and coffee.

'Sorry to interrupt your break.' Mearns smiled politely.

'Not at all. It wasn't a break as such. To be honest, I haven't done anything since . . .'

'I'm sure. It must have been quite a shock. Are you happy for us to ask you a few questions here, or would you rather go somewhere else?'

'Here's fine for me but I have to apologize, I can't offer you both a seat.'

Mearns put him at ease. 'We spend enough time on our backsides as it is, don't worry. Please, don't let your drink go cold.'

George bent to pick up his cup but chose to stay standing instead of hogging the only seat.

'Did you find the woman?'

He swallowed a mouthful before pouring the dregs of his cup out on the grass. 'No. One of the regulars did. Tom Bradshaw.' His eyes were pained, watery. 'I've not long called the hospital. Looks like a heart attack.'

'I'm sorry to hear that.'

'They reckon he's going to be OK. Old guy's in his eighties but he's in good nick.'

'He must be if he's a regular here. Can I ask you to run us through what happened?'

'I was raking the bunkers, waiting for Tom to take his next shot. I couldn't see him, only his clubs, and, as I got closer, I realized he was on the ground. I ran over to him. He tried to tell me something, but I was unable to make it out. He managed to point and that's when I saw her.'

'Did you recognize the woman?'

George was tapping the empty cup against his thigh. 'No, and there's not a lot of folks I don't know around here, even the dog walkers.'

'Would you say it's a reasonably accessible part of the course?'

'Yeah, there's paths around the whole course regularly used by people walking, horse riding and so on. Where she was is a decent distance from the car park; it would've been a pitch-black walk. There's no lighting or anything along there.'

Mearns pictured the scene, what had been bothering her about it. 'Is there any chance someone might've seen her, you know, before she got herself up there?'

'There wouldn't have been anyone golfing after seven p.m. Too dark. But a lot of the local kids come to hang out here. The usual – underage drinking, away from the prying eyes of parents or the police.' He paused. 'Actually, I moved cans off the course this morning, so I assume some of them may have been mucking about last night.'

'Close to where the woman was found?'

'Not too far. I know she wasn't there when I finished last night because I worked that green.'

'What time did you finish?'

'About eight p.m. I would've been off the green by seven p.m.'

Mearns paused. 'Can I ask, did you see anything positioned against the tree? Move anything before officers arrived?'

George shook his head. 'I never touched a thing.'

Mearns nodded. 'OK, thanks. These kids you mentioned. Do you know them?'

'Not by name, but it tends to be the usual faces. They're here most nights. I could come and check if they're here again later if you wanted me to.'

'That would be helpful.' Mearns passed George a card. 'I appreciate you talking with us. If you remember anything else, or do manage to track down the kids, would you give me a call, please?'

'Sure.' George pocketed the card and shook the hand Mearns offered.

They walked away before Mearns turned to Ferguson. 'I guess it's time to get back to the station. Hunter will kill us if we're late for the morning briefing.'

Ferguson tutted. 'If that comment was supposed to make me quake in my boots, it failed. I'm well aware Eve would happily kill me for a lot less at times.'

Mearns didn't grace the comment with a reply, her mind busy.

Ferguson studied her. 'What?'

'We need to get MacLean up here.'

'Why?'

'That woman can't have got herself up that tree.'

Chapter 7

COOPER STOOD AT THE open door to Hastings's office, knowing why he'd been summoned without needing to be told.

Hastings sat at his desk. 'Take a seat.' His voice was gruff, pissed off already. 'I wanted a word in private. How long will she be?' Hastings leaned back, splayed fingers and thumbs touching to form a pyramid in front of his face.

'Not long, I dropped her at Costa across the road on the way back to the station. We're both needing the caffeine hit.'

'Has she said anything about what happened with Colin Robertson on Friday?'

Cooper shifted in the chair. 'She didn't need to. I was there when it happened and here when you pulled her into the office.'

'He threatened to press charges over the weekend.'

Cooper tutted, anger spreading in his chest. 'Are you kidding? The guy we know is guilty of battering his wife

34

black and blue is threatening to press charges for what amounted to a hard shove?'

Hastings frowned. 'So you're denying Hunter got in his face, cornered him, and shouted so aggressively that spittle flew all over his face?'

Cooper shifted in the seat. 'No, sir, but he goaded her.'

Hastings's face remained hard. 'You know as well as I do that, in this job, we're goaded every day. It's our responsibility to do the right thing. To follow procedure. But most of all to remain professional.'

'It was bad, sir. Mearns called to say Laura Robertson had left the shelter with the kids, no explanation. Colin was there by the time we got to their home. Smirking as Laura broke the news she was dropping all charges against him. It was obvious he'd threatened her. The kids were in the room next door, crying.'

Hastings ran his hand through what little hair he had left, white whiskers twitching at his top lip and chin. 'I'll be honest, I would have wanted to hit the bastard myself but—'

'She didn't *hit* him, sir, it was—'

'Yeah, you said. It's still an officer using physical force. And it's not the first time with Hunter. Far from it.'

'I'm sure she regrets her actions, sir. But you know how Eve gets about men mistreating women.'

Hastings didn't look convinced. 'The bottom line is she needs to keep a lid on that temper of hers.' His hands grasped the arms of his chair and he pulled himself straight. 'Do you think she's got too much workload?'

Cooper scratched at the fake leather on the thin arm of the chair. 'If anything, you're not giving her enough since . . .' There was no need to say it out loud.

Hastings looked over his shoulder as he heard a door opening down the hall, around the corner, the familiar sound of Eve's almost military footsteps echoing along.

Cooper stood, eager not to be caught coming out of Hastings's office.

'Keep an eye on her. If there's anything, anything at all, you let me know.' Hastings shuffled paper about his desk.

Cooper left the room, feeling like a traitor. Even though Hastings was supposed to be on the same side.

Eve stood at the front of the incident room, the white-board behind her already displaying a photograph of Dean Johnstone in life, alongside the images of him in death. They'd gleaned little about him, even after talking to his father. The photo from his security pass had been blown up to A4 size, the image grainy as a result, although clear enough for their purposes.

Eve's gaze lingered on Cooper, who'd been acting sheepish since she'd returned with the coffees. She'd chosen not to ask why he'd been in Hastings's office, pretended she hadn't clocked him darting out of it and across the hall to the incident room.

Eve banged on the desk in front of her, once, and turned to the whiteboard. 'Dean Johnstone. Twenty-five years old. Found at home early this morning. A neighbour called in a complaint of loud music and responding officers found him dead.'

Eve paused a second to let the information sink into those in front of her. 'Dean was found on the floor of his front room, a blow to the back of the head, the weapon still at the scene and with forensics now. However, according to MacLean, it appears Dean may have died as a result of being smothered.' Eve clocked the collective frowns around the room.

Ferguson spoke. 'Any idea when we'll have firm confirmation?'

Eve tucked her hair behind her ear. 'MacLean is looking at your golf course body first.'

One of the officers up the back coughed. 'Surely murder takes precedence over suicide?'

Eve hadn't shared the suspicions about the woman who had been found hanging but, deep down, she knew from the photos Mearns had captured on her phone that the DC's appraisal of the scene was accurate. No ladder or means of reaching the branch where the woman had been found – unless she'd possessed uncanny climbing skills – indicated this wasn't a straightforward suicide. In the meantime, Eve would keep those facts between herself, Cooper, Mearns and Ferguson, until they had confirmation of MacLean's findings.

'We all know how MacLean works. Every body belongs to someone and that someone deserves answers as much as the next person does. In this case, MacLean probably knows the hanging should be an easy autopsy and one he'd rather deal with before setting to work on Mr Johnstone.' Eve understood the logic, but it wasn't the truth.

'Anyway, back to Dean. He worked in IT up at In-Serv in Altens. His father, Robert Johnstone, owns the company. Cooper and I met him at the airport this morning. Something's not quite right there. Everyone reacts differently but his was definitely not the reaction you'd expect from a parent told their child is dead. If anything, he was cagey. When we requested a visit to his workplace to talk with colleagues, he resisted. We won't be leaving it at that.'

Eve came around the desk in front of the whiteboard and placed her backside against the edge, a hand propped either side of her. 'At present we have no idea who was in the flat with Dean when he was murdered. No CCTV within the property either.'

'What about the drugs?' Cooper steered the conversation where Eve was already going.

'Cocaine. That much we know. One rolled note at the scene but it's possible whoever was there with him was using too. Only enough in the flat for recreational use.'

Mearns interrupted. 'If he was a habitual user, that may be why Robert Johnstone doesn't want us sniffing around at work?'

Eve shifted her position against the desk. 'Could be. It's something we need to explore. We're awaiting word on whether we have any fibres or fingerprints on the note – ones that don't belong to Dean.

'We spoke to his next-door neighbour who made the noise complaint, Lisa Taylor. According to her, Dean fancied himself as quite the expert with women. Chances are he had a woman there with him last night.' Eve didn't say she thought the same could probably be said of Lisa with men. 'Plenty for us to be looking at. We have a laptop and other devices found in the property in our possession. But no mobile phone. Maybe his attacker took it. So now the digging starts.'

Her team straightened, ready for the task list ahead.

'Cooper and Ferguson, I want you to head up the door-to-door inquiries.' Eve didn't miss the groan under Ferguson's breath. 'Problem?' She glared at him. Their relationship had improved tenfold over recent months, but he still liked to push back at times, perhaps as much as she enjoyed keeping him in his place.

Ferguson shook his head, his face telling a different story.

Eve continued: 'The whole block and surrounding flats: find out everything and anything the residents know about Dean Johnstone. There's also a designated secure parking space underground. Forensics have the car, but I want you to scope out the car park, check which neighbours were parked closest, who may have seen him come and go day to day, apart from Lisa.

'Mearns, you start by going through his laptop, check if anything unusual flags. Diaries, emails, anything.'

Ferguson put his hand up.

'I'm not your teacher, Ferguson.'

Ferguson muttered, 'Act like it most of the time.'

Eve's eyes narrowed, her attention distracted by her mobile ringing. 'Wait a sec.'

She moved off to the small office in the corner of the room as she pulled her phone out of her inside pocket. *MacLean*. As she stepped into the glass office and nudged the door shut behind her, she prayed he'd been able to move on to Dean's autopsy.

Cooper yawned, watching as Eve closed the office door behind her, trying to gee himself up at the thought of working with Ferguson.

He was shattered. He'd tried to chat with his wife, Louise, when he got home last night, but, as she lay balanced on the edge of the sofa where their son Nathan had finally fallen asleep, she'd offered nothing but one-word answers. She'd thawed a little when he told her to get off to bed and he'd see to their son – lying when he said he wasn't tired. And then the early-morning call from Eve.

He stifled another yawn, rubbed at stinging eyes, and forced himself to look alert. The rest of the team were already moving about, getting organized. He stood to join Ferguson, and jumped as the office door opened. Eve walked out and towards Mearns.

'Mearns, you're with me.'

Mearns stood, and took her jacket from the back of the chair. 'Where we headed?'

'Downstairs.'

Cooper and Ferguson watched Mearns trying to match Eve's pace as she left the office. 'Downstairs?'

'To the morgue.'

Cooper stiffened, more awake; Ferguson looked as intrigued and confused as him. He heard Mearns shouting after Eve in the corridor.

'Has MacLean begun work on Dean already?'

Eve's voice drifted back. 'If only. Seems you were right about our Jane Doe.'

Chapter 8

THEY FOUND MACLEAN IN the position they were used to seeing him: standing hunched over a metal gurney, a dead body beneath a white sheet in front of him. Eve and Mearns stepped up to the other side of the trolley.

'Welcome.' MacLean said it as if they were arriving at his home. Which, with the hours he worked, the morgue almost was.

Only the woman's head was visible, the outline of her shrouded body painfully small. Dark, greasy hair scraped back from her face disappeared into a tangled mess beneath her shoulders.

MacLean must've noticed the look on Eve's face. 'You should've seen her before I cleaned her up.' He lifted the sheet at the woman's neck, pulled it back, taking his time, honouring the dignity of the woman even in death. 'Going by skeletal and dental development, I'd say she was around twenty-two to twenty-five years of age.'

Eve's breathing hitched as the painfully thin naked form was unveiled. She noted the absence of the

Y-shaped incision on the torso, something that usually accompanied any post-mortem they were involved in. The deep indentation in the skin around the neck was clear. Purple and red in colour, badly swollen either side. All the signs of a hanging. But what wasn't were the scabs covering her knees, and the raised lumps of old wounds, many silvery white, others an angry crimson, that appeared to run everywhere. 'What exactly are we looking at?'

'One thing's for sure, we're not looking at a woman who killed herself.' MacLean moved to the top of the table, in line with the woman's head. He bent over, pointed to the neck. 'This mark is typical of a hanging.' MacLean trailed his gloved finger along the indented line, running upwards at an angle, V-shaped on her skin. 'It's the other one that isn't.'

Eve hadn't noticed another mark. She moved closer as MacLean moved his hand.

'Here. Not nearly as visible as the first one but there, nevertheless. A straight-line bruise.'

Mearns brushed against Eve, trying to get closer. 'What does that mean?'

'Ligature strangulation. She was dead before the hanging.'

Eve heard Mearns's sharp intake of breath. The mark was clear, nowhere near as pronounced as the other, but definitely there. 'How can we be sure? Could it have been a botched first attempt at hanging herself?'

MacLean's finger ran the length of the wound again. 'No, the angle is all wrong. The straight mark was made by someone pulling on something from behind.'

Eve's mind played with what-ifs. 'An old wound? Or an injury that happened not long before the hanging that didn't kill her?'

'Absolutely not. And here's why.' MacLean moved, and gently lifted the woman's fingers. 'If there was any way she hanged herself, there would be fibres under her nails. There aren't. She never touched that rope. However, I did find a deep cut to the back of her head. A messy one that should've been stitched at the time. Looks recent although definitely not related to the cause of death. Cause of death was strangulation from the said force from behind.'

Eve's gaze locked on the woman's thin fingers and then a mark on her wrist as MacLean lifted her hand a little higher. 'Is that a tattoo?'

MacLean nodded. *'Mamica.* Not sure what that means. Maybe foreign.'

Eve made a mental note to look it up as MacLean moved up the table to the woman's head. Eve and Mearns silently mirrored his movements on the other side.

MacLean pointed to the woman's mouth. 'Hanging compresses the veins, but arterial blood flow continues, causing small bleeding sites on the lips, inside the mouth and on the eyelids.' MacLean's hands swept above the woman's face as he spoke. 'None of that is evident here. Which means no blood flow when this woman dropped from the tree.'

Eve studied the woman's congested face and neck, both dark red in colour. 'There's no doubt someone strangled her then attempted to make it look like a

44

suicide?' Everything MacLean had said made it clear. She was stating the obvious. But she wanted to hear it said out loud.

'Exactly.'

Mearns stepped back from the gurney. 'How the hell would they've managed to get her up there? Bit of a job to stage, isn't it?'

MacLean pulled at the wrist of one of the gloves he wore, latex snapping back against his skin. 'Yes and no. As you can see, this woman wouldn't have weighed much. It appears she'd had a tough time of it. She's got a fair amount of scarring.'

Eve forced herself to memorize the woman's knees, the scars that ran over the rest of her body.

MacLean stood back from the gurney in his turn. 'Not only there . . .'

Eve stiffened. 'Internal?'

'Yeah and pretty bad. Either into rough sex, unbelievably so, or forced.'

Eve turned to Mearns, who she noticed had shifted her gaze from the woman. When Eve spoke, it was gentle. 'Are the wounds recent, or old?'

'Both. Some recent, like the one on her head. But there's scarring that suggests the damage goes back years. The scabs you see on her knees are carpet burns. All the rest are cuts, evidence of being tied both by her wrists and ankles. You name it.'

Eve studied the woman's face, Mearns taking longer to do the same beside her. Beautiful. High cheekbones. The skin on her face smooth, both blemish- and wrinkle-free. The ugliness of what she'd been through hidden beneath the clothes she wore when she'd lived. *Inside* her, where only she'd known of the pain. The question was, who had inflicted that pain?

'Do you think this is the work of one person?' Even as she said it, she knew it wasn't a question MacLean could answer.

'If it is, it's one sick individual, but I found something else that makes me suspect not.'

Eve was surprised but hopeful as MacLean placed a hand either side of the woman's head, gently turning it to the side so the back was exposed.

Eve and Mearns stepped sideways, further up the gurney, as MacLean dragged his gloved fingers through the tangle of dark hair at the base of the woman's neck, holding back the thick clump to show her neck.

'Here.'

His finger pointed to a blurred black mark. Small, no more than a couple of centimetres wide, on the woman's neck. Right beneath the hairline.

'Another tattoo?' Eve leaned in, Mearns's shoulder brushing against hers, as they both craned their necks, peering closer. Vertical black lines, with numbers beneath.

'Jesus.' Eve straightened. 'Is that a barcode?'

MacLean let go of the hair, returned the woman's head to centre. 'Not an uncommon choice of tattoo amongst the youngsters these days, I know, but, given her injuries, and what appears to be the latest trend, I'm thinking there may be more to it.'

Human trafficking. Prostitution. It was no secret the people controlling these girls had recently been known

46

to brand them. Like cattle. Pieces of meat. Eve was aware it wasn't long ago that the trade in human trafficking had operated largely south of the Central Belt. But it had steadily been trickling up north. More officers on the force being assigned to deal with it every day.

'We could be looking at her pimp. Or a punter?'

'Maybe. All I can tell you is she didn't put that rope around her neck herself. Now I'm sure it wasn't a suicide, I'm going to have to open her up to find out more.'

Eve imagined the invasion to the tiny body the incision would cause. She looked at the unkempt dark hair, the skeletal body that seemed too small for the head, ribs jutting upwards, pelvic bone visible above legs that seemed as if they might snap. The procedure was inevitable, and it might give them something to work with. Eve fought the lump in her throat at the thought of what this woman had seen and felt in the run-up to her death. What had happened before she was hoisted by that noose.

Mearns inhaled beside her before she spoke. 'Let's say someone moved and lifted her into that tree, wouldn't it have been difficult to set the rope and get her up there?'

MacLean stared at the victim. Eve knew he saw her as a person, not his next job. It would be easy to slip into that mindset doing the job he did, day in, day out. Choosing to switch off to death and all the cruel and unexpected ways it came to people. But she also knew MacLean found solace in humour. Gallows humour. Like so many working in these jobs. A shield to protect themselves from death and all its evils working its way inside you, no way back once you let it in.

Eve cast her eyes over the small thin body once again, and all its scars marking the brutality of the woman's life, thinking of those evils in death; thinking, too, about Mearns's question. 'It wouldn't have been that difficult to get her up there. Especially if whoever did it had help.'

Mearns's mouth dropped open. 'You think there were two people involved?'

'I don't think it can be ruled out.'

And in that moment, Eve knew she wouldn't allow anything to be ruled out, especially whether she'd be taking this case alongside Dean Johnstone's. She reached out and clasped the cold, bony hand of the woman, not caring that Mearns and MacLean were standing silent, staring at her. She couldn't take her eyes off the wounds covering the young woman's body, evidence of the horrors she'd endured. She thought of her own mother. Dragged down a dark alley at knifepoint. Attacked. Used and abused by a total stranger. *Her father.*

No, nothing would be ruled out. Not with this woman. Not this time. And not until she'd caught the person responsible.

Chapter 9

EVE AND COOPER SAT in front of Hastings's desk. Eve felt like a wayward kid called to the headmaster's office. She hated they had to be in here at all; hard to believe it had only been three days since she'd last been dragged in.

'There's been a development, sir.' Eve shifted in her seat, getting ready to fight her corner, knowing Cooper would back her up. Always. It was the reason she'd pulled him in here with her.

'On the Johnstone case?'

'Not exactly. It's about the suicide. Or what we thought was a suicide.'

'Eh?' Hastings gripped the desk edge.

Cooper took the lead. 'MacLean's confirmed it. The girl was murdered before being strung up.'

Hastings lifted his hand, dragged his fingers over his eyes. 'Christ,' he sighed. 'OK, I'll assign it to—'

Eve jumped in. 'Ferguson and Mearns have already been to interview the greenkeeper who found the body.

Or rather, the second person to find the body. The old guy that saw her first is in hospital after suffering a heart attack with the shock. They were there before we knew it was a murder.'

Hastings tutted. 'The responding officers that dealt with it will have taken statements, Eve.'

'I know, I've spoken to them. But Ferguson and Mearns were close by when the call came in. I didn't see the harm in them checking things over. A good call now we know what we're dealing with.' She hardly stopped for breath, keen not to let him interrupt until she'd said her piece on this. 'Now it's a murder inquiry I want to double-check we have the go-ahead.'

'We?'

'The team.'

'Hunter, your team are already working on the Johnstone case.'

Eve tried not to let her irritation show. There was a time Hastings would have thought nothing of her working multiple cases at a time, never mind two, but these days, since what had happened last year, he treated her like a rookie. She would have to play the one card she had.

'Sir, you know how short-staffed we are. My team are more than capable. If you assign extra civilians for the office-based tasks, anything you can manage, we can take on both, no problems.' She'd seen the woman in the morgue, could still see her, and that made her Eve's responsibility, as much as Dean Johnstone.

Hastings didn't look convinced.

'Sir, give us a chance. Let us look into this one, at least, before taking things any further.'

She could tell Hastings was thinking about it, probably also imagining the headache in getting another team involved with the workload they already had across the force.

He leaned back, elbows on the armrests of his chair, fingertips pressing against one another in front of his face. His go-to stance and one Eve had been party to more times than she cared to remember. 'Do we have an ID on the hanging victim?'

'No, sir. Not as of yet. But we believe her to be Eastern European. She has a tattoo on her wrist saying "Mamica". It means mother in Romanian. We'll run her prints through the system but I'm about to re-delegate tasks to the team in light of the extra case. I thought I'd check in with you beforehand.'

Hastings tapped his fingers against each other. 'Looks as if you've already called the case as your own before you came in to give me this so-called update.'

Eve said nothing.

Hastings looked between them, his gaze resting on her colleague. She saw something pass between them, not sure what.

'What's happening with the Johnstone case?'

Cooper shot in, probably keen to stop Eve from losing the small advantage they appeared to have. 'Looking like a headache, to be honest. But we'll get on top of it.'

Hastings turned to Eve. 'I trust taking on the extra workload won't interfere with your appointment with Dr Shetty this Thursday?'

Eve bristled at the mention of the police psychiatrist in front of Cooper, even though he was aware of the appointments. She straightened, composing herself and managing to hold the deep sigh that wanted to escape.

She'd had to agree to psychiatric assessments when she returned to work after six months' enforced leave due to injury, after she ran a suspect off the road in a high-speed car crash. She and her then-partner, DS Nicola Sanders, had later been violently attacked by the suspect's father, leaving Eve with a limp and Sanders paralysed.

If only that had been the end of it. But Eve had returned to work straight into a high-profile case that saw a string of women murdered – Sanders being one of the victims. It was enough to break anyone.

And it had almost broken Eve. She hadn't planned on returning to the force after that. But Mearns and Cooper had not let that happen – even Ferguson had fought for her to come back. So had Hastings. Eve had been under the illusion her boss's desire to keep her on the team would give her clout when it came to the psychiatrist sessions. She'd bluntly asked if her return could be on the condition she stopped having to meet with Dr Shetty. No such luck, but at least they were now monthly visits instead of weekly. Although still the kid gloves from Hastings.

But she couldn't be angry with him. She understood his position; she owed her job to him. 'No, sir. It won't affect anything.'

Hastings went to speak, but stopped when his desk phone rang. He glanced at the display, frowned, and picked it up.

Saved by the bell.

Eve stood, almost dragging Cooper with her, keen to escape. Hastings didn't stop her as he barked into the receiver, which Eve took as an agreement. She rushed to the door before he changed his mind.

Early evening and Eve stood at the front of the incident room for the second time, wondering how it could possibly be the same day.

She gave a general update, everyone now aware they were going to be handling the two cases.

'OK. Let's start with Dean Johnstone.' She looked to her right. 'Ferguson, what have you got?'

Ferguson sat forward, happy to hog the limelight. 'We did a door-to-door of the block Dean lived in, all six floors. A lot of residents, mainly professionals, were out at work. Those we did manage to talk to didn't have anything of importance to share with us. Most interaction anyone had with Dean was a passing hello in the lift from the car park from time to time. None of them knew him more than that.'

Ferguson paused. 'We've posted incident cards through any unanswered doors. The flat to the left of Dean's is empty. Tenant hasn't moved in yet. You've already spoken to Lisa Taylor, his neighbour on the right-hand side.

'We also did a door-to-door of all the surrounding blocks, including the one looking on to Dean's block. Unfortunately, and as expected, nothing was seen due to his curtains being drawn.' Ferguson, pleased with himself, sat back, nothing more to offer.

Eve turned to Mearns. 'What've you got?'

'I've managed to override the password on his laptop and started going through it. Appears it was professional use mainly. Work documents, and emails. All old. I expect he used a separate device for personal stuff. No sign of that in the flat. Could be he kept an email account on his mobile phone, same with a diary.

'As we already know, the phone wasn't found at his home address. I'm looking through his internet search history on his laptop next.'

'OK. Thanks, both.' Eve surveyed the room. 'MacLean will be making a start on the autopsy of Dean Johnstone. If not tonight, tomorrow. Let's see what we get from that. Meantime, let's hope we get a hit from those incident cards posted through the doors.'

Mearns nodded.

'Which brings us to our Jane Doe.'

Everyone shifted in their seats, ready for the next onslaught of information.

'Ferguson, I want you to lead going through the missing persons reports, check if anything flags.' Eve waited for the familiar groan from him, pleased when it didn't come. 'Get all the details we have for her to the Missing Persons Bureau. Her prints are currently being run through the system. MacLean is going to try dental records.'

Eve tucked her long fringe behind her ear, remembering the angry welt on the woman's neck. She gathered herself.

'I have to admit we're at a loss on this one at the moment. We know now this wasn't a suicide. Someone killed her and that has to leave a trail somewhere. What we need to do now is to find it, follow it, and hope the sonofabitch who did it is waiting for us at the end.'

Chapter 10

Tuesday

A<small>NDREEA</small> <small>FROZE</small> <small>AT</small> <small>THE</small> sound of the flat's front door opening.

Daria.

She stole a look at the clock on the wall. Six a.m. An hour earlier than usual. Andreea balled another dress into the all-black load in the washing machine, wanting to look busy; she sensed rather than heard Daria as she came up behind her in the kitchen doorway.

'Everything OK?'

Fear shot through Andreea at the sound of the woman's voice, not dampening as she turned to look at her. That smile. The same one that had been painted on her face when she'd met her and Elena at the airport. A new friend. Eighteen years old – four years older than Elena; six years older than her. Daria had seemed so cool and fearless. An alliance. One they'd made whilst hanging about the streets of Bucharest, and someone who had offered them hope. Both of them feeling so grown up, lured from Romania to the

UK with the promise she would find them a better life, a good job.

They were barely a week in the country before they realized the last thing Daria was, was their friend. The luxury flat she'd brought them to, the shopping trips, the home-cooked meals, the shoulder to cry on, all a ruse of the early grooming before Bogdi and Vlad came to visit.

Andreea lowered her gaze to the floor, knowing what Daria was capable of. The bruise on Andreea's left cheek was still visible from the previous week when Daria had found the cleanliness of the flat not to her liking. Hate coursed through her body for the woman.

'I asked if everything was OK?' The smile was gone now, the edge to her tone slicing through the space between them.

Andreea nodded slowly, her head still lowered, wondering if Daria already knew Elena was missing, if this was some kind of test.

'All the girls asleep?'

Andreea dipped her chin again. True in that at least the ones who were here were.

'Is there anything you want to tell me?'

Andreea swallowed, the sound loud in the silence. Not unusual for Daria to ask the question, but in light of what Andreea knew, she thought she heard the threat in her voice.

Tears sprang to her eyes. She didn't risk raising her head. Daria stepped forward, Andreea shuffling away until the back of her thighs were pressed against the washing machine.

'You seem rather skittish this morning.'

She knew. She must.

Andreea tried to be brave. Even if she were to tell Daria about Elena, she couldn't know about Andreea's involvement; she only knew it was Andreea's job to keep an eye on the girls, to cook, clean and launder for them. To report back to Daria on every aspect of their lives – Daria in turn passing any pertinent information to Bogdi and Vlad. She would be doing no wrong by telling the truth of Elena's disappearance.

She took a deep breath, raised her head an inch, her gaze still short of Daria's. 'Yes. There is something I must tell you. Elena didn't return.' Andreea braced herself, the floor tiles swimming in front of her, ready to be struck in Daria's misplaced anger.

'Does anyone else know?'

Andreea was surprised by the softness in Daria's voice. Her voice cracked as she replied. 'No, hers was a private hire. The rest of the girls all returned in the early hours and went straight to bed.'

'Good. Let's keep this to ourselves.'

Andreea's head shot up. The last thing she'd expected to hear.

'What about Bogdi and—'

'Leave them to me. At least until I can find out what has happened. You know how they will be once they get hold of this news.'

Andreea whispered a yes in reply, not understanding how they couldn't already know. She cast her eyes downward again, never sure who was most dangerous – Daria or the brothers.

She remembered the first time Daria had introduced them. She'd told her and Elena two colleagues were coming to meet them for some potential work. Not entirely untrue but a far cry from what they had imagined that to be. She and Elena were asked to wear black, tight mini-dresses and heels – not something they would've picked themselves. Daria urged them to treat the meeting as an interview, to act nicely, wearing the perfect outfit.

Andreea remembered the look on the men's faces when they saw the birthmark on her cheek. Bogdi had slapped Daria across the face for not telling them she was soiled goods and at first Andreea had wanted to go to her, to comfort her. Daria had apologized profusely, saying the girls were young, a quality men wanted regardless. He'd slapped her again, said something about Andreea being kept indoors for use with the girls, but that he would sample the goods regardless.

Andreea had screamed as Bogdi lifted her, clawing at the doorframe as he carried her through to one of the bedrooms. Begging Daria to help her. But no help had come. She'd wept as he threw her on the bed. He had forced himself on her, taking her virginity, clamping his hand over her mouth, muffling her screams and cries, which were being echoed in the room next door, where Vlad had taken Elena.

Andreea closed her eyes at the memory, confused as to why Daria would be trying to save her from being harmed by them now.

Daria smiled, the gesture ugly. 'Say nothing to no one. This will be our secret. If any of the girls ask, tell them she has been hired for a longer-term client.'

Andreea didn't argue. It happened occasionally. Elena was one of the most requested girls; the others wouldn't question it.

Daria reached out. Andreea flinched before the woman cupped her face, the touch like fire on her skin, flames licking at the old bruise there. Andreea stilled, all the while wondering whether the small round of her stomach was as hidden in the baggy top she wore as she hoped.

'Do not worry.'

Andreea chewed at the inside of her cheek. Everything felt wrong, especially the worry in Daria's eyes. Because the only person Daria worried about was herself.

Chapter 11

SHE'LL BE HERE SOON. *I'm sure I can hear my heart thumping in my chest. I lie and wait, pretending that, when she does arrive, she won't see me lying here on the bottom bunk. But I know in real life she doesn't miss a thing.*

Beneath the thin, scratchy sheet, I clutch the grubby small square of material – once a large fluffy blanket, but cut down again and again as if one day my need for comfort will disappear. And so I won't, and don't ever, dare to stroke my cheek with it before it is dark. Until she is gone.

After all, it's my one comfort here . . . Apart from El.

I turn my head sideways on the lumpy pillow. The bunks are in rows. Children, because that's what we are, as young as eleven and twelve, squeezed in alongside teenagers and beyond. No room for privacy, no space for any kind of freedom.

My heart skips as I hear the heeled footsteps, the ones I'd once idolized but now fear. Quickly, I shove the square under the bumpy mass of a pillow and press my head down, keeping my secret safe. I can't be made fun of in here. Life's bad enough.

I don't breathe as I hear her weave throughout the metal frames, the stick she carries gently clanging. Bodies shaking beneath paper-thin sheets, an involuntary yelp if the stick skims over the top of their scrawny bodies.

I'm light-headed with the lack of oxygen as her legs pause by my bunk. El gasps in the bunk above me, the stick finding its way to her tonight.

I squeeze my eyes shut, willing the woman to move away, imagining being brave enough to kick out from beneath the sheets, right into her shins as she stands there. Imagination is a great thing. My protection from reality.

'Lights out,' she barks.

I duck beneath my sheets at the voice.

No one moves, no one argues as the flick of the light switch is heard.

After all, darkness is all we know now.

Chapter 12

DI Daniel Portman, portfolio lead for human trafficking in the north-east of Scotland, had a ruddy complexion, a kind face and an easy smile. Qualities that didn't hurt the fact Eve respected him as a fellow officer. Dedicated to the job but humble about his successes, Portman had been involved in a sting the year before that had led twenty-five Hungarian girls to safety and freedom. Eve hadn't once heard him talk about it.

'Thanks for making the time to see me.' She took a seat opposite him at one of the canteen tables, making sure both of them grabbed breakfast over their early-morning meet.

'No problem.' Portman closed and rolled up the *Aberdeen Enquirer* he'd been reading. This morning's edition carried a full-page spread about Dean Johnstone, headlines shouting about the young, affluent man murdered in his own home. Minimal coverage had made it into the late edition yesterday. Their Jane Doe also got a mention in yesterday's paper, a mere filler on about page six. Old news by today.

Portman slid his breakfast towards him and cut through the bacon and egg butty, yolk oozing across the plate. 'Haven't seen you around here in ages.'

Eve spooned her cereal, wondering whether Portman was referring to her times away from the station over the last year or so or whether she was reading too much into it. 'I know. We probably miss each other here in the canteen by minutes every day.'

Eve meant it. Sometimes it felt as if the seven-storey building was full of stand-alone businesses on separate floors. Months passed without setting eyes on someone who worked two floors up from you.

Portman lifted the bun to his mouth and took a bite before speaking around the mouthful he was chewing. 'What can I do for you?'

Eve didn't muck about. 'As I mentioned on the phone, I'm looking to find out more about the human trafficking scene.'

Portman took a gulp of the glass of water in front of him. 'Shoot.'

'I'll get right to it. Do you know if it's common practice to brand these girls?'

Portman's nose crinkled as he thought about it. 'Yes and no.' He mopped at yolk on his plate with his forefinger. 'We've heard of stories nationwide where it has been and, from my personal research, it's common practice globally.'

Eve put down her spoon. She wanted to concentrate on every word Portman said. 'Have you ever seen it?'

He nodded. 'Wish I hadn't.'

Eve's heart sank. 'What's the point of it all?'

'It's an ownership thing, proof of status. These men want to show people they have a stable of girls at their disposal.'

Eve was glad she'd picked a light breakfast. 'What kind of markings have you witnessed?'

Portman licked at the yolk on his fingers. Eve didn't mind; it was hard trying to grab a half-decent meal on the job.

'All sorts. Some use their initials. A nickname. Others are brazen and will go with their names scrolled across a woman's chest, or perhaps her thigh. I've heard of girls who have had a pound sign tattooed by their crotch.'

'Christ.'

'Yeah, not nice.'

Eve dug into her pocket, took out a folded sheet of paper. 'What about this?' She opened and flattened the photocopy of the enlarged picture that had been taken of the barcode found at the base of the woman's hairline.

Portman clicked his tongue. 'Yeah, this is classic. A tattoo that identifies the woman as being available for purchase.'

Eve grimaced. She tapped a fingernail against the photocopy sitting upside down in front of her. Twelve numbers: 333 777 2 8 444 2. She pushed the paper closer towards Portman. 'Any ideas?'

'Well, they've stayed true to form.'

Eve looked blankly at him. 'You've lost me.'

'Universal Product Code. All barcodes usually consist of twelve digits, uniquely assigned to each trade item.'

'Tell me more.' Eve picked up her spoon again, on safer ground now.

'Sure, but this is where I get geeky. Blame my days of working as a supermarket supervisor in Somerfield.'

'Your talents are endless but you're showing your age. Does that place even exist any more?'

'Nope, it hit retail heaven, maybe around the same time as Woolworths.'

Eve cocked an eyebrow. 'OK, tell me what you know. Get as geeky as you like.'

'Right. In its standard version, a barcode consists of a five-digit manufacturer number followed by a five-digit product number. In addition to that there's a one-digit number system identifier at the beginning, as well as a check digit, which makes up the last digit of the code. Twelve numbers in total.'

Eve studied the numbers. 'But not this one. Although still twelve numbers, the layout of the numbers are different from what you describe. Is that common in these types of tattoos?'

'God, yes. Sometimes people get smart and make sure it fits; other times the artwork is the lines of a barcode but it's letters rather than numbers beneath, maybe spelling out a name or a word – easily identifiable by others and I don't think folk care if it matches twelve characters or not.'

'Any idea what these numbers might mean?'

Portman's expression was as if she were asking him to change water to wine.

Eve tried again. 'I mean as in, do you know if any of these numbers relate to anything to do with trafficking?'

'Not as far as I'm aware but I guarantee that, in some way or another, they'll relate to the men who own these girls.'

'In some way?'

'Yeah, as I said, a name, a nickname, an in-joke. I've even heard of it being co-ordinates.'

Eve slumped beneath the weight of the task ahead. 'Endless possibilities. Where would I even start trying to figure it out?'

Portman picked up his bun again. 'I'm not sure it'll help, but I'll put out feelers, ask around. Apart from that, there's not much else I can do, except to say I'm glad it's you that has to figure it out and not me.'

Chapter 13

Eve looked up as Mearns knocked on the glass door of the fishbowl where she sat – an office of sorts, which amounted to a partitioned corner of the otherwise open-plan space.

Eve motioned for her to enter. 'What you got?'

Mearns stood in the doorway, a laptop in her hand. 'Not much on our Jane Doe. Fingerprints have been run through the system. Nothing. Ferguson's still cross-referencing the mispers list. MacLean's had no luck on the dental records.'

Eve tried not to show her frustration. She knew the team were working hard. 'Have details been logged with the Missing Persons Bureau and circulated to other forces?'

'Yes.' Mearns stepped further into the office. 'You have any luck on the barcode?

'No. Portman's going to ask around. Meantime it's a guessing game or a puzzle to be solved, let's say.'

'There've been no callbacks on the door-to-door at Dean Johnstone's. But, if it's any consolation, I've found

68

interesting reading on there.' She laid the laptop on the desk between them. Dean's laptop.

'Enlighten me.' Eve sat back, pen in hand.

'Internet search history definitely points towards a love of porn. All kinds of kink.'

'No surprise there.'

'I guess not. There's nothing in the Outlook calendar. If he used one it must've been on his phone, which isn't linked. Nothing unusual in the saved documents. Appears to be mainly work-related.'

'Where's the interesting part?' Eve tapped the black biro against the edge of the desk.

'Instagram. Only social media he appears to have been on.'

She stopped tapping. 'I would've had him down as a Tinder man.'

Mearns patted the laptop. 'No sign of it, but again the laptop isn't linked to his mobile. He may have been.'

'What's his Instagram saying, apart from updates on what old school pals are having for their breakfast?'

'Loads of that, but I think you'll be more interested in who his school pals were.'

'Let me guess, the kind of twats that were part of the popular crew? Sporty. Laddish. A harem of googly-eyed girls in tow.'

Mearns grinned. 'More or less. And rich. Stinking rich.'

Eve scrunched her face. 'Of course.'

'They're loaded. I mean as in Peter Miller rich.'

Eve groaned. Peter Miller, local businessman extraordinaire. She'd clocked him the other month driving down Union Street in his mid-life-crisis soft-top super-charged Jaguar F-type. His tanned arm perched on the wound-down window, brown quiff blowing above over-sized shades, the personalized reg screaming out his identity.

Last she'd heard he'd moved into the hotel and casino market, still keeping a couple of pubs and clubs in his portfolio. The grown-up version of the school twat.

'I hear he's a big deal in Aberdeen. Or was.' Mearns, being from Bolton, had been saved the torture of his mug all over the press as she ate her tea as a teenager.

'You could say that. I'm sure he thinks so anyway. Where does he come into it?'

'He doesn't as such, but his son, Finn, does.'

Eve wasn't sure she'd heard right. 'A son?'

'Yup.'

'Never knew he had one. I remember hearing about Peter losing his wife to cancer years ago and being heart-broken. Surprising, given how well known he was for not being able to keep it in his pants on the party circuit.'

Mearns wrinkled her nose. 'I'm assuming that was Finn's mother. He's twenty-five. Went to the same school as Dean. He's on Facebook as being a PR and advertis-ing man with a bit of performing thrown in. There's no mention of who he works for.'

'Probably his dad. What school did they go to?'

'Heritage School for Boys.'

Eve curled her lip as she pictured the enormous pri-vate school on the outskirts of Aberdeen. 'Of course they did.'

'Anyway, there're loads of pictures of Finn and Dean. Most of them taken with another guy up until a year ago, and then nothing.'

'A fall-out?'

'No.' Mearns placed a piece of paper in front of Eve. 'Andrew Shirriffs. I clicked on his profile. Timeline is a screed of RIP messages from friends and family. He died a year ago.'

Eve looked at the photo in front of her. She remembered reading something about him in the papers at the time. Not that she'd paid much attention to it when her own life was spinning out of control. 'Same school?'

Mearns nodded.

'How did he die?'

'Suicide. Found naked with a tie around his neck, hanging from the handle of a bedroom door.'

'Bloody hell. OK, get me everything you can on him.'

'I'm on it already.'

Eve bolted forward in her chair. 'Wait a minute. Andrew Shirriffs. Was he not the son of *the* Shirriffses?'

Mearns took her time, seemingly enjoying the suspense. 'You mean the Shirriffses who own a restaurant chain in Aberdeen?'

'Yes.'

She nodded. 'The very ones. Patricia and Kirk Shirriffs. Not that I knew before I saw a picture on his Instagram of his folks and the restaurant they own in Union Street.'

'And Holburn, as well as Thistle Street.'

Mearns whistled. 'Not short of a bob or two.'

71

Eve looked at the photo. Three boys. Andrew Shirriffs sitting centre, his dark brown eyes staring up at her; Dean Johnstone and Finn Miller either side of him. 'No, and we all know money tends to stick together.' Eve sat back in her chair again, leather squeaking. 'Sounds as if Dean and Andrew were into similar kinds of kink. Which begs the question, what's Peter Miller's son, Finn, into?'

Eve walked into the chaos of the incident room with Mearns and the laptop following closely behind her.

'Listen up.'

Ferguson, Cooper and the crowd of bodies working the room stopped what they were doing.

'First, anything to report?'

Ferguson stretched his neck after too many hours at the computer. 'Nothing on missing persons matching our Jane Doe. On the plus side, the Hazlehead grounds-keeper called. School's out for lunch and the usual kids that hang out at the course have wandered down from Hazlehead Academy and are there now.'

Eve's head whipped towards Ferguson. 'How long do they get for lunch?'

'An hour.'

'OK. You and Mearns get up there. Fast. Find out if they saw anything. If they did, get on to the head-master for his and parental permission to get them in here for interview. They're minors, so will need an adult present.'

Ferguson and Mearns were already out of their seats and heading for the door.

72

Eve turned back to the room. 'The rest of you, as well as looking into missing persons, I want a little background on the Heritage School for Boys. Who owns it, who goes there and who went in the past. Particular attention to the years Dean Johnstone attended and who he hung around with. Where they are, what they're up to, and into.'

Everyone in the room had their attention fixed on Eve as she barked orders. 'One thing we know for sure is he hung around with Andrew Shirriffs of the Kirk and Patricia Shirriffs restaurant chain fame, and Finn Miller, son of Peter Miller.'

Cooper straightened at the desk. 'Didn't Andrew Shirriffs commit suicide?'

Eve nodded.

Cooper whistled low. 'And Miller's son. Is he as much of a twat as his dad?'

Eve wasn't surprised Cooper held the same opinion as her. 'I intend to find out. See if you can get hold of Peter Miller and I definitely want to speak to the son. My main aim is to find out why the hell he's the only one left out of the three of them.'

Eve stopped as her phone rang. MacLean. She didn't move off into another room, knowing her team were waiting on this call.

'Hunter.'

'I know. I called you.'

Eve didn't grace him with an answer.

'Thought you'd want the result from Johnstone's autopsy.'

'You bet I do.'

'I was right. Blunt-force trauma to the head would've knocked him out but he was smothered to death before he regained consciousness.'

'How do you know?'

'Small red and purple splotches in the eyes, neck and face. Common in the lungs too in this event but not as many as I expected.'

'Why would that be?'

'He'd have been out cold, so didn't gasp and fight for his life as much as he would've had he been able to.'

'Thanks, MacLean.' Eve hung up and relayed the information to the people in front of her.

'Get me something to work with, guys.'

Chapter 14

FERGUSON AND MEARNS TOOK it in turns to shake George Christie's hand outside the same shed where they'd found him before, although the man looked decidedly better than the last time they'd met.

'Thanks for calling. How's Tom?' Ferguson hadn't forgotten about the old guy who had collapsed and been hospitalized after spotting the woman hanging from the tree.

'Good, thanks. I visited him last night. Says he's expecting to get home in the next day or two.'

Ferguson nodded. 'Glad to hear it.'

George motioned towards the clubhouse and walked as he spoke. 'They were down by the woods before I came here to meet with you.'

Mearns strode to keep up with the two men. 'We could've met you there.'

George turned. 'They didn't see me and wouldn't have stayed if they had. Let's say we've had a couple of run-ins over the past year about their behaviour and

75

the mess they leave. I'm not their favourite person. Add the fact you guys are coppers and they'd be out of there faster than a speeding golf ball. Here. We'll take the buggy.'

Ferguson and Mearns hoisted themselves into the back of the four-seater buggy and held on to the metal handrail down by their sides as George started the engine and made his way across the concrete car park before bumping on to the course.

Ferguson squinted against the midday sun, which seemed out of place with the nip in the air. The kids that hung out here definitely had it made. The place was beautiful. A real step up from the usual street corners, or the local chippie, where kids were typically found congregating. Poles apart from his upbringing. The kids here wouldn't be coming to scrawl graffiti around the place, but they'd no doubt be having the same sneaky fag he might have had. Ferguson didn't blame them. A little freedom away from the prying eyes of adults, a chance to look cool alongside their peers before heading back to school.

Ferguson looked ahead, nudging Mearns as he saw a group standing by the dry-stone dykes lining either side of the wide, rocky and mud-packed lane that separated the course and wound its way around it, a popular walking path. Thin plumes of smoke rose between the heads of the four boys that stood there, laughter carrying on the breeze. Definitely partaking of a sneaky fag.

The group turned at the sound of the buggy and began to move off as one, a defiant stroll rather than a run. George accelerated a little, shouted from the buggy. 'We want a quick word.'

The kids stopped. Ferguson asked George to wait before jumping from the buggy as it came to a stand-still, going around to help Mearns down, though she refused the assistance. Ferguson spoke softly, avoiding his voice carrying over to the kids. 'Thanks, George. No offence, but the kids might be more willing to talk with-out you getting involved.'

He walked towards them, Mearns by his side. 'Thanks for stopping.' Ferguson tilted his head in George's direc-tion, his voice louder. 'Like he said, a quick word.'

The tallest of the group, a gangly kid with a rucksack slung over one shoulder and skull badges adorning the green school blazer he wore, stood with a fag pinched between his forefinger and thumb. Looking awkward, as if he'd ended up with it after it being passed around the group. Ferguson was glad he didn't smell weed. He pointed to the fag, almost burnt to the filter.

'You want to get rid of that?'

The kid's face coloured as he dropped it to the ground and placed a trainer over the top, grinding it into the dirt. He ran a hand through his shoulder-length greasy hair and glanced at his pals before looking back at them. His gaze lingered for a second too long on Mearns. Ferguson's gut told him these kids weren't any trouble. If anything, they were probably the school mis-fits, preferring to hang somewhere like here as opposed to the places where the 'popular' or 'troublemaker' cool kids hung out.

'I wanted to talk to you about Sunday night. George over there thinks you may have been here.'

'How'd he know that?' The question came from the same guy who'd stubbed out the fag. Apparently he was group leader.

Ferguson looked at the ground where the spent fag end still smouldered. 'Reckons he found beer tinnies on the course yesterday morning. I'm not saying it was you lot. It's no concern of mine.'

The youth appeared wary but didn't break eye contact.

'I'm sure you'll have heard about the woman we found up here.'

'Yeah, but we didn't see her. We don't know nothing about it.' The quiver was clear in the boy's voice as his eyes darted between Ferguson and Mearns.

Mearns reassured him: 'I'm sure you don't. No one's in any trouble. We're interested in whether you saw anything else that night, anything that seemed unusual or out of the ordinary.'

Ferguson knew Mearns was keeping it vague on purpose, aware they had to be careful about questioning these kids without an adult present.

The boy turned to the group, long hair flicking over his shoulder. The other three boys waited, as if for instruction on what they should do next. He looked at Mearns, who had asked the question. 'One thing . . . We spoke about it the day after, when we heard what happened. It didn't seem all that important. Not enough to report anything.'

Ferguson saw fear rippling through the group. Scared they'd made the wrong call, that they should've spoken up.

'Look, as my colleague and I said, you're not in any trouble here but we do need to know anything you saw or heard. The smallest detail can help us sometimes.'

'It honestly wasn't anything. We were heading down from the course. It was dark, must've been about eleven p.m. There's a car park of sorts up from the golf clubhouse one and the Hazlehead Park overspill one. It's a clearing, bit of a mud bath.'

'I know the one.'

The boy swallowed. 'We were walking along the road, towards the clubhouse, rather than through the park. We heard a car coming up the track and stepped into the bushes at the side – thought it might've been old George over there. But it went into that car park and the engine was shut off.'

This could be useful.

'OK. Before I ask you to say anything else, it's best we get in touch with your school, let your parents know we'd like to take you down the station for a formal chat.'

Pale-faced and wide-eyed, the boys looked amongst each other, the leader being the one to speak. 'You're arresting us?'

Ferguson smiled. 'Not for a few tinnies and something you might've seen. But you're minors and we need to do things properly. That means bringing you in and having a responsible adult there with you. Let's go back to the golf club, be somewhere warm until we make arrangements.'

The collective groan didn't stop the boys from following Ferguson and Mearns on foot back to the club, George happy to head back on the buggy alone.

Chapter 15

EVE LOOKED ALONG THE corridor to where Mearns and Ferguson stood chatting with a tall, slim, sharp-suited gentlemen. If the four boys seated and slouched against the wall in silence by the man's side were anything to go by, it was Hazlehead Academy's head teacher.

The boys were pretty much what she'd expected: spotty-faced and young – a hint of bum fluff signalling their impending adulthood. The head teacher, however, was much younger than she'd imagined. She held out her hand.

'Mr Buchanan. Nice to meet you. Thanks for coming down with the boys.'

'Of course.'

He must've done a good job of convincing the parents their kids were not in trouble and he'd ensure they were OK. Eve was glad; the small corridor was cramped enough, and she didn't want the boys clamming up because Mummy and Daddy wouldn't like to know the finer details of what they got up to at the golf course.

Eve studied the faces in front of her. 'We'd like to interview each of you separately. Mr Buchanan will be in the interview room with you, as will DC Ferguson and myself. DC Mearns here will sit with the three not in the room until we've spoken to you all. That OK?'

One of the boys nodded. The gesture was slowly followed by the other three in turn.

Eve clapped her hands together. 'OK, let's work along the line.'

The first boy stood, looking nervous. The leader of the four. Eve had worked that much out in the small time she'd been in their company.

Mearns took the boy's place on the bench. Eve walked briskly, leading Ferguson, Mr Buchanan and the boy into the interview room a couple of doors down. Mearns would be OK with the arrangement – good with people of all ages whilst keeping an air of authority. Ferguson would be too tempted to try and be their best mate, all flexing muscles and chats about girls. He'd be better suited in with her.

Craig Mutch turned to his head teacher for the third time in the five minutes since they'd sat down at the table in the interview room. Each glance taken whilst divulging details Craig maybe thought wouldn't go down too well with the school principal. Hanging out at the course in the early hours of the morning . . . Smoking a sneaky fag or two whilst they were there . . . None of the boys proving popular with George the greenkeeper . . .

Eve doubted Mr Buchanan would be too hard on them. She studied Craig's face and body language as she let Ferguson lead the interview.

'The car in the car park. Were you close enough to see who was driving?'

Craig shook his head. 'It was pitch black and, with the headlights shining towards us, I couldn't see anything.'

Ferguson thought a second. 'Did you see the make of the car? Any details of the registration?'

'Nope. But I think a large car. The headlights were wide apart, not like a Mini or something.'

'Colour?' Ferguson was clutching at straws. The kid had already said it was too dark.

'I can't be sure. I'd say a dark colour.'

Eve didn't doubt he was telling the truth; unfortunate they hadn't been able to see more.

'We heard them, though.'

Ferguson turned to look at Eve. Both of their interest piqued. 'Them?'

Mr Buchanan stared at his pupil.

'Yeah. A man and a woman. The doors and windows of the car were closed, but it's dead round there at nights. We heard them arguing.'

'Definitely two people?'

'Yeah. For sure. As we got nearer, they got out of the car. Still arguing but not as loudly. They hadn't seen us.'

Ferguson paused, Eve knowing he was figuring out where to go next. 'Could you hear what they were saying?'

'Nah, but it was pretty obvious they weren't happy. She was muttering, crying. He was silent, with the odd grunt.'

'In English?'

The teenager focused on a spot above Ferguson's head, thinking. 'I couldn't make out anything they were saying.'

Eve wanted more. 'Can you describe them?'

'Not in detail. Too dark and, to be honest, I didn't take much notice.' He paused. 'The thing I remember is the guy seemed pretty big next to her.'

Eve was glad of something, no matter how small. 'Did they move away from the car at all?'

'That was the weird thing. They kinda danced around it, as if they couldn't decide or agree what they were doing.'

Eve tried to picture what might have been going on. 'Did they take anything out of the car?'

The teenager rubbed at his chin. 'Not whilst we were there. She touched the boot a few times but never opened it. They spotted us and both got back in the car.'

Something definitely off. 'Who was in the driver's seat?'

'The man.'

Ferguson's arm brushed against Eve's before asking the next question. 'OK. Did it look like she was forced into the car or unhappy about getting in?'

'Nope. He got in his side and she got in hers.'

Ferguson scratched at his forehead as Eve took a turn. 'Did they start the car? Drive away?'

'No. They sat there in the dark. We walked past and headed to the golf club. We didn't see them again.' The youth eyed them nervously, perhaps making sure they weren't disappointed with how little he could tell them.

'OK. Thank you for coming in to talk to us. I'll see you both outside and we'll get the next one in.' Ferguson stood, letting Craig and Mr Buchanan go to the door before him.

Eve took advantage of the brief silence. Anything might've happened before and after that car left. But what she wanted to know, regardless of how long the car had stayed there, or which way it had gone, was whether the woman had still been in the car when it left.

Chapter 16

EVE BENT-TO PICK up the wet leaves that her boots had dragged from the garden into her shed, stopping half-way as the cork noticeboard on the wall in the corner caught her eye. She straightened, remembering the photographs and newspaper clippings that had been pinned there less than a year ago. Hard to believe the anniversary of Sanders's death was coming around.

Thank God they'd got to Mearns before she'd been taken too. Eve closed her eyes, remembering the show-down at Mearns's old flat in the Bastille, the killer's cries as he'd fallen from the balcony to the concrete car park beneath. Cries she'd heard in her sleep many times since.

Going back to work, yet again, had been tough; the only thing making it easier was that the whole team had taken the same hits this time. Different from the previous times when Eve had felt she was sinking alone. They'd all suffered the same doubts: whether they could've done more; if any of those women might've been saved.

But the last few months, together, they'd slowly found a way to relieve that guilt for one another. Working tirelessly on cases and making sure they did everything they could to bring justice to the people who had been hurt. All of them needing to immerse themselves in the job. Not to forget. Never to forget those they'd lost. But to move forward.

And Eve had moved forward too, but the grief and guilt had moved with her. Hanging around her neck like the noose around their Jane Doe.

She tried to hide that at work, almost sure they all were doing the same. But she couldn't at home. She couldn't hide from herself.

She stepped over to the garden waste bin that she kept in the shed whilst she worked, and binned the rotting leaves. She opened one of the cupboards by the window, sighing as she pulled out a box of two-ply cord, not knowing what she wanted to do with it but needing to keep her mind and hands busy. She reached for small, plain boxes bought from Hobbycraft down at Union Square, each one a blank canvas to be given life, an idea forming in her head about decorating them. She grabbed the glue, but her gaze kept wandering to the board.

She laid the materials out on the workbench, tried to get herself in the zone. This concrete shed was her haven. Built by her grandfather in the back garden of the cottage where she'd always lived.

Usually, discarding her work clothes and changing into her paint- and varnish-splattered dungarees transported her mind to another place before she even set foot in the shed. Once here she would lose herself in projects, shaking off the stress of the day, working long into the night if she needed to. And she often did.

Eve closed her eyes, reliving the case gone by whilst her mind fought with the case at present. That angry welt on their Jane Doe's neck swimming in her mind, the thin black lines of the barcode on her neck, the grubby beige soles of Dean Johnstone's socked feet. Pressure mounted in her temples. They'd achieved next to nothing today. Time had disappeared, a large chunk of it spent talking to the schoolboys who had ultimately been able to give them next to nothing to go on.

She took a deep breath. The bubbling would only be held down for so long before it rose to the top. Last Friday one of those bubbles had popped. Laura Robertson's husband, everything she detested in a person. Manipulative. Violent. Dangerous. She'd managed to stop herself before it went too far. But when she let those bubbles build, when her temper had nowhere to go, it was in danger of erupting when she least expected it. Her actions hurting those around her.

She picked up her mobile, wanting to do something, anything to divert her frustration. Her thumb flew over the keys as she unlocked the screen: 6886. The same code she'd had since she'd owned her old Nokia brick, each key having to be hit anywhere from one to three times to get the desired letter when texting: 6886 spelt MUM. It would always be her security code.

As the mobile screen sprang to life, something pricked the back of her mind. She stood still, trusting the feeling, forgetting about the phone for a second.

What if the numbers on the barcode were transferable to letters? Eve's heart raced, adrenaline pumping at the possibility, her mind already working at it before she went to get the paper photocopy of the barcode. A problem to solve.

All other problems forgotten for now.

Chapter 17

Wednesday

EVE MADE HER WAY along the corridor towards the incident room, balancing three large lattes in the carton in her hand, car keys still in the other. She bumped the office door with her shoulder, today's newspaper under her armpit, surprised to find Cooper there before her.

'Bed on fire this morning?' She handed one of the disposable cups to him. Cooper took the coffee from her, not quite meeting her gaze. 'Are you OK?'

'Yeah. Louise was in a mood, so I left early.' He offered nothing more.

She set down the drinks tray and newspaper on the nearest desk. 'You look shattered. Any sign of Mearns and Ferguson?'

'Haven't seen either of them yet.'

Eve pulled her arm free of her jacket, threw it over the back of a chair and took one of the two remaining coffees out, sipping at it hungrily, as tired as Cooper looked. 'Didn't get much sleep myself last night. Got to thinking about that bloody barcode.'

'And?'

'And I'm not totally sure if it's something or nothing.'

Cooper waited for Eve to elaborate.

'Remember back in the day with the old-style push-button phones?'

'Yes, as much as I'd like to be young enough not to.'

'You'll remember when texting you had to press a number a certain number of times to get the letter you wanted?

Cooper nodded.

'I use the same for my Nokia screen password. Punch in the number keys that spell out a word.'

'You need to be getting an iPhone. Much easier to use,' Cooper ribbed her. 'What's the word?'

Eve wasn't giving that titbit away. 'Wouldn't you like to know? Anyway, it got me thinking that might be the case with this barcode. Numbers coded to be a word or words.'

'Seems feasible.' Cooper took a swig of his coffee.

'I had a bash at it.' Eve took the piece of paper out of her inside pocket, her handwritten scrawl of last night clear beneath the barcode image. 'So: 333 777 2 8 444 2. I took each space to mean every group of numbers represented a letter. F – R – A – T – I – A.'

Cooper ran his finger around the mouth of his coffee cup. 'New one on me.'

Eve agreed. 'And me, but going by the tattoo on our Jane Doe's wrist being "Mum" in Romanian, I googled to see if "FRATIA" translated to anything in the same.'

'And?'

'And it does. "BROTHERHOOD".'

Cooper didn't look overly impressed. 'Good thinking, although I'm not sure it leaves us with much more than we already had. I guess the guys peddling these women do consider each other as some sort of force, a kind of brotherhood. Of course, we could be looking at actual family ties.'

Eve knew they might be looking at countless things. 'It's worth running past Portman again. Find out if there's anything like that on his radar.'

She turned as Mearns walked into the room. 'Morning.'

Mearns walked over and helped herself to the remaining coffee, knowing it was for her, the three of them always first in, their dynamic improved beyond recognition from a year ago. Ferguson wouldn't be far behind her with whatever God-awful protein shake he'd made that morning.

They took seats around one of the rectangular tables, thirty minutes before Eve was due to give the morning briefing to the rest of the team. Eve filled Mearns in on her barcode theory.

'It's great, but a pity it's so general.'

'I know. Anything new from your end?' Eve wasn't expecting there to be.

'Nope. I tried to get hold of Peter Miller again last night on the phone on the way up to the golf club. Only contact I have is for Miller's Hotel. I eventually got put through to his secretary. According to her he was out on business, not to be interrupted.'

Eve tutted. 'Not even by the police when one of his son's best friends has been murdered?'

Mearns's mouth was tight. 'Appears not. I asked if it would be possible to contact his son, Finn, instead. She didn't have contact details for him.'

Eve snorted. 'I find that hard to believe.'

'Me too. I've left a message for Peter Miller to get back to us as a matter of urgency.'

Eve doubted it would make any difference. 'Thanks. I updated Cooper on the kids' interviews all checking out the same.'

Cooper rubbed at his neck. 'We need to find out who the man in that car was.'

Mearns looked at him. 'You reckon the woman must've been our Jane Doe?'

Eve bit the inside of her index finger, a habit she'd picked up when thinking, the dry ragged skin testimony to how deep in thought she'd been these past few days. 'The kids said the woman walked round the back of the car and touched the boot a few times, but she didn't open it. Maybe she was our Jane Doe, but I'm more inclined to think that she, and the guy in the car with her, might've been the ones responsible for getting her up in that tree.'

Cooper's eyes were owl-like. 'You reckon the body might've been in the boot?'

Eve leaned back, her team studying her. 'Nothing at the moment to suggest it wasn't.'

*

Eve knocked twice in quick succession on Hastings's door and pushed it open. DCI Hastings bolted upright behind his desk, banging his knee.

'For God's sake, Hunter. I guess "come in" would be a little late.' His sunken cheeks coloured as he dropped the last of the bacon roll on to his desk. Eve eyed the windowsill, the packed lunch box his wife sent him off with every day sitting unopened there. She wasn't sure if the roll was breakfast or an extra snack, but she knew one thing for sure: his wife, Sheila, wouldn't know about it.

Eve found it hard to figure how he stayed stick-thin with the food he managed to shovel away. The consistent greenish hue to his skin was a possible sign of how his insides were doing. 'Thought you'd want an update.'

Eve explained the connections they'd discovered between Dean Johnstone, Kirk and Patricia Shirriffs and Peter Miller, watching her boss's expression harden.

'Shit.' He threw his napkin on to the desk. 'Hunter, you're going have to go easy with this one. No charging in like you usually do. We can't have anything like your last bull-in-a-china-shop moment.'

Eve said nothing. She'd heard it all already last week when he'd dragged her into his office to berate her for the incident with Colin Robertson.

'A lot of feathers are going to get ruffled. I'm surprised the press haven't made the connection yet.'

Eve, grateful he was letting her off relatively easily, muttered, 'I'm afraid they have, sir. This morning's edition references Andrew Shirriffs's death a year ago. I'm sure Andrew's parents, Kirk and Patricia Shirriffs, will be feeling the pain right now at it all being dredged up again.'

'Great.'

Eve agreed it wasn't ideal, but it would've been worse if it had been Claire Jenkins covering it. Eve tried not to give too much thought to the dead reporter, who had lost her life in the case they'd been working last year. They'd never been friends – quite the opposite when Jenkins had gone out of her way in the past to make Eve's life a living nightmare – but no one deserved what had happened to her. Eve still felt guilty that she hadn't been able to save Jenkins. Her replacement, Marcie Wade, seemed to be a kitten in comparison, but Eve wasn't easily fooled.

She looked across at Hastings. 'We'll do our best to keep control over the press reports.' Eve was still getting used to HQ's new press guy and hadn't had too many dealings with him to date. 'We're trying to track down Peter and Finn Miller. No luck yet. But I'll be mindful.'

He said nothing, as if he severely doubted Eve had any idea about how to be mindful. *Here we go . . .*

'You do know you have to keep a lid on that temper of yours with these guys?'

Eve clamped her back teeth together, loosening her jaw only to speak. 'It's fair to say that should be the case with anyone. Just because these twats have money and some clout in the city, doesn't mean they deserve special treatment. Anyway, I held it together when Robert Johnstone was being an obstructive prat out at the airport the other day. I'll do the same when I go to see him again.'

Hastings glowered at her. 'This is true, but we both know that's not always the case with how you operate.'

Eve relented, not wanting to push her luck. 'Look, I know these guys wouldn't hold back on making things difficult if I stepped out of line. And I also know they're surrounded by people, important folk, who would listen. For the record, I have no personal vendetta with Peter Miller. Or Johnstone. I hate any kind of abuse of power.' Eve swallowed. 'But, like I say, I'll behave.'

She stood, nothing else to say.

Hastings's facial expression made it clear he didn't believe a word she was saying but he wasn't stopping her from leaving.

Eve turned towards the door, her teeth clamped together again. The thing was, she couldn't promise herself, or him, that she believed it either.

Chapter 18

ANDREEA WILLED THE GRAFFITI-STREWN elevator of the block of flats to move faster. She fixed her gaze on the thick black marker scrawled across the steel doors as the small box she stood in groaned past each floor, oblivious to what the vandals had written, used to it all, and to smelling stale urine in the tight space.

The lift shuddered to a stop. Andreea's nose almost touched the doors as she waited for them to part. Her foot was through the space before there was enough room for her body to follow. She burst out into the ground-floor entrance hall, clutching the blue velvet purse she held on this day every week.

The heavy intercom door banged shut behind her as she stepped out into the rain, glad of fresh air against her wet skin. She didn't look back, or up. They'd be watching her from the fourth-floor window: Bogdi, Vlad and Daria. They liked to be there on a Wednesday to drop the money, to ensure the weekly shop got done, but, most of all, to check the girls were in order.

Daria used to shop with her, but stopped when she decided Andreea could be trusted. Andreea darted around the corner on to the sloping pavement of Deer Road in the city's less desirable area of Woodside, clutching her long woollen cardigan around her waist. Her feet moved down the narrow lane between buildings to Great Northern Road.

She broke out on to the main road, turned right, safer now traffic zoomed past her either side of the dual carriageway, keeping back from the edge and the water being sprayed on to the pavement every time a bus or lorry thundered by. She kept her head lowered against the downpour, the grey fluffy hairs of her cardigan turning darker, clumping together against the black T-shirt and leggings beneath.

People scurried along the pavement towards her. Some with knock-off designer baseball caps keeping them dry as their trainers squeaked in the rain; an old woman taking her time as she pulled a battered tartan shopping trolley through puddles behind her. Most of them doing a double take of Andreea's face; the greasy-haired drunk standing outside Iceland the only one to shout an insult. Andreea didn't react, either with words or by raising a hand to cover her eye and cheek; after a lifetime, she was immune to it.

She passed the long row of run-down shops, not looking in the dirty windows of any of them, knowing the one she was headed for, its windows protected by security mesh. The rusty bell above the door jangled as she stepped in off the street. A muggy warmth and the inviting smell of spiced meat caused tears to form in the corners of her eyes. She'd made it.

Andreea walked up the side aisle towards the cash desk of the Eastern European mini-market, the place like a home from home. Yearning for the life she once knew.

She couldn't see him. Her heart pounded.

'Bună.'

His voice. She sobbed as she saw him. His solid frame, chestnut-coloured eyes beneath curls she'd always loved, and soft smile making her heart leap as he stepped out from behind the curtain that led through to the back of the shop.

'Marius.' She bolted to him, grateful the shop was empty, for the safety of his embrace enveloping her.

'What is it?' Concern filled his voice as his words muffled against her hair. He moved his hands to her upper arms, gently pushing her back to make eye contact.

'Elena's missing.'

The safety dissolved as she saw the panic in his eyes. Andreea whipped round towards the door at the sound of the bell. She jumped away from Marius, her chest tightening. The woman who entered the shop stopped, confusion on her face, and said hello before she browsed the nearest shelf. English-speaking. Andreea put a hand to her chest, breathed deeply, trying to calm herself. Marius guided her towards the counter and lowered his voice even though they would not be understood by the woman.

'Do they know where she went? What she was doing?'

Andreea focused on Marius's eyes. 'I can't be sure.'

Concern filled his face. 'Do you think they found out what Elena was going to do? Or that you knew her plan?'

Fear shot across her stomach again as Marius said the exact thing she'd been asking herself. They both knew what Bogdi and Vlad were capable of, of all they'd done to the girls and clients who hadn't kept their side of a deal. She looked for the customer but the woman had disappeared down the next aisle.

'They came this morning, gave me the purse as usual. Said nothing. Seemed the same. Maybe they want to see what I do next.'

Marius looked at the purse in her hand. 'They know you're here?'

'Yes.' Same time, same day every week. The same list of essentials she was sent to buy to keep the girls in food, to keep them clean. Marius perhaps hoped this one time she'd run.

The woman walked past them to the door. They watched her go. Marius was used to the visits out of curiosity that usually resulted in no sale. He waited for the door to close before putting his forefinger and thumb to Andreea's chin. He tilted her face towards him. Looking at *her*, not the angry purple birth stain on her face. 'Maybe it wasn't them. Why would they let you out?'

She turned towards the door, not trusting it to stay closed. 'Maybe they want to be sure. But maybe they want to mess with me.'

Marius pulled her close, said nothing.

Her hand fluttered to her stomach.

'Are you OK?'

'I think so.' They looked down at the tiniest hint of a bump. That the time would come when they would be forced to do something had never been in doubt. But they'd hoped it would be on their terms.

'My uncle is away at the suppliers all day.'

Marius's uncle owned the shop. He'd once almost been part of the fittings, to be found behind the counter day and night. But he was an old man now. He'd fought against Marius's pleas to step back, to let him work the shop. Pride partly, but fear too. Knowing what some of their clientele brought into the store. Bogdi and Vlad selling them protection but ultimately stealing a chunk of their livelihood.

Marius had finally managed to convince him it was time to step back, to let him do the long shifts, and that he could handle it. Now his uncle only visited the shop from time to time, accepting it was easier for Marius to do the paperwork, to deal with the suppliers and all the other things that came with running the mini-market. His uncle's absence had suited Andreea and Marius's situation well.

She didn't know what he meant by his uncle being away. 'I can't stay here. They'll come looking for me.'

'No. I meant I'll take you to his for now. I can't let him know about you. Not yet. It's too dangerous for him to know if Bogdi and Vlad come looking. We'll go there now, then I'll get you to the shelter.'

'I don't want to go to there. I want to be with you.'

'You will be, I promise, but for now you need to be safe. The people at the shelter will look after you. Bogdi and Vlad won't find you there. Please, Andreea. I understand why you didn't want to before, why you wanted to stay with Elena, but now . . . This might be the one chance we get.'

Andreea buried her head against his chest, letting the tears fall before a thought made her catch her breath. 'But they'll come looking for me. Here.' The circular cracked clock above the curtain showed they were already running out of time.

'It doesn't matter. I can handle it. Let's go. Now.'

He walked to the front door, taking her along with him by her hand. He flipped the open sign to closed and locked the door.

She pulled at his hand. 'But I have nothing. The other girls. I—'

'You have me. And this.' He placed a tender hand against her stomach.

She covered his hand with hers. 'What about you? They'll want answers and they'll do anything to get them.'

'Let them.'

That same grip of fear which had been squeezing at her since Elena had left. What if Marius disappeared too? 'I can't. I—'

'You can and you will. You have to.'

Andreea gripped his hand again, letting herself be led through the back of the store, terrified of what waited beyond for her. But even more for what lay in store for Marius.

Chapter 19

EL'S BRAVER THAN ME. *Always has been. She yearns to break the rules, to escape the confines.*

Me? I want to curl up inside myself, invisible, where no one can hurt me any more.

El says I mustn't let them win. Sure, let them believe they've broken me but I must make sure I stay whole, true to myself.

I don't know how that can be possible when the people who keep watch over us spend every hour of every day smashing any hope I have left to pieces.

El calls me 'Kid'. Not in a cheeky way, like I'm annoying or whiny. More that she wants to protect me, that she knows I'm not as strong as her. I like that she calls me that. I pretend we are sisters. That I have someone in the world. If it weren't for El, I might not have survived any of it. At least not as long as I have.

El says we're going to get out of here, experience what life has to offer. Take what should have been ours.

I can't help but think El knows as well as I do that'll never happen. That this is the only life we'll ever know. But neither one of us wants to be the one to say it out loud.

Chapter 20

MEARNS TAPPED ON THE DOOR. 'Can I come in?'

'Of course.' Eve waved her in.

Mearns sat and placed a thin manila folder on the desk. She sat back. 'What were you chewing over?'

Eve straightened. 'Spoke to Portman about the tattoo, whether he knew of any family-run organizations. He said they were aware of brothers who were persons of suspicion a while ago. The Rusu brothers. It's been some time since any activity's been flagged up and they've all but fallen off the radar. But every chance it could be them.'

Eve spread out the paperwork on her desk until it uncovered what she was looking for. Mearns blanched at the close-range morgue photos of their Jane Doe as they came into view, even though she'd been there to witness it first-hand.

Eve picked up the closest one. 'I haven't been able to get her wounds out of my mind.'

Mearns knew exactly what she meant. 'Me neither.'

'We need to speak to someone in the trade. I suspect Rosie might be able to help us.'

Rosie was a prostitute who had helped them with the case the year previously.

Mearns agreed it would be a good place to start. 'Any ideas on how to find her?'

Eve paused, mulling it over. 'Shouldn't be too hard. Last I heard she has a support worker, got herself set up in a flat.'

'Go Rosie.'

Eve wasn't surprised to hear the pride in Mearns's voice. That Rosie had come out of her experience last year relatively unscathed and, even better, made a life for herself on her terms, was something they could all take comfort in.

Mearns beamed. 'Let me look into it. In the meantime, I did as you asked and looked into Andrew Shirriffs's death. Mainly the newspaper coverage and social media around the time.'

'What about the police report?'

'I couldn't access it online.'

Eve put down the picture in her hand. 'Paper copy?'

'I requested it but got a call back saying it was missing from the archives.'

'And nothing digitally at all?'

Mearns shook her head. 'Both appear to be missing.'

Eve's hand hovered where she'd laid the paper down. Mistakes happened, but unusual for both files to be unavailable. 'Keep looking. Find out who worked on it – maybe they still have the file for whatever reason.'

'Will do. I did manage to get MacLean's post-mortem report.' Mearns placed her hand on the manila file. 'That's in there too.'

'Good work. And?'

'Pretty tragic. Facts are Andrew was found hanging from the door in a flat he rented in the city centre. On his knees, naked and leaning forward. The tie he'd been wearing at work that day wrapped around his neck and the door handle. High levels of cocaine and alcohol in his system.'

'And everything pointed to him being alone?'

Mearns nodded. 'Single twenty-pound note on a tray by the bed and the remnants of coke beside it.'

'Same as Dean, at least with the single note and cocaine.'

'Yeah, and it appears he'd been drinking straight from a bottle of vodka.'

'Party for one?'

'Seems so, according to official findings.'

'And the unofficial line?'

'It's fair to say it was a shit storm at the time. Being the Shirriffses' son attracted a fair amount of attention from the media, plus who he was friends with. The connections he had. To be expected, I guess, especially when Claire Jenkins headed up the local reports.'

'And what did she have to say?'

'Formal finding was suicide. But the papers, Jenkins, hinted at all sorts. And not exactly subtle in her hints. Andrew being found the way he was, I guess it goes without saying.'

'Solo sex game gone wrong?'

'Yup.'

'Anything from Andrew's parents, Kirk and Patricia?'

'The father requesting understanding and privacy. Much the same from the mother, apart from saying she didn't believe the rumours, or that it was suicide. The standard thing that any parent says when they lose a child in such tragic circumstances.'

'Was it something Patricia tried to follow up?'

'No, not in anything I read. Appeared to be the only statement she made. Never repeated, even once the findings of his death were released.'

'Anyone come forward to support any of the speculation?'

'Jenkins had an "unnamed source" reveal details about how Andrew chose to spend his spare time. That he was often seen partying hard with Dean and Finn. A lot of things being said without actually being said.'

'Anything damning?'

'No. I think the press were fully aware of the clout these families have in the city. Any gossip seemed to be historic stories rather than current. Tales from school days, that sort of thing.'

'Interesting. Was this source an old school friend?'

'I think it's fair to say a school enemy. Didn't say much. Sort of that he wasn't surprised after some of the goings-on at school. He hinted at Andrew's love of the extreme, and I don't think he meant sports. Seems evident way back.'

'Identifying that source will be nigh impossible with Jenkins no longer with us.'

'Where do we start?'

Eve paused. 'We look up the Heritage School for Boys' yearbook.'

'Yearbook?'

'A school like that is bound to have one. Pictures of their esteemed soon-to-be alumni – with bullshit blurbs about their lifetime achievements.'

'You don't like private schools, do you?'

Eve didn't make eye contact. 'Not true. I don't like many of the things they stand for – or a lot of the people they spawn. But I don't have a problem with the schools as such.'

Mearns failed to cover her smile. 'Sure you don't.'

Eve tutted. 'Let's start with the yearbook, find out if we can get contacts for any of them now. We'll need to arrange a visit to the school itself too. Has Peter Miller called back?'

'Nope.'

'Chase that too. And keep looking for that file. Do a bit of digging.'

Mearns took it all on board. 'I guess I better tell Ferguson and the team to get our spades ready.'

Chapter 21

Mearns slammed down the phone. 'Something's not right.'

Ferguson's gaze fell to the phone receiver that had been crashed back into its cradle. 'I never would've guessed.'

'Second day running I've tried multiple times for Peter Miller, to be told by his PA that he's out on business again and not to be interrupted. Must be a hell of a busy guy not to be able to return a police call in the last twenty-four hours.'

'What about the son?'

'She doesn't have contact details for Finn, apparently.'

'I find that hard to believe. Is there not another way of contacting him?'

'Not that I can find. Appears to work for Daddy.'

Ferguson shuffled the paper on his desk. 'He does look like a daddy's boy, right enough.'

Mearns craned her neck and peered over at the piece of paper Ferguson was looking at. She made out the upside-down photo. One of the many Ferguson had printed off from the online Heritage yearbook. 'The question is whether Daddy is protecting him for some reason.'

Ferguson picked up the photo. 'You suspect Finn Miller had something to do with Dean's death?'

'No evidence to say he did, but the more they avoid talking, the more I'm thinking they've something to hide, or at least one of them has. In fact, I'm wondering if anyone linked to those three kids *doesn't* have something to hide.'

'Why?'

'I still haven't been able to track down the case file on Andrew Shirriffs's death. I did, however, manage to trace it back to the DI who worked the case, a DI Phil Crawford, and it so happens he's retired. Then there's Robert Johnstone; Eve wants to meet him again. And guess what?'

'Busy?'

'Yeah, also with a secretary guarding the gates.'

'You told Eve yet?'

Mearns hadn't, knowing how it was going to go down. 'I thought I'd save it for when she got back from Rosie's.'

Mearns hadn't had to look far for Rosie. The support worker had been happy to help.

Ferguson chewed at his lip. 'What about the Shirriffses?'

Mearns looked at the phone. 'Eve hasn't asked me to go there yet but I bet they'll be on the list at some point.'

Ferguson agreed. 'I guess it'll really start to stink if they happen to be just as busy.'

'For sure. In the meantime, I'll keep on trying. You never know, their secretaries might get sick of me and beg them to call back.'

Chapter 22

PETER MILLER AND ROBERT JOHNSTONE sat, silent, looking down on Aberdeen Harbour from the Torry Battery.

'I'm not sure he can be trusted.' The words were slow, quiet, the leather upholstery of the driver's seat creaking as Peter pushed back.

Robert sat rigid, staring at the sea and the city in the distance. 'Kirk wouldn't say anything. There's too much at stake.'

Peter searched his face. 'Maybe he's reached a stage where that's no longer of importance to him.'

Robert didn't turn. 'He has no proof the boys were there.'

'We still can't be sure that slut didn't tell him.'

'I don't think she would have done. This will have come from Patricia. She's never believed the story about Andrew's death.'

Peter's eyes bored into Robert. 'Is Patricia a problem?'

Robert paused. 'She's a good woman. But there's no doubt she's caused us trouble.'

Peter nodded once. 'Elena's death should've put an end to this.' He rested his forearm on the window, put his hand against the side of his head. Weary. 'These detectives are an issue. My secretary is being hassled around the clock for contact details for Finn.' His fingers pressed against his scalp. 'I never saw us being in over our heads like this. The press is sniffing about too.'

'I know. I've managed to avoid them so far. I always saw the day coming where we'd be in the shit. But you wouldn't listen. You never did. Yet you're the one left with a son.'

Peter tutted. 'Yeah, well, it's too late for all that. Too late long before any of this.' Peter turned towards Robert again, hesitated. 'Do you believe we would've been tight, no matter?'

'Friends? Life never let us find out.'

Regret was clear in Peter's tone as he answered: 'I guess not. Anyway, we have nothing to tell us it was the brothers.'

'We have nothing to say it wasn't. Who else, if not them?'

Robert said nothing at first, eyes directed forward in the dark. 'Have you considered Finn?'

Peter spun towards Robert, taking time to recover before answering, the shock at the betrayal in his tone. 'Think carefully about what you're saying. What you're asking.'

Robert turned towards Peter, eyes glinting in the darkness. 'I have. The question is clear. Do you think your son killed mine?'

Chapter 23

EVE LOOKED AROUND THE meagre bedsit and decided the place would be easier on the eye with a pair of sunglasses on.

Nothing matched. Anywhere.

But to Rosie it was home, something she hadn't known in a long time.

Eve struggled to take it all in. Everything was loud in colour or, worse still, floral. Some of it probably left by the landlord – disposable things they were willing to let out to a Department of Social Services tenant. Other pieces perhaps cobbled together out of donations from the local Shelter and Instant Neighbour charities, or the likes.

Rosie sat in the armchair in the corner of the room, feet tucked beneath her; she seemed relaxed. She wore leggings and a jumper, fluffy slippers on her feet. Looking like the young girl she was, compared to the heavily made-up one who had worn the skimpy top, miniskirt and heels the last time Eve had seen her.

'You're looking well.' Eve meant it. Rosie was almost unrecognizable from the year before. She sat across the room, next to Cooper.

'Thanks.' Rosie didn't smile, the old attitude still there, providing a safety blanket.

But, since escaping the clutches of a man who had kept her under lock and key and available for his every whim, brainwashing her into a kind of sick infatuation, and, after that, getting away from the pimp who had been working her, Rosie had put on weight. It suited her. The scabs and sores on her face and hands gone; fingernails that had been bitten to the skin now manicured. She'd started taking care of herself.

Eve wished Rosie had also managed to get out of the trade altogether, but at least she was doing it on her own terms and had a better chance of staying safe via contact with her worker. One step at a time and all that.

'Thank you for agreeing to see us.'

'I figured I owed you.'

Eve heard gratitude in her voice. She didn't draw attention to it. It would be as big a deal for Rosie to say it as it was for her to hear it.

'I'm glad you're doing well. As I said on the phone, we hoped you might be able to help us with a woman we've been unable to identify.'

'This the girl found up Hazlehead Woods?'

Eve wasn't surprised Rosie knew.

'Saw the mention in the paper. A lot of girls been talking about it, and some of the regulars.'

'Did anyone know her?'

'Hard to tell. Not much to go on when there's no name.'

'No one on the scene is missing?'

Rosie ran a thumb over her bottom lip. 'Nope. We would've heard about it.'

Eve took the post-mortem photograph out of her pocket. 'We've been unable to identify her. There were definitely signs on her body she may have been involved in the sex trade, as the rumour mill may have already got hold of.'

Eve went to pass the photograph to Rosie; then she stopped. 'It's not pretty but I'd appreciate if you would take a look, tell us if you recognize her.'

Rosie bent forward, took the photograph, moving her legs from beneath her. She put both feet on the floor and baulked at the photo. 'Shit.' She was keen to hand it back to Eve. 'I've not seen her before. A lot of these girls are private rentals – operating out of flats, taken to and from the client. A certain kind of clientele. She's Eastern European, I take it?'

Eve told Rosie what she knew. 'As far as we can tell. She had a tattoo on her wrist saying "Mum" in Romanian. And a barcode on her neck.' Eve kept details of the barcode to herself.

'Figures. Branding isn't uncommon with their lot. They've been pissing off a lot of the local girls. All these women coming in and taking our business. Regularly. Last month especially.'

'Why last month especially?' Cooper smoothed the throw that covered the sofa arm beside him.

'Offshore Europe. Biggest annual oil exhibition there is. Brings the money into Aberdeen from all over and a lot of these hotshots are looking for a little extra entertainment on the side. Used to be a huge earner for girls like me. It's difficult to get a look-in now. There're whole groups of girls being drafted in for it, and the guys running the show have their contacts to get the business.'

'Drafted in?' Eve understood there would be a lot of bad feeling on the local patch but had not appreciated exactly how much it affected the local girls' livelihood.

'Yeah. Loads of them are a permanent fixture in the city with ongoing business but they take in extras this time of year. Make sure all bases are being covered, if you know what I mean.'

'Have you ever heard of the Rusu brothers?'

No flicker of recognition. 'Nope, but it wouldn't surprise me if it were brothers running the show. Family ties run deep – even if you're sick fucks.'

Eve was in no doubt that sick would run in this particular family. 'The sad thing is these women would rather be doing anything else but what they're being forced to. For a lot of them it's not a choice, by any stretch of the imagination.'

'Maybe. Doesn't make it any easier for the girls losing business. Competition is competition, whether they're willing entrants or not.'

Eve couldn't dispute that.

Rosie folded her legs beneath her again. 'I doubt any of the girls I know would know her. As I said, she's probably a private rental. The best I can give you are places I know of where the girls might be set up in accommodation. You may already know.'

Cooper leaned forward. 'Not necessarily. Anything would help.'

Rosie pushed back into the chair. 'Airbnb has a lot to answer for. Cheap rentals and short-term options have led to a lot of pop-up brothels. But there're those who will buy property – a lot of the Romanians make a permanent base for these girls they're bringing into the UK. And a lot of the Eastern European set-ups tend to not stray far from the mini-markets.'

'Mini-markets?'

'Yeah, they tend to stick to their own cuisine, their own people. Cheap too. I know for a fact there are girls operating in the George Street and Summerhill areas, both with these markets nearby. I doubt it's co-incidence.'

'So, they keep themselves to themselves, apart from when it comes to clients?'

'Yeah. But that's not to say the Romanians don't like to make connections. They'll run their businesses online mostly but the big players try to muscle in on the local patch too. Get already established players here on board.'

'Established players?'

'People who have the means to grow their business. Accommodation rentals and ownership. Links to entertainment and the rich high-flyers.'

The likes of Peter Miller. Rosie wasn't telling them anything Eve hadn't already suspected. Only making it all the more real.

She pictured the mini-markets she knew of in the city. As good a place to start as any. Eve was aware of the two shops in the areas Rosie had mentioned. But she needed to know about all of them in the city. And fast.

Ferguson and the team would be getting a further break from tracking down the Heritage boys.

Chapter 24

MEARNS PUT DOWN THE phone and stretched back in her seat. 'Longest day ever. This is proving to be a bloody nightmare. I'll take looking up Aberdeen's mini-markets over trying to track down a load of ex-school pupils any day of the week.'

'How many pupils have you tried to contact now?' Ferguson sat opposite on the computer.

'Twenty. You?'

'Coming up to the same before I was tasked with finding these shops.'

'Can't be too many of them.'

'Not in the grand scheme of things. Think I've got them all. I've sent through details. Enough to be getting on with.'

'Cool, because I could do with you back helping with the school stuff.'

Ferguson groaned. 'I can hardly wait.'

Mearns smiled. 'I'll bet. Why's it so difficult to find someone Dean went to school with, or at least someone willing to speak?'

Ferguson picked up a pen, held it by its ends with his forefingers, elbows propped on the edge of the desk. 'Doesn't help that half of them have sodded off overseas with their fancy jobs. Private education served them well. Most of the last-known contact details for them in the city are bringing up jack-shit.'

'Same here. Two hits out of twenty and both of them said the same thing – weren't close friends, haven't stayed in touch. Which chimes with the total lack of response to the news of his death.'

'You think it's true?'

'Maybe. Although being the school it is, plus Andrew's death not long ago, wouldn't you have thought all that might've jogged their memories?'

'I guess . . .'

Mearns rubbed at her earlobe. 'Life's busy. As you say, a lot of them have left for high-flying jobs and success abroad. Folk like that are driven; maybe they look forward and rarely look back.'

'Maybe they don't look back for a reason.'

Eve stepped out of the Polski Sklep in Summerhill Shopping Centre, leaving the smell of raw meat behind, and walking into the aroma of hot dough wafting out from the Domino's next door instead.

'That was a waste of time.' She strode around the corner and through the dark alleyway that led to the car park. Cooper pocketed the picture they'd shown the guy behind the till.

'Where to next?' Cooper quickened his step to catch up with her as she sped past the glass front of Farm-foods, narrowly missing a dishevelled old guy who stepped from the shop rambling about the injustice of something or another. She didn't apologize as he swore and she made her way down the small cobbled embank-ment to the car.

Eve scrolled through the list Ferguson had sent. They'd already ticked off four places. 'One in Woodside.'

'It's getting late. Not sure what time they'll be open until.'

Eve glowered at him over the roof of the car.

'Woodside it is.'

Eve unlocked the door, climbed in and slammed it behind her.

The ring of the bell above as the door knocked against it echoed throughout the cramped, dark store.

Eve and Cooper stepped around each other as Cooper closed the door behind them; rows of shelves made three narrow aisles, immediately in front of them. Lights buzzed at the back of the store – Eve assumed it to be the chiller section. She took three steps sideways to the right and peeked around the end of the last aisle, locating the shop counter.

'Hello?' She had no doubt the sound of the bell would've alerted the owner to their arrival, but no one had appeared. She motioned Cooper to follow her to the counter, hearing a groan and shuffling from the curtain behind it as they approached. A hand appeared at the curtain's edge, pulling it back to reveal a young man.

'*Bună.*' He did his best to raise a smile but the bruising to his cheek and the deep cut to his top lip prevented it.

'Hello.' Eve did her best not to stare at his wounds. They looked fresh. He part-shuffled, part-limped to the counter, one forearm held tight against his ribs. Eve was reminded of a time not so long ago when she'd limped as badly, surprised every time she caught her reflection in a window or mirror that the woman staring back was her.

'Can I help?' The words were laboured and broken. Eve was unclear how much that was to do with a poor command of English and how much the pain he was clearly in.

'Yes. Can I ask your name?'

The man seemed surprised to be asked. 'Marius.'

'Marius. I'm DI Hunter.' She turned to Cooper. 'This is my colleague, DS Cooper.'

The man behind the counter rocked on his feet before straightening.

'You may have heard about a woman found dead at Hazlehead golf course. We're trying to find anyone who can help us identify her, who might've known her. Would you mind looking at a picture of her?'

Marius paled. 'I wouldn't know about someone found there.'

'I know it's a different area of town but we have reason to believe she may have made use of stores like this.'

Cooper placed the picture on the counter and slid it towards the man.

Marius didn't touch it, didn't even raise a finger to try to. His eyes flickered over the image, the Adam's apple in his throat bobbing against the hard swallow.

'I'm sorry. I don't know her.' His gaze didn't quite meet theirs as he spoke. He pushed the photograph back towards them.

Eve pressed her forefinger against the photograph, stopping it in its tracks. He lifted his hand, which almost touched hers, watched the photograph as she slid it back towards him.

'Are you sure?'

He looked past them towards the door. Something else in his eyes. Panic.

'Marius, are you sure? What if I told you she had a tattoo on her wrist that said "Mum" in Romanian?'

His eyes darted as his body moved, rocking on those heels again as if he wanted to step away from them. He tried to maintain eye contact.

'Can I ask how you got your injuries?'

Now Marius did step back from the counter. 'I'm sorry, I . . .'

'Don't worry. You're not in any trouble.'

'Shoplifters, earlier this morning.'

Eve wasn't buying it. 'Did you report it?'

He hesitated. 'I didn't see them. It was dark.'

'That shouldn't stop you reporting the incident. I hope you've had those injuries seen to, at least.'

Marius's silence continued.

'Have you ever heard of the Rusu brothers? Perhaps served them in here?'

A definite flicker as he shook his head – faster than his injuries were able to keep up with, if the grimace on his face was anything to go by.

Eve didn't press. 'I'm going to leave my card, in case you should hear anything, or even if you come up against any trouble in the dark again.' She placed her card on the counter.

Marius seemed keener to touch that than he had been the photograph. But as he hid it under the counter, it was maybe more to do with getting rid of it as quickly as possible.

'Thanks for your time.' Eve turned and headed towards the door, Cooper following.

She waited until the door had shut and they were clear of anyone on the shabby street. Happy to be out on it, with daylight and air. 'What's the bets he's on the phone to someone already?'

'My thoughts exactly.' Cooper once again placed the photograph in his inside pocket. 'He definitely knows something.'

'I'm not saying he has anything to do with it but I'm willing to bet those injuries are linked somehow. Maybe these Rusu brothers are a shot in the dark – they were a mere mention from Portman – but, going by Marius's reaction, my gut says not.'

'What're you going to do?'

'The question we need to be asking is what's *he* going to do.'

Chapter 25

Thursday

'I'M SORRY. ELENA'S DEAD.'

Andreea almost dropped the phone, barely awake and functioning before she'd taken the call.

'What?' Silence on the other end, Marius giving her space to process it. 'What happened?'

'I don't know.'

'How did you find out?' Andreea's voice almost a whisper.

'Police.'

She let hope creep in at the edges. 'The police? Has something happened with Bogdi and Vlad?'

'No. The police were here.'

'At the shop? Why didn't you tell me last night?' Hope was quickly replaced by panic.

'I didn't want to worry you or stop you sleeping. They had a photograph.' Marius sighed.

'How would they have got a pho—' Andreea stopped, realizing the answer to her own question.

'It was only of her head and shoulders but there was bruising . . . They mentioned her tattoo.'

Andreea closed her eyes, picturing the word on her friend's wrist; the times they'd wished life was simple once again, with their mums. Their families. But even as she yearned for her dead friend, for a life she once knew, something else pulled at her. 'Marius?'

'Yes?'

'What's wrong with your voice?'

A pause on the line, forced lightness to his tone. 'Nothing's wrong.'

'You sound different. Mumbling, as if something's wrong with your mouth.'

'Don't be silly. I'm in the shop. I don't want anyone hearing me.'

Andreea put a hand to her stomach. 'Marius. Please don't lie to me.'

Silence.

'Have Bogdi and Vlad been there? Have they hurt you?' Andreea looked at the carpet, tried to concentrate on the swirl of the pattern, not wanting to imagine what Marius might have gone through for her.

'I'm OK, baby.'

She began to cry. 'Are you hurt?'

'I'm a bit tender.'

'Did they come to the shop?'

'Yes.'

Andreea gasped, tears running down her cheeks. 'What did they say?'

'They asked if I'd seen you. I told them I had. That I knew you from the weekly shop, but you'd shopped and left.'

'Did they believe you?'

'Judging by the hit I took to my face and my ribs, my acting needs practice.'

Andreea heard the smile in his voice, teasing her, trying to make light of a horrific situation. She pictured his eyes, the soft curls that framed his face. Her breath caught as he spoke again.

'I told them nothing. Someone came along and they scarpered. I haven't seen them again.'

'What if they come back?'

'I'll deal with that as and when. The police know their surname.'

'How?'

'I don't know. I said I didn't know of them, but since the police have been making themselves known, and are aware I'm injured, it'll be too close a call for them to make a repeat visit.'

'OK. Please, be careful.' She swallowed. 'Did . . . Did Elena look bad?' She didn't know why she was asking. Death couldn't be made to look good.

'Looks like she was hanged.'

Andreea gasped. 'Hanged?'

'They never told me that. But the bruising around her neck . . . like some sort of rope had been there. I couldn't see any other injuries.'

'Why would they hang her?'

That wasn't the way the brothers disposed of those who had betrayed them or were no longer needed.

'Maybe they wanted it to look like she'd committed suicide.'

'I can't imagine them taking the chance of any slip-ups. No trace is usually left.' Marius was aware she didn't only mean forensics.

'Then the alternative is that she did do it.'

Andreea gripped the phone. 'No, she never would've done that.' The only other possibility played on her lips. She hesitated before saying it out loud. 'What if someone else killed her?'

Chapter 26

THAT WOMAN AND HER stick are gone. Lights off. Every girl in bed. El is tossing and turning in the bunk above me, and I know she has something to say, the way I do when she seems unsettled. I wait, giving her time to think how to say it, to make sure those closest are sleeping and no one else will hear. I don't have to wait long.

'Kid?' Little more than a whisper.

'Yeah?' I hear the bed springs creak above me, see El's long dark hair cascade over the bunk and into view, her face looking strange upside down in the little light there is.

'I have a secret.'

This is a new one. Hard to believe any secret could be kept in this place. I prop myself on my elbows, eager to hear what she's managed to keep to herself. 'What is it?'

'You promise not to tell?'

'Always.' And I mean it.

'I've met someone. People, in fact.'

My eyes widen in the dark. 'How? Where?'

She giggles softly, and I'm aware it's one of the first times she's acted her age. Carefree. 'That's not important. I want you to meet them too.'

I let my head fall back on to the pillow. A mix of excitement and terror flooding through my body. Already wondering if I'd dare. The thought of sneaking out. What would be out there waiting for us. But, even more, I think about the woman, the stick and the beating that would be here waiting if we were found out.

El whispers again. 'Aren't you going to ask who they are?'

I close my eyes, squeeze them tight, fighting against wanting to ask, knowing if I do I'm setting something in motion that I might not be able to stop. 'Who are they?' There. I've said it. Brave like El for once.

'Three boys.'

My heart is hammering. Boys. I've never known a boy who doesn't want to hurt me. 'Boys?'

El giggles again. 'Yes. They're rich and dreamy.'

El sounds like some princess in a book, as if she believes she's found her fairytale, the knight in shining armour who's going to save her. For the briefest of moments, I let myself believe it could be true. But only for the briefest of moments ... 'I can't. I—'

'Don't be scared, Kid. You know I'd never let anything happen to you. You don't have to do anything you don't want to do.'

I wonder what she means by that, but I don't want to know. It might burst the bubble El is trying to wrap around it.

A bubble and a fairytale that seem too good to be true. But, when I think of the alternative, I'm happy to be led by El. To climb inside and float away – up, up and away in that bubble.

Chapter 27

COOPER CREPT BACK INTO bed after leaving the room to read a text from Eve. Six a.m. and already time to go back into work.

He was dog-tired, almost jealous as he heard Louise snoring softly. But grateful she was getting rest and that she'd gone to bed rather than waiting for him last night. He couldn't stand to see the tiredness on her face, or the disappointment that, yet again, he hadn't been home to tuck the kids in. Enough guilt without that.

He lifted the edge of the duvet and attempted to get into bed quietly, wanting to be next to her for a bit longer – his body freezing as a bed spring creaked. Louise stirred, lying on her side and facing away from him. He shoogled across the mattress, snuggled in behind her and draped an arm over her waist. 'Sorry, honey, didn't mean to wake you.' He was surprised the kids weren't awake yet.

Louise mumbled, but didn't turn.

He pulled her closer to him, wanting the comfort, needing her to know he was there for her.

She placed a hand over his and he warmed at the gesture, until she pushed his arm away from her body.

'Too hot,' she muttered.

Cooper didn't answer as he turned on his back, eyes directed at the ceiling, the crack in the plaster above him visible in the glow from the hallway light. A view he was getting used to.

Eve pulled up parallel to the car parked kerbside outside Cooper's home. Blocking the road, not a space to be had in the crammed ex-council-estate street. It was still too early yet for the normal folks to have left for work.

Eve switched off the engine, the car still freezing after the five-minute drive from her place in Rosemount. Better to sit shivering than wake the neighbours, or Cooper's kids inside.

Light spilled from the kitchen window of her colleague's two-storeyed terraced home and out over the small patch of leaf-strewn grass. She imagined Cooper would be moving about behind the closed roller blind, attempting to leave the house unheard if the kids weren't already up.

The kitchen window disappeared into darkness, the front door opening seconds later. Cooper stepped out, dragging himself away from warmth and normality as he locked the door. His silhouette bobbed beneath the orange hue cast by the streetlight as he made his way down the path.

She straightened and started the car as the passenger door opened.

'Missing me or something?' Cooper got in and fastened his seatbelt.

Eve tutted, turned the heating up full and pulled away from his home. 'Hope I didn't wake Louise or the kids.'

'Hannah would sleep through a brass band. Hard to believe Nathan came from the same womb but he's still conked out. Louise too.'

'Bet I'm popular with the wife when she wakes to find you gone.'

'More popular than me.'

Not the usual jokey tone that accompanied such comments but now wasn't the time for marital confessions or counselling, not that she'd know the first thing about it even if it were. She turned to the windscreen, indicated left at the bottom of Cooper's road, bringing four-storey shabby tenements into view on Cairncry Road and the six roads roundabout. She signalled right on the approach to the roundabout and, within seconds, passed by Westburn Park en route to the city centre.

'As I said in my text, Mearns phoned late last night. She got a callback from one of the guys that used to go to school with Dean Johnstone.'

Cooper peered out of the window. 'What does the guy do for a living to have us out this early?'

'Social worker. He's appearing in court first thing this morning but offered to meet us for a coffee beforehand.'

'And do Mearns and Ferguson get to lie in their beds?'

'No. I've sent them to Miller's Hotel, hoping they catch Peter Miller before yet another incredibly busy day of his – given he's been far too run off his feet to return a phone call.'

Cooper chuckled. 'Nice. OK, but make sure that coffee of mine's a strong one.'

Chapter 28

ANDREEA SAT ON THE edge of the bed watching the slim grey-haired woman, Jean, who had shown her to the room yesterday, fuss with the window blinds.

'I hope you slept well. As I said, it's a shared bathroom and kitchen but the room is yours.'

Andreea didn't understand everything Jean was saying, but it was something about a toilet and kitchen. The woman appeared unaffected, unaware even, of the birthmark on Andreea's face. She'd most likely witnessed much worse working here. Andreea pulled the small rucksack on the bed towards her. She'd searched it out as soon as she woke and now placed it on her lap. She fingered the canvas drawstring fasteners as the woman spoke again.

'I know this is all strange. Take your time. I'll go and find you spare clothes and some toiletries now you're awake.'

Andreea didn't move. Jean repeated what she'd said but, this time, she pointed to her checked shirt and leggings, pretended to brush her teeth. Andreea wanted to cry at the woman's kindness.

She swallowed the lump in her throat and looked around her, daylight alien to her in a bedroom. A room with a single bed, not a bunk. Cream walls, clean sheets and a comfy pillow. No smell of sweat. In a house where she had no idea where she was.

Marius had taken her to his uncle's flat and called her a taxi. They cried as they stood on the pavement waiting for the car to arrive, clinging to one another. Andreea didn't want to let go. She pleaded for Marius to come with her, but he told her it was best she go alone, that the shelter would frown upon a male being there for fear of unsettling the other women. She eventually agreed, influenced by the disgruntled taxi driver growing tired of waiting.

She slumped in the back of the car, watching bustling streets, buildings and traffic flash past through the blur of tears as she clutched the small rucksack Marius had given her. Nothing out of the window was familiar to her. She had no knowledge of Aberdeen other than the block of flats she'd been kept in, and the walk to and from the shop.

She ignored the glances from the taxi driver in the rear-view mirror, grateful he made no attempt at conversation. She paid the fare with money Marius had given her, legs shaking as she stepped from the car, the taxi driver jabbing a chubby finger against the window towards the building she was looking for. Knowing only that the area was called Ferryhill.

The building resembled every other drab grey box on the street, except this one had a security system out front, and a buzzer around the back to gain entry.

They'd taken her in, no questions asked, but she expected they were still to come.

Andreea opened the rucksack, containing the velvet purse she knew well. There was also a small, dog-eared photograph of her and Marius she'd been too afraid to keep at the flat but he had given her, and a new pay-as-you-go mobile phone and charger that Marius had left his uncle's to get from the local supermarket. The only number in it was his.

She held the phone in her hand, desperate to hear his voice again. Being able to spend time with Marius had been the first time in her life she'd ever been grateful for the affliction on her face.

Bogdi and Vlad's intention to use her for cleaning the house, shopping and cooking for the girls had worked out well, even though they, or Daria, beat her regularly when they decided she wasn't doing enough.

They didn't mind not earning daily from her, not when she was useful in other ways. Having her at the house every night whilst the girls were out with punters meant someone there for security when they were not. They trusted her to be there. To report anything out of place – including the girls' movements – and she had to let the girls believe that would happen. If she didn't and they tried anything that broke the rules, she would be the one who received the most brutal beating.

Andreea had wrestled with guilt as the girls left one by one each day and night, a lot of them not hiding their resentment towards her – that she wasn't forced into doing what they were. Alone even amongst her own.

She'd thrown herself into ensuring things were comfortable for the girls. Making beds and washing sheets without being asked. Cooking the best meals, trying to provide variety from the weekly shopping list. She listened to them if they needed her to. Became whatever they needed her to be. And slowly their bitterness dissolved.

She was glad of that, and of the weekly half-hour of freedom when she was allowed to the mini-market. Especially because she got to see Marius.

She always made an effort on her visits. Not too much, nothing that would draw attention from the other girls. A clip in her hair, a smudge of gloss borrowed from Elena's make-up bag. She loved those half-hour windows of freedom with him, wanted desperately to stay longer, but knew better than to be late, to chance raising any suspicion. The threat always there, looming over her, that they'd stop her from going out.

He'd always told her he would help her. Promised for so long that he would get her out of there. But she wouldn't leave the other girls. Couldn't.

Being the only girl left in the house at night had its advantages. They began sneaking out to meet each other, feelings between them becoming stronger all the time. Both of them getting carried away. Not caring.

Until she missed a period.

She'd been terrified to tell him. Afraid what Bogdi and Vlad would do to her if they found out, or when she started to show. Sick at the thought Marius would reject her. Knowing for sure by the dates and the length of time since Bogdi or Vlad had last touched her that the baby was his. Instead he promised they would work it out, that they'd be together. He'd tell his uncle, who'd understand. He'd accept her, and the baby too. And she'd seen the truth in his eyes. But she also knew that Bogdi and Vlad would always be there. Hunting her down. Not willing to take the risk she would talk.

When she told Marius of Elena's plan, the one thing that would be sure to bring the brothers down and ensure all the girls were free, Marius supported it all the way. Like her, he believed it to be the only way out. The only way they could be together. Safe. With their child.

Andreea placed a hand on her stomach, the secret still hers and Marius's. Tears spilled down her cheeks as she thought about Elena, how she'd never see her friend again. She lived in constant fear Bogdi and Vlad would find out she'd known about Elena's plan, and would come for her.

She brushed her thumb across the phone screen, wanting to know Marius was at the shop and safe. Desperate to know if Bogdi and Vlad had been there again. But it was too dangerous whilst the shop was open, the risk they'd be there. She'd have to wait until tonight. When Marius was home at his uncle's, and alone in his bed.

She had to hope Marius would make it home. That he'd manage to return when Elena hadn't.

Chapter 29

DAVID CARNEGIE WAS A small man. He sat opposite Eve and Cooper in the lounge area of the Marriott Hotel in the city centre's Marischal Square. His muddy-brown piggy eyes peered out at them from behind thick horn-rimmed glasses, blond side-slicked hair looking wet beneath the overhead lights. He wore an immaculate navy suit, a white shirt and a large polka-dot bow tie which he fussed at and straightened, having done so several times since sitting down two minutes ago.

'Thanks for agreeing to meet with us, Mr Carnegie.'

'Please, call me David.' His voice soft, kind and most likely of great use in his job as a children's social worker. 'You'll have to excuse the formal attire. As I said to your colleague over the phone, I have a hearing first thing this morning.' He smiled. 'You'd usually find me in jeans and a T-shirt. I can't quite buy into the whole tie thing though.' He pointed at the bow tie, the multi-coloured spots reminding Eve of a circus clown.

Eve assumed the bow tie was for the benefit of the kids he would be meeting throughout the day. She looked sideways at Cooper. 'You look smart. I believe my colleague, DC Mearns, explained why we got in touch with you?'

'She did. But, as I said to her, I'm not sure how I can help if it's anything to with Dean's death? I haven't seen him since the day we left Heritage.'

'That's OK. We wanted to get more of a picture of who he was back then. We're finding it hard to get anyone who knew of him in recent years to talk.'

'I'm not surprised.'

Cooper clasped his hands between his legs. 'Why?'

David smoothed his hand against his thigh. 'The way he was at school. I can't say I'm sorry that I haven't seen him since.'

'I take it you guys weren't friends?'

'Friends?' David curled his lip. 'Definitely not. He was two years above me. He and the guys he ran with made my life hell back then.'

'They bullied you?' Cooper didn't have to ask the question.

David exhaled sharply. 'Me and anyone else they saw as fair game.'

Eve studied the man in front of her. She could easily imagine how someone like Dean might've tormented him. 'Who were the others that hung around with him?'

David's face looked as if it had all happened yesterday. 'Andrew Shirriffs and Finn Miller. The Trinity. At least that's what they were known as.'

Eve's mouth dropped open. 'The Trinity?'

'Yeah. Because there were three of them but I always thought more because they strutted about the place like some kind of gods.' David dropped his gaze to the glass coffee table dividing them. 'For me it began right from my first day. I was awarded a scholarship to attend Heritage. For my musical abilities. Violin. Add a council-estate kid to a scholarship and, well, you can imagine.'

'What happened?'

'Daily jibes, tripping me up in the corridors, stealing my bag. The usual. But things changed in my second year. They decided they wanted me to prove myself to them. Initiation. At least that's what they called it.' The memories appeared painful. 'They stripped me in the showers, tied my hands behind my back to the pipes and stuffed a bar of soap in my mouth.'

Both Eve and Cooper inhaled sharply.

'How old were you. Twelve?' Eve didn't hide the shock from her voice.

David avoided eye contact. 'Just thirteen. They made everyone stand there and watch as the water ran down my face and the soap bubbles ran down the back of my throat. They removed the soap when I started being sick but only because one of the other boys got vocal about it.'

Eve's voice was low. 'Did they let you go?'

'No. The soap got replaced with a gag.' David closed his eyes. 'And a girl was led into the shower stall.' He opened them again, focusing directly on Eve. 'Not a shy, scared girl. As bad as it sounds, I wish it had been. No, this was a woman used to providing a service, if you know what I mean.'

144

'A prostitute?' Cooper's voice rose in pitch.

David nodded. 'Finn stood there, the head of the Trinity, Dean and Andrew either side of him, and what seemed like the whole school filling the shower room. He said for me to be accepted into their group, which, roughly translated, meant they'd leave me the hell alone after that, I had to last a minute.'

Eve closed her eyes, knew where this was going.

'I had to stand there, watch her drop to her knees in the soapy water in front of me and let her touch me. Get me excited. I tried to close my eyes, to make all those people go away, to pretend it wasn't happening, but Dean stepped forward – ordered to by Finn – and forced my lids open. Told me he'd stand there holding them if he had to. I had to endure everyone laughing at me as she gave me a blow job.'

Eve struggled to find words. 'I'm sorry.'

David's Adam's apple bobbed, his voice cracking as he spoke. 'I'd never been . . . I'd never been intimate with anyone before that.'

How that experience must've affected him. How it must have shaped his life going forward.

David laughed, a brittle, hollow sound. 'Needless to say, I didn't last the minute. Stood there, naked and gagged as she moved back – when I couldn't stop it from happening – making sure the audience got a full view.'

Eve and Cooper sat stunned.

Eve broke the silence. 'How did they have access to prostitutes? They must have been, what, fifteen?'

David nodded. He hadn't fussed with his bow tie once during the whole sordid tale. Perhaps the nerves had gone now he'd shared the worst moment of his life. His voice croaked when he spoke again.

'Those boys had access to whatever they wanted. Rumour had it Finn's dad got him a prostitute for his birthday that year. I mean, what kind of father does that?'

Eve and Cooper had no answer.

David sat back. 'Anyway, that's my experience of them. I expect there are hundreds more stories from others. Of course, no one spoke about it, same as no one wants to talk about it now, by the sound of things.'

Eve was beginning to think the same thing.

David straightened. 'The worst thing was, it wasn't only the bullying of other students. It was the power the three of them had over the teachers. Disruption in class; blatant lack of respect in the corridors. Their ever-present influence over what went on in the school. And no one did a damn thing about it.'

Eve felt sick for the kids who had suffered. 'No one? Not even the head teacher?'

'Definitely not the head teacher.'

'Why?'

'The usual. Money. Their parents supported sports events, field trips, entertainment – all positive advertisements for the school. It paid to keep them onside and to shut up about the boys and their behaviour.'

'Why wouldn't the school expel them? Surely they could source their funds elsewhere? It is a private school, after all. Lots of strong links and families who can afford to splash the cash.'

'Maybe, but this was different. These were big players in the city. But it wasn't about that. It was about history.

Tradition. The way it often is. All those things that matter to the prats that run these schools.'

'What tradition?'

'Don't you get it? Family tradition. Their fathers were the Trinity before them. Most likely their grandfathers before them.'

'Peter Miller, Robert Johnstone and Kirk Shirriffs were the Trinity before their sons?'

'Exactly. Money and power handed down through the generations. Privilege that translated to exemption from real life's rules. Things that didn't seem to apply to them.'

'Surely the buck had to stop somewhere?' Eve was disgusted.

'Nope – and I learned that quickly. I may have been from council roots, but I had been brought up to respect others, to muck in when times were hard.'

David lifted the cup again, sipped, before laying it on the table. 'My experience of those people – materialistic and obsessed with greed and status – made me determined to help other kids like me. But once I started, I found all too often no one looks at the ones who do live in grandeur. The supposedly privileged ones.'

Eve studied him. 'What do you mean?'

David went to fuss at his bow tie but stopped. 'I help the kids living in squalid conditions. The ones the neighbours call in about after hearing the abuse being dished out – verbally or physically – through the walls. Those kids that are lucky enough, if that's even the word, for the schools to sit up and take notice of one too many bruises or breaks. And I manage to make myself feel better that at least I'm helping. At least I'm trying to do something.'

David wiped at his top lip. 'But I'm acutely aware of those rich kids. The ones whose suffering is never reported, whose neighbours turn a blind eye in the same fancy street, whose schools do everything they can to cover up anything that might harm their statistics.'

They all sat silent for a moment before Eve spoke. 'Is that why you agreed to see us today?'

David looked at her. 'People like that shouldn't get away with it.'

'No, they shouldn't.' The words sounded meaningless as Eve said them, but behind the statement they were looking at something much bigger than Dean's murder. Actions, past and present. Had those actions, the cruelty of these people who hid behind their power, resulted in Dean's death? Andrew's death? The possibility couldn't be ruled out, because it seemed there might be people out there who believed they'd had a price to pay.

Chapter 30

Dr Shetty's office felt as claustrophobic as ever. Impossible not to in a room beneath street level.

The basement. A space used in countless fictional and real-life horror stories. Being here was Eve's own nightmare. Pretty much the way she felt every time she came here, expected to bare her soul.

'It seems such a long time since our last session.' Dr Shetty put down the obligatory two mugs of coffee on the table that separated the two armchairs where they would sit for the next hour.

To Eve the time between her sessions here would never be long enough. Still, she was grateful for the small mercy that she now attended monthly, instead of weekly.

Dr Shetty lifted her mug. The rising steam fogged the gold-framed glasses that were perched on the end of her nose. She took a sip, cradled the mug in her hands, the condensation clearing enough to show huge brown eyes staring out at Eve. 'How have things been?'

Such a pointless question but one the doctor asked every time. Bound by confidentiality in her job, Eve couldn't relay case details and wouldn't want to. The fact her job was her life left little in the way of other 'things' to feel either way about.

'Fine.'

The stock answer Dr Shetty had come to expect. She showed no impatience or annoyance as she took another sip. 'It's coming up to a difficult time of year for you.'

Eve clenched her teeth. There was certainly nothing subtle about the doctor. 'Is it? I hadn't noticed.'

Dr Shetty smiled knowingly. 'Maybe. I guess that comes with being busy but, as much as you believe you're not aware, subconsciously you will be.'

Eve didn't comment on the psychobabble bollocks. Especially when she was acutely aware of what time of year fast approached – and struggling to believe it was.

If she was being honest, the way she was supposed to be in these meetings, she would admit she still hadn't found the answers, and it was debatable whether she ever would. She certainly didn't expect to find any solutions here.

'I guess on some level I am aware.' Eve held eye contact with the doctor, determined not to be read.

In truth, there'd been a time when she'd questioned whether she'd return to the job. Ironically, the worst events of her career, and that was saying something given her history, had shown she was capable of doing the job, had sealed her return to the force – if she wanted it. And she had wanted it. Eventually.

In fact, she'd craved it. She might still question her capabilities for the job but nothing compared to asking herself who she was without it.

Dr Shetty's look bored into her skin. 'I wanted us to try and visit that time.'

Eve stiffened.

'I'm not talking about reliving the events over those six weeks. I mean high level. In the sense of those you lost.'

'I'd say that's damn close to reliving things, wouldn't you?' Eve felt like a petulant kid.

'Would it be fair to say that, to a large extent, you already felt as if you'd lost Sanders before you did?'

She nodded once, not willing to give Dr Shetty any more.

The night her colleague had been injured, resulting in paralysis from the neck down, had definitely been a loss. A gut-wrenching one, to lose the woman who had been her friend and such a valued member of the force. But nothing compared to what Sanders had lost. Her job, her independence, her identity. All brutally ripped from her. And, ultimately, her life, because Eve hadn't managed to catch the bastard in time.

She accepted that. But not the need for Dr Shetty to pick apart her feelings. Her moods. Her actions. These sessions were purely to tick a box. For top-level management to keep their noses clean, making a show of following procedure – and Hastings's hands were tied. But Eve didn't appreciate her life being a box that needed to be ticked.

'OK. Let's say we ease in gently. How about you tell me if there's anything you want to share with me?'

Eve figured Dr Shetty already knew that answer. 'Not that I can think of.'

'How's the workload?'

'Manageable. The usual trying to put the pieces of the puzzle together.'

'And how's that working out?'

Eve fought not to tut. 'Not too well.'

'How so?'

'I can't go into much detail. Let's say it's the same old story. Men believing they have a God-given right over women.'

'Can you expand?'

Eve hadn't meant to say it. Hadn't thought of what it meant when she did. Realizing now that Dr Shetty was connecting dots, trying to draw a line back to her father, the man who had raped her mother.

'Nothing to expand on. Rich self-entitled dickheads and women too vulnerable to fight back.'

'Is their financial status important?'

Eve bristled, not comfortable with where this was going. The truth was that, no, it didn't matter. She had no idea whether her father had money or not. But he'd felt that same God-given right, and her mother hadn't been able to fight back. As the years passed, Eve's hatred and bitterness had grown, encompassing anyone who thought they had power over others, male or female, rich or not. Making others feel less. Not good enough. Unimportant. Something she'd felt all her life.

'Is money the problem?'

Eve blinked, back in the room. 'Sometimes. Let's say we're working on the jigsaw. There are days we're making progress, others it's like the box is missing a good few pieces.'

'And how does that make you feel?'

Jesus, she thought she'd moved them on. Did every statement have to be linked to an emotion? 'That it's my job to find them.'

Dr Shetty shifted in her armchair, smoothing her long pleated skirt as she crossed her legs. 'And what about the other things missing from your life?'

'What, like good food, a decent TV or the time to watch it?'

The doctor said nothing. Waited.

'Look, this is no reflection on you or your job, but we both know I find all this to be a load of bullshit.'

'I appreciate your honesty.' A smile on the doctor's lips.

Eve's temples pulsed at the doc's sing-song voice and patronizing tone. 'Not everything has to be boxed and labelled. Shit happens. To us all. People deal with it. Without coming to something like this. I would do the same, if management didn't make this compulsory.'

'That's the thing. You do have to come here and it's my job to make sure you keep yours.'

Nothing threatening in the statement. It just irritated Eve that it was true. She grasped the arms of the chair, releasing her fingers too late as she saw the doc clocking the movement.

Eve tried to calm herself, feeling as if she was being held hostage. 'Other things missing from my life?' She knew she sounded tense. *Goddammit.*

Dr Shetty didn't answer. Annoying Eve further. But there was no point in refusing to answer. The doctor's report would reflect her resistance and Hastings would make something out of nothing.

'You want me to talk about my so-called father? About colleagues I've lost?' Attitude clear. Eve fighting to hide it.

'It's good you're willing to admit they are under the surface when I ask about things missing. That you'd do that.'

Bullshit. Eve did tut this time. 'I wouldn't exactly say I'm willing or admitting anything. We both know I'm acutely aware of the loss of my colleagues. I don't have to voice that here or anywhere else to feel it. As for my father, he's not worth my breath.'

'Perhaps not talking about them is affecting you more than you realize.'

Eve wanted the doctor to cut the crap. Her hands tightened on the chair again.

The doctor looked down at the chair. 'How's the temper?'

Chapter 31

'HEY.' MEARNS TRIED TO sound as bright as possible down the phone, knowing Eve would be in a foul mood. She heard traffic in the background, pictured Eve striding down the street.

'What you got? Any luck with Miller?' The growl in Eve's voice was clear above the din.

'Eh, I hope it went OK.' Mearns was met with frosty silence. Wrong thing to say. She grappled with a replacement. 'The meeting with David Carnegie, I mean.'

Eve's reply was clipped. 'Yeah, an eye-opener. I'll tell you about it later.'

Eve's reluctance to talk would be as much about getting her thoughts in order after the counselling session as it was about confidentiality as she walked down a public street.

Mearns answered Eve's original question. 'Ferguson and I turned up at Miller's at eight thirty a.m. to be told he was out on business. We refused to leave until the receptionist phoned his mobile. It went through to voicemail. She eventually gave us the number but we are getting the same.'

'What the hell is he playing at?'

'Beats me. Anyway, I got hold of the school since we've not had much joy with talking to actual ex-pupils other than Carnegie.'

'Good work. Not sure how much it'll help though. I mean, are any of the same teachers even still there?'

'Better than that. Same head teacher.'

'Did he have dealings with Dean?'

'That's a definite.'

'Why?'

'It appears they like to keep things close.'

'Close? In what way?'

'As in within the family.'

'Mearns, is it a slow day at the office or something? Spit it out, will you?'

'OK, OK. Let me enjoy the small finds. So, the current headmaster is a Mr William Henderson but the headmaster before *him* was none other than Dean Johnstone's grandfather.'

'You're joking.'

'Even better, the actual founder of Heritage was Dean's great-grandfather.'

'Bloody hell. Now I know why they were untouchable.'

'Eh?'

'Nothing, something David Carnegie said. I'll fill you in later. Anyway, how did you find out about the family connection?'

'I read a blurb about the history of the place, thought I'd do a quick search on the founder. Kind of fell down a rabbit hole reading about his family – daughters, granddaughters. Turns out it was worth it though, as one of them ended up marrying none other than Robert Johnstone.'

'Interesting.'

'Anyway, what about the current headmaster?'

'They definitely like to keep things close. Mr Henderson was at school with Dean's father.'

'He was at school with Robert Johnstone?'

'Yeah, and Kirk Shirriffs and Peter Miller were in the same year.'

What David Carnegie had told them, about the clout Dean and his friends had, all clicked into place. Their interest in kink and their use of girls even back then. Had their fathers been the same? Were they now?

Eve was breathless not only with the brisk walk to her car, but also with so many revelations in one phone call. 'It's fair to say my eyes are well and truly opened. When can we get into the school to meet with this headmaster?'

'I've arranged for you and Cooper to go tonight.'

Eve remembered her earlier chat with Cooper, the suspicion that things weren't too rosy for him at home at the moment. 'Listen, it was your breakthrough. How about you join me tonight?'

Chapter 32

HERITAGE SCHOOL FOR BOYS wasn't visible from the road. Nestled in lush greenery on the outskirts of Aberdeen, the only sign it was there as you drove past were two large granite and brick pillars that interrupted the hedgerow, bold black lettering reaching up in a metal-arched frame from one pillar to the other, creating a sombre rainbow above the road between them.

'Shit.' Eve braked, checked her rear-view mirror and reversed. Quickly. The winding country road didn't lend itself to such a manoeuvre. She indicated right, for no one in particular, and turned off South Deeside Road.

'La-dee-dah.' Mearns admired the manicured lawns either side of the speed-bumped road as they left the pillars behind. Orange, brown, yellow-leaved trees as far as the eye could see.

'Wouldn't fancy the janitor's job here.' Eve checked the dashboard, sticking to the designated ten m.p.h., the road stretching into the distance before the school finally came into view. 'La-dee-dah, indeed. Holy shit.'

Mearns crouched beneath her visor, looking up at the turrets perched upon the building's edges, which appeared to scrape the sky. She looked at the central console as Eve's phone rang.

Eve was still taking in the surroundings through the windscreen. 'Get that, will you?'

Mearns picked up and answered the mobile. She listened, saying little, Eve not sure what was going on, and then hung up.

'Well?'

'HQ call handler. Took a call from a taxi driver.'

'About what?'

'A woman he saw who seemed distressed. Running.'

'And why call me?'

Mearns turned. 'He's calling on the back of the information released about Jane Doe.'

Eve's head whipped round. 'You're kidding me.'

'He's available to meet tomorrow.'

Eve saw the main entrance as the long drive finally came to an end.

A lone figure stepped into view at the top of the stone steps that led to yet more pillars and a rather grand double door, one side open.

Mr Henderson had been more than affable when they'd called earlier, and it seemed he wanted to make sure they felt welcome.

'I guess we get on with this for now.' Eve let the car roll from the road on to the gravel car park, crunching to a stop. The headmaster was waiting at the bottom of the leaf-strewn steps by the time they got out. He lifted his hand as they approached and smiled as he shook both of their hands. Eve noticed the gesture didn't quite reach his eyes.

'Find us OK?'

Eve answered. 'Yes. Some grounds you have here.'

'Thank you.' He spread his arm wide and motioned to the steps. 'Please, be my guest.'

Eve made her way up the stairs to the doors, Mearns by her side. If Eve didn't know better, she would've thought they were about to enter a luxury spa, not a school.

The busy entrance hall was vast, sweeping staircases either side, a reception desk straight in front which dominated the space. Eve imagined the boys who would grace the space during the day. Looking like clones in identical tailored blazers, pressed trousers, polished shoes and sharp haircuts. Their chatter would be low. Nothing like Eve's old school where the kids wore an approximate version of the school uniform or none at all. Piercings, coloured hair, graffitied school bags marking those who wanted to stand out from the crowd. The noise in any part of the school deafening. Here, you probably strived to be part of the crowd.

'Please, follow me.' Mr Henderson turned right, heading for a doorway at the foot of the staircase that led into a wide bright corridor with rows of over-sized gold-framed portraits interrupted by huge windows giving stunning views over the grounds. He strode along it.

Eve clocked the portraits as she went by them, slowing and nudging Mearns as she passed a familiar face in one of them. Eventually they were led into a smaller hall, a gold nameplate on a wide mahogany door marking the headmaster's office.

'In here.'

The office was cluttered and smelled stale. Old books lined two walls as well as countless others balanced on every available surface. A window the same size as those in the hallway rose behind the large desk Mr Henderson sat at. Eve and Mearns took the two seats in front.

'How can I help?'

A surprising question given they had called in advance stating the reason for their visit. She'd even offered her condolences for Dean Johnstone's death. Mr Henderson was acting like a different man from their earlier telephone conversation.

'As I said, we'd like you to help us build a better picture of who Dean Johnstone was. The dynamic between him and the boys he was friends with during his time here.'

Mr Henderson shifted in his chair. 'I'm sure you're aware it has been some time since Dean was a pupil of this school. I can't see why it—'

'That's strange, Mr Henderson, as you seemed to fully understand how it might help us when we spoke earlier today,' Mearns commented.

The headmaster's face reddened. 'Yes, well, I've had time to think about exactly what I can tell you and I doubt it would help your investigation.'

Eve stared at Mr Henderson and thought about the portrait in the hallway. She was willing to bet he'd since

161

spoken with someone who had told him what he was allowed to tell them.

'I believe you were a student here at the same time as Dean Johnstone's father? The same year, in fact?'

'Yes . . .'

'It seems Mr Johnstone is held in high regard here, going by the fact his portrait hangs in one of the school hallways.'

'Robert Johnstone was a high achiever here.'

'And a good friend?'

'He had time for everyone.'

Eve was in no doubt the same would be said about his son. David Carnegie, stripped in the shower rooms in front of a baying audience and forced to stand there whilst a prostitute performed oral sex on him, had certainly been given plenty of Dean's time.

'And what about Peter Miller?'

'Peter? Also a high achiever and generous with his time.'

'Quite. I'm sure he has a portrait here too.' Eve paused as Mr Henderson fussed at his tie. 'Does Kirk Shirriffs?'

'Inspector, I'm not sure what you're driving at. Or what this has to do with Dean Johnstone's death?'

'Apologies. Perhaps I should explain a little more clearly. Maybe it would help if I told you about the Trinity?'

Mr Henderson's face coloured as if the room had got four shades hotter. 'You don't have to tell me about the Trinity. I'm aware it was the term bandied about for the friendship between Peter, Robert and Kirk, but, I assure you, it was a thing of positivity and a great presence within the school.'

'I'm sure it was. Especially with Dean Johnstone being the great-grandson of the founder of Heritage.'

'How did you—?'

Mearns cut in. 'I believe it was a term also "bandied about", as you say, for their three sons, who followed them into this school?'

'Yes, but not a term their sons exploited. Finn, Dean and Andrew were typical of how things are at Heritage. Generations of the same family are educated here. Other boys in the same year as them would've heard of their parents through their own fathers, who I expect would've told them of the Trinity. The use of the same term by the next generation would've been a case of respect.'

'Yes, and it appears in Robert Johnstone's case they definitely kept things in the family and its generations. I'm surprised he didn't keep more of an active role in the school. That he's not in your role.'

'Robert excelled in engineering and wanted to follow that. As I'm sure you know, he's done well in the field.'

'Yes, a high achiever in his career as well as his school years.'

'For sure, and he still has an active role within the school. He's on the board. His company sponsors a lot of our events.'

Mearns took over the questioning. 'Are Peter Miller and Kirk Shirriffs also on the school board?'

'Yes. They were keen to give back to the establishment that had given them much in the way of preparing for life.'

'Of course. Look where it's got them – Kirk Shirriffs running a chain of restaurants within the city and Peter Miller . . . well, Mr Miller entertains the city.'

Mr Henderson seemed to relax a little now they were on positive ground. 'Peter liked a good time. He had a knack for organizing events within the school and getting the backing to make them a success. It wasn't his chosen path, but he developed a love for it and had a vision for how his skills could be used to enhance the city and, of course, be a money-spinner for him.'

'He is indeed spinning a lot of money these days,' Eve remarked.

Mr Henderson didn't show if he was bothered by the comment. 'Quite, and I guess you could say Kirk followed in his footsteps in a way. Still providing an entertainment of sorts to the community with his fine dining. All skills that have lent themselves to the school and the wider community. They are well respected in both.'

'And I assume the original Trinity must've had a lot of respect for you, what with you being given this role?'

Mr Henderson's eye twitched. 'I wasn't given this role. I applied like everyone else.' The edge was back in his tone.

'Apologies. Of course you applied, and I'm sure you got the job fairly. Do you know if there were applicants who *weren't* ex-pupils of the school?' Eve said innocently.

'I wouldn't know.'

'Perhaps not. I guess that's something Robert Johnstone *would* know, what with him being on the school board?'

'Why would it even matter?'

'I guess I'm exploring how close they like to keep people they know and trust.'

'Isn't that the case for anyone?'

'You could say that. Questionable if you don't ever let anyone else in, though.'

'What is that supposed to mean?'

'It's not supposed to mean anything. It's a fact. Two young men are dead within a year of each other and the one left behind is being guarded around the clock by his father.'

Mr Henderson flinched. 'Wouldn't . . . wouldn't you be doing the same if your son had gone through the trauma of losing his two closest friends?'

'I'm sure I would be. I'm not sure that would include keeping him away from talking to the police. Though that seems to be common behaviour amongst anyone linked to the boys.'

Mearns was staring at her.

'Inspector, you have to understand that the nature of Andrew's death and the surrounding gossip and hearsay made us all protective of those boys. Protective of the school and its reputation. Of the generations who have invested heavily in making the name for it that they have.'

'I'm sorry for that, but in order to catch Dean's killer, we need to know everything about him, the good and the bad, so we can identify whether he had any potential enemies. Judging by what we've learned about the so-called Trinity, it's as if you're purposely obstructing us from finding the truth about what they used to get up to.'

'I take offence at such a claim. I'm sure they have no wish to hide anything I'd—'

Eve interrupted. 'You mean "he". There's only one of the recent Trinity left.'

'Quite. I'd be interested to find out who it was that spoke with you?'

Eve wouldn't be giving that away any time soon. 'I'm afraid we won't be able to share that information.'

'I'm not sure why it has to be kept a secret. Regardless, certainly as a school we are an open book and proud of our former and current students, irrespective of their struggles or, dare I say, failures in life.'

'To be commended.' Eve let the sarcasm drip.

Mr Henderson seemed unaware. 'Yes. In fact, we are having an evening in memory of the two boys. Saturday week. It will coincide with our centenary, which I'm sure you agree will be fitting. Ex-pupils and teachers, parents, members of the wider community.'

'Members of the wider community?'

'Yes, those who have supported the school over the years. Providing sponsorship, work placements for leavers, employment.'

Eve was willing to bet there would be no ex-Heritage boys on the police employee roll. And no link between Police Scotland and the school. So there definitely wouldn't be an invite in the post for her, or Mearns. But she wasn't afraid to crash a party.

Chapter 33

Friday

JIM MILNE LIVED IN a one-bedroom maisonette in Cove and looked as if he'd lived in it thirty years too long. With a greying comb-over to rival a 1980s Arthur Scargill, teamed with grey flannel trousers and a chunky knit cardigan, he bucked the trend of the single twenty-something Eve had imagined would live in this type of home.

'Thanks for phoning in.' Cooper spoke to Mr Milne from the two-seater sofa where he sat next to Eve.

The man carried two mugs of tea out of the box-sized galley kitchen, a slight shake to his hands. Mr Milne had to duck a little as he passed beneath the winding stairwell that led to the bedroom and bathroom upstairs but also took up a large part of the downstairs living room.

Cooper took the cup being offered to him and rested it on his lap. Eve had declined.

Mr Milne stepped over to the remaining seat in the room: a cheap-looking recliner; there was little space for much else apart from a low unit that housed the telly. 'Hope you didn't have too much bother finding me.' He sat.

'It's a bit of a maze. The taxi in the driveway gave it away,' Cooper said heartily.

'Of course.'

Eve coughed, bringing the conversation back on track. 'I know you made a statement over the phone, but could you tell us again what you saw?'

'Sure.' Mr Milne took a sip of his tea and cradled it in his hands. 'I was on shift, would've been about twelve thirty a.m. Sunday into Monday.' He leaned forward and put his cup on the floor, the waiting coaster signalling this as his regular seat. 'I was driving down North Anderson Drive when I saw a woman.'

Eve nodded. 'Did anything in particular make you notice her?'

'She was running. Across the opposite side of the dualler. Nothing unusual in that as it was pouring with rain. At least I didn't think it was at first.'

Cooper ran his finger around the edge of his cup. 'Did you stop?'

'No, but I had to brake as I thought she wasn't going to.'

Eve's mind worked overtime. *What had made this woman run so fast?* 'Did she see you?'

'Yeah, she stopped on the central reservation, briefly, to let me pass before she was off again.' Mr Milne stared at the floor as if he were seeing everything that night again.

'Did you see her face?'

He looked up at Eve. 'Yes. My headlights were on her on the central reservation as I approached. After I passed her, I couldn't get her face out of my mind. Even days later. I needed to say something.'

'Why?' Eve asked, even though she guessed what he'd say.

'She looked petrified.'

Cooper took a hand from his mug and rested it on the arm of the sofa. 'Did she not try to flag you down?'

'No. But I feel guilty for not stopping anyway.'

Cooper pushed a little more. 'Kind of doesn't make sense, does it? If you're scared and running and you spot a taxi, surely you'd be begging for it to stop?'

'You'd think. But I didn't see any sign of anyone chasing her either. Even once past her, I had to stop at the roundabout for a car and when I looked in my rear-view mirror she was darting across the other side of the dualler.'

Eve wanted specifics. 'Whereabouts on North Anderson Drive were you?'

'The roundabout where the old Egg and Dart pub used to be.'

Eve's heart skipped. 'Did you see what she was wearing?'

'A short, tight-looking black dress.'

Eve uncrossed her legs. 'Are you sure?'

The taxi driver didn't hesitate. 'Positive. I remember thinking it was an odd thing to be wearing in the rain.'

Eve looked at Cooper. 'Would you remember it if you saw it?'

'I . . . I think so.'

They needed a firmer answer. 'You can't be sure?'

'It was dark, and only a matter of seconds that I saw her. If anything, it's more the shoes I remembered.'

'The shoes?' Eve didn't imagine shoes were something men normally noticed. Not within seconds of seeing someone. Unless that's what they were into, of course. Maybe Mr Milne here had a foot fetish.

'Yes. Purely because they weren't on her feet.'

Eve's mouth went dry, those small feet on the morgue table clear in her mind. Caked in dirt, bloody cuts to the soles even though she'd been found with her shoes on. 'Where were her shoes, Mr Milne?'

'She was clutching them in her hands. They were a dark colour with straps of some kind hanging from them.'

'Did you notice where she came from?' Eve's mind whirred, trying to work out where the woman might've gone.

'Yes, I was coming over the brow of the hill of Rubislaw when I caught sight of her. She came bolting around the corner from Queen's Road.'

'And when you checked your rear-view mirror, did you see where she went?'

'Up the Drive. Away from the roundabout.'

Eve pictured the other side of the dual carriageway. Houses. Big houses. Rubislaw Den, also described in the property pages of the local press as Millionaire's Row. Where was she running to – or whom?

'Can I ask why it took you so long to report the incident?'

Mr Milne opened his palms skyward on his lap. 'Because at first it didn't seem to fit.'

'Why?'

'Because of where she was found.'

'But you changed your mind?'

'Yeah, when I heard more about the woman found hanged. I've no idea if it's related or not but, like I said, I couldn't get it out of my head. I didn't want to think I hadn't said anything when it might be that same girl.'

Eve reached inside her jacket pocket.

'I want to show you a photograph we have of the dress that girl was wearing. Would you be willing to take a look?'

'Of course.'

Eve passed the photo across, searched his face for a reaction. She didn't have to wait long.

The shake in his hand got worse as he studied the photograph. 'Yes, that's the dress.'

Eve took the picture, reached inside her pocket again. 'Mr Milne, we have a picture here of the woman that we found. I'd like to warn you it was taken in the morgue. Would you be willing to look at it for us, see if you recognize her?'

Mr Milne sat silent as Eve passed the second picture across.

Those shaking hands again – no need for him to speak as the single tear ran down his cheek.

Eve let the taxi driver have his moment, wondering if Cooper was experiencing the same realization she was: that Dean Johnstone's flat was around the corner from the direction Jane Doe had been running from.

Chapter 34

EVE POINTED THE REMOTE control towards the television screen the four of them were huddled around and pressed pause.

'So, we have our confirmation.' Jane Doe's image stared out at them, the black tube dress and shoes clear on the footage they'd lifted from the taxi's dashboard cam. Eve swallowed. It was difficult seeing the woman in life against how she'd been on that morgue table.

Cooper pointed to the top right corner of the screen. 'Captured at twelve thirty-three a.m. Sunday into Monday, exactly as the taxi driver said.'

Eve bubbled with excitement. 'I've sent a copy of this through to the press office and told them we need this out in the press and local news as a matter of urgency. Last-ditch attempt to ID her as nothing else seems to be working.'

Eve turned as Mearns's mobile phone pinged. Her colleague stretched back from the television to reach the table behind her, lifted her phone and read the message. Mearns growled in frustration, slammed the phone back on the desk and turned around again with a face like thunder.

Ferguson stared at her. 'As bad as that?'

'My bloody parents have decided to descend unannounced. Right now, they're checking in to the Marcliffe and asking if they can pop by tonight.'

Eve knew little about Mearns's parents, other than what she'd gathered from the small titbits she'd dropped. Mearns had a rather strained relationship with her father, who hadn't approved of her career choice and decision to move to Aberdeen. He'd wanted his only daughter to follow him into the oil industry.

Ferguson grinned. 'As your regular chauffeur to and from work, I reckon I should get to escort you in and meet them. Since you never tell me much about yourself before coming here.'

Mearns didn't hide the distaste in her reply. 'Ferguson, it's a lift. Nothing more. Certainly doesn't grant you access to my home and, believe me, you don't want to be bombarded by my parents and their woe at their only child leaving the nest.'

Eve interrupted. 'Doesn't your father work in oil?'

'Yes, why?'

'Is there any chance he would have been to any Offshore Europe events? Maybe he came across Peter Miller, in light of what Rosie told us.'

Mearns pinched her bottom lip. 'I guess he might have. I can ask him if you'd like.'

Eve nodded. 'Not outright. Maybe see if you can get a feel for things. We need to take a further look into Peter

Miller's presence in the city. His businesses, and the properties he owns.'

Mearns snapped to attention. 'I'll get on to Companies House. See what I can find.'

'Good idea.' Eve rubbed at her eyes, frustration and tiredness weighing heavily on her, trying to assess what else they should be looking at. 'Any update on the two people in the car that the kids at the golf club mentioned?'

Ferguson looked at the image of their Jane Doe still up on the screen. 'Nope, no CCTV, no other sightings. Might as well have not existed.'

Eve was getting pissed off with the lack of progress and the fact people who might be able to help her appeared to want to remain as non-existent as the couple at the golf club. 'I need to see Robert Johnstone again. Maybe the way to do that is to turn up at his work and stay until he has to talk. Ask him about our Jane Doe.'

Cooper coughed. 'I'm looking forward to that.'

Eve didn't smile. 'Mearns, I know you have your folks tonight, but if you and Ferguson keep trying for Miller too. Up the pressure. Demand it, if you need to. And not a phone call. One-to-one. If I have to do the same and turn up unannounced, I will.'

Ferguson tutted. 'I'm wondering if the guy is actually still alive, so you're not asking much.'

Eve shrugged. 'You have to earn your keep somehow. Meantime, I've asked for our Jane Doe's prints to be checked against the ones found on the ornament at Dean Johnstone's flat. We should hear back pretty quick.'

Ferguson spoke. 'What if they match?'

'Something tells me it's going to be a case of *when* they match. And when they do, and we can place her there for sure, the question will be whether it's possible our Jane Doe killed Dean Johnstone.'

Chapter 35

'IT'S CERTAINLY COMPACT.' Mearns's father made an exaggerated show of exiting the bathroom of her flat. She ignored the comment and let him help himself to one of the coffees off the tray she was clutching as she made her way through to the living room from the galley kitchen. To think she'd rushed home for this.

Mearns nudged her foot against the bottom of the living-room door and walked in, her father right behind her. Her mother sat upright on the sofa, laughing and looking as if she was enjoying Ferguson's company a little too much. Ferguson. Who had feigned surprise at her parents standing outside her flat door as he pulled up in the car. The megawatt smile charming her mother and leading to an invitation inside. Mearns passed her a coffee.

'Thanks, dear.'

She gave the last coffee to Ferguson, whose amusement hadn't yet faded, and slid the tray down the side of the sofa before perching on the arm. Her father surveyed the room, a look of disgust on his face at the remaining chair in the room taken up by dirty clothes she hadn't got around to moving. Ferguson was grinning like a loon as she stood, bunching the dirty clothes in a ball and moving them on to the floor so her father could sit.

She ignored her father's look of despair as she spoke. 'How long are you here for?'

'Trying to get rid of us already?'

'No, Dad.' Mearns wasn't in the mood for her father's constant ribbing and negativity. She hated the way that, within five minutes of being in his company, she was transported back to her childhood. Hated that Ferguson was here to witness it.

Her mum must've sensed the tension. 'How're you settling in, dear?'

It had been almost a year since she'd moved, but with her parents living abroad, time seemed to disappear in between visits.

'OK. I like how central it is.' She'd bought a one-bedroom flat in Holburn, a ten-minute walk from the city centre but with its own shops, pubs and entertainment nearby. A fair comedown from the executive penthouse she'd previously lived in at the Bastille, an old converted factory that was a boastful attraction for the city when newly done. Not something she could've ever afforded on her own.

Her parents had bought it to 'keep her safe', which loosely translated meant they still had a little control over her life once she'd upped sticks and transferred from the force in Bolton. Their belief the flat would keep her safe when she faced the danger she did every day in the job had been ironic to say the least. Especially when she'd nearly died at the hands of a serial killer in her own home.

Her dad tilted his head to the ceiling as her neighbour announced her arrival home from work. 'What the hell is that?'

'That is Chloe. A penchant for high heels and a total disregard for the fact she has wooden flooring.'

'I wouldn't be putting up with that.' Her father shuffled to the edge of the sofa. 'Let me go speak to her.'

Mearns stopped herself from snapping. 'I'm more than capable myself. I've got used to it. To be honest, I like hearing it.'

'It would drive me insane.'

Mearns studied her father. 'Actually, it's silence that drives me mad.'

Her father sat back, his glare softening as he realized what his daughter meant. More than likely reliving what he'd been told about her time alone in that flat with a madman. And she'd told him the soft version.

Ferguson was no longer grinning.

Her dad put his coffee mug on the floor, clapped both thighs with his hands, 'Anyway. We're here for a week. The Marcliffe is lovely, you know, now you don't have the space.'

He couldn't help himself.

'Your mother and I are looking at a couple of rentals. Possible business opportunities.'

'Dad, don't you earn enough?' Her father ran a successful pipe business, supplying to the offshore industry.

'Sure, I do, day to day, but your mother and I aren't getting any younger. We have our retirement fund to consider.'

Her parents were loaded. Her father was simply incapable of doing nothing. Moving into property was the perfect way to keep his hand in once he did shut up shop.

'Why Aberdeen?'

'European oil capital. Professionals come here from all over the world. And when it comes to Offshore Europe you can make an absolute killing in rentals.'

Mearns looked at Ferguson at the mention of Offshore Europe, so timely with what Eve had said earlier. Her father was right about the rentals. She'd heard of folk moving out of their homes and in with friends and family to get the sky-high rental fees that came in the days before, during and after that one week.

She tried not to look overly keen. 'Have you ever been to it?'

'God, yes. Vital when I was trying to get the business off the ground.'

Ferguson was staring at her.

'I presume it's a bunch of stuffy businessmen selling their services?' She was aware of confidentiality in her job, regardless of the fact she was talking to her parents.

'A lot of them, yeah, but once the drinks are flowing even the worst ones can be known to loosen their collars.'

'I take it any entertainment laid on is in-house?'

'What, within the exhibition centre?'

179

'Yeah.'

'Christ, no. Don't get me wrong, you won't struggle for a drink there, but some of the best dos are back in the city centre.'

Mearns already knew that to be the case from her online searches after meeting with Eve earlier. Historic Facebook images and listings from well-known cocktail bars in the city advertising parties to coincide with the global event. A big money-earner and anyone worth their salt in the entertainment business locally would be making the most of it.

'Did you ever go to any of the events?'

'Why're you interested?'

'You're so suspicious. It's conversation. You brought Offshore Europe up.'

'Yeah, I did as a matter of fact, and I bet you had me down as one of the stuffy ones.'

Mearns didn't miss the look on her mum's face that said he was delusional to believe otherwise.

'I went to one at Soul Bar. The drinks were coming at me faster than I could finish them. Networking off the scale.'

'So were the hangovers the next day, I bet.' Mearns could only imagine.

'You're right there. For a lot of them it's one week-long hangover. They've travelled a long way for seven days off the leash.'

Mearns's mother bristled.

Mearns's father spluttered. 'Apart from me, dear. I didn't see it like that.'

Ferguson coughed to cover his bark of laughter.

Her dad recovered quickly, remembering the good old days. 'Long time since I was in the city for it though. Not sure how much it's changed. The days of doing business in the pubs seems to be a thing of the past. Gone are the days when folk would recruit roustabouts from a tour of the pubs.'

Mearns knew, at least, that a roustabout was the bottom rung of the ladder offshore and these days those jobs were like gold dust.

Her father sighed. 'Things are different, for sure, but if anything's still the same on the entertainment side, the party everyone wanted a pass to was always run by Peter Miller.'

Mearns hoped the excited look between her and Ferguson had gone unnoticed.

Chapter 36

Saturday

EVE COULD ALMOST TASTE the grandeur as she stepped into the entrance hall of Peter Miller's city-centre hotel. Sunlight shone through stained-glass windows, casting fragmented rainbows across the flagstoned floor.

The woman behind the mahogany reception desk smiled. 'Good morning, madam. How can I help?'

'We're here to see Peter Miller. He's expecting us.'

'Certainly. Your name?'

'DI Eve Hunter.'

The smile vanished from the receptionist's face.

The thinly veiled threat made earlier by telephone – that Eve would have no other option but to come to the hotel and wait until Peter Miller was made available, and that she wouldn't be turned away like her colleagues – no doubt had something to do with the agreement to finally meet. The receptionist didn't hide her scowl as she picked up the phone, jabbed at one button and mumbled into the receiver. Clearly the place didn't attract the police often and, even more, she was keen not to attract the attention of other guests. The woman put down the phone.

'Mr Miller will be with you immediately.'

Eve turned as a door the other side of the stairwell opened. The receptionist wasn't wrong. Peter Miller strutted out into the hallway. Exactly how Eve remembered him from all the press coverage over the years. He didn't appear to have aged at all, the way school teachers still looked the same years later, although he was wearing better than some of the dinosaurs who had taught her. She was willing to bet his age-defying appearance wasn't achieved without a little help.

'Ah, DI Hunter.' He raised a tanned hand towards Cooper.

'I'm DI Hunter.' Eve stood rigid, no offer of a hand, enjoying the look on Miller's face. 'This is my colleague, DS Cooper.'

Miller regained his composure, lifting a hand to Eve, which she took grudgingly. He shook firmly, smiling all the while, as if pleased to see her and he'd willingly offered his time. A two-faced shit or a show for the guests who sat reading papers and drinking coffee within the foyer.

Miller motioned them both towards the door he'd come out of.

He closed the door behind them, held the smile. 'Please, sit.'

It wasn't your typical office; this place was something else. A suite. A large sofa, double bed, television and pictures all over the walls, famous faces staring out from gold-leafed frames, Peter Miller shaking hands, laughing, patting backs alongside them.

Mr Miller made his way around his desk, sat in the mammoth chair and leaned back, resting one ankle above the knee of his other leg. Casual.

'Can I get you something to drink? To eat? Must be a nightmare working the weekend.'

Eve ignored the offer. 'You'll know plenty about working the weekend, I'm sure. Quite the place you have here.'

Mr Miller spread his hands wide. 'My personal sanctuary. I figured the hours I spend here, I might as well make it a home from home.'

'Yes, it seems a lot of important hours. You're not an easy man to pin down.'

Miller appeared ruffled, as if he hadn't expected such an abrupt start to their chat. 'I apologize. A busy week in the hotel calendar.'

Eve didn't hide her disdain. 'Must have been a real inconvenience with your son's best friend dying.'

Miller didn't flinch. 'Such a sad thing. Terrible state of affairs. What can I do to help?'

'We understand your son, Finn, was good friends with Dean?'

'Yes, that's right. They went to school together.'

'I'm sure you'll be aware we've been trying to track down your son. According to your secretary, she has no contact details for him.'

Miller's expression showed he didn't actually care whether they'd been trying to talk to Finn or not. 'He hasn't been here. I sent him to my timeshare in Aviemore. To get a little time away to deal with the loss. As you can imagine, it's been a real shock.'

'Thoughtful of you. The shock is to be expected but wouldn't he like to help? Feel that he's providing assistance in the search for Dean's killer?'

Perhaps Finn wasn't shocked at all. Maybe the search would end with him, rather than their Jane Doe.

Miller said nothing.

It didn't put Eve off pushing. 'When do you expect him back?'

'I'm not sure.'

Eve didn't believe it for a second. 'Had Finn seen Dean recently?'

'I'd expect so. I believe they saw a lot of each other.'

Eve paused. 'Did they still see as much of each other after Andrew Shirriffs's death?'

Miller's eyes darkened. 'Yes, I believe they did. A form of comfort for them both. The three of them had been terribly close.'

'And now your son is the only one left.'

Miller looked at his desk.

'Do you know where Finn was on the evening of Dean's death?'

Miller didn't hesitate. 'He was with me. At home.'

Eve didn't respond to the alibi, instead pushing on with the next question. 'Would you be able to put us in touch with Finn?'

Miller picked up a pen and rolled it across the desk beneath the flat of his palm. 'My son needed to take time out. Is it so important you talk with him?'

'Yes. As you said yourself, they were close friends and I think it's fair to say Finn would be integral in helping us build a picture of who Dean was, what he was into and perhaps his last movements.'

'What he was into?' Miller was rattled.

The belief the boys were untouchable – as David Carnegie had said. *Not on her watch.*

'Perhaps I worded that incorrectly. What he liked to do in his spare time, Mr Miller. You know, his pastimes and hobbies. Anything Finn may have also enjoyed.'

Miller squirmed. 'Dean worked in the IT department for his father's company. I'm sure you already know that.'

'I'm more interested in their personal time.' Eve hoped her message was hitting home.

'Personal time? Well, they both liked music.'

For sure, after Lisa's complaint to the station that led to them finding Dean in the first place.

Miller seemed more animated, getting into his subject. 'Finn craves it, in fact. He plays in a band – guitar but lead singer too.'

Eve cocked an eyebrow. 'I bet that attracts the ladies.'

Miller managed to raise a smile.

'Does Finn have a girlfriend?'

'Not that I know of. Why do you ask?'

'I was interested if perhaps Finn and Dean also shared a love of the ladies. Perhaps the same one? If they'd ever had a friendly spat over a lady they both liked?'

Miller's mouth was a thin line. 'I don't know what you're getting at.'

Eve took her time, ready for her next move. 'It's come to our attention that a woman may have been in Dean's apartment the night he was killed.' She said nothing about the woman being the same one found hanging shortly after Dean's body was discovered.

Miller was doing a fine job of looking shocked. 'A woman. Who?'

'We're not at liberty to divulge that in an ongoing investigation. Do you know if Dean or your son regularly had women over to their homes? Women who weren't girlfriends?' Eve hoped, if Miller did know what the boys were into together, that he was sweating right now.

Miller composed himself surprisingly quickly. 'It wouldn't surprise me if they did. Nothing wrong in that. Men and women can be friends.'

Eve smiled. 'Quite. So, you don't know who the woman at Dean's flat may have been?'

'No. Why would I? I wouldn't expect to know the ins and outs of my son's life, never mind his friends'.'

Somehow, Eve didn't think that was the case, but she'd said enough to plant the seed. She decided to change tack, taking Miller by surprise. 'Does Finn play in public?'

'Excuse me?'

'The music. His band.'

'From time to time. Plays a couple of the local bars.'

'He must be good.'

Miller took his time nodding. 'Yes.'

As with Robert Johnstone, Eve wasn't going to be getting anything of value from Miller. She took out her card. 'I would appreciate if you'd have Finn call us.'

'I'll try. I can't promise.'

'I understand.'

Miller looked relieved at her acceptance, and stood to show them out.

Eve walked to the door with Cooper, but turned as she was about to open it.

'I expect before long Finn will want to make a return to his music. I'll have to try and catch him performing. What's the band name?'

Miller stood, struggling to find a reason not to answer. 'Parallel.'

'Sounds right up my street.'

Miller said nothing as they left, but Eve was sure he knew they'd be speaking to Finn with his help or without it.

Chapter 37

Eve ANSWERED HER RINGING mobile as Cooper drove them back to the station.

'Can you speak?' Mearns spoke fast, as if she had news. Unexpected, even when they'd all come in, more than willing to work overtime at the thought of moving the case forward.

'Yeah, about ten minutes away and my knuckles are still twitching to punch Miller.'

'Not a productive meeting?'

'The guy knows how to avoid a question. He'd make a good politician. What's up?'

'Forensics came back on those prints.'

Eve held her breath.

'You were right. Our Jane Doe was at Dean's murder. On top of that, as far as Dean's mate Andrew's death goes, we may have a way of finding out more about those missing files. Marcie Wade from the *Aberdeen Enquirer* called.'

'How can she help?'

'I'm not sure, but you'll want to see her. She says she has information about Andrew Shirriffs.'

Eve wasn't expecting that titbit. 'When's she free?'

Marcie Wade possessed none of the brashness that her predecessor, Claire Jenkins, had.

Eve and Mearns sat at the four-seater Costa table watching her at the counter exchanging chit-chat and laughter with the barista who was serving her. The coffee house had been the perfect place to meet. Tucked at the bottom of the Marischal College retail and office development where the *Aberdeen Enquirer* offices were housed, it was also a two-minute walk from the station.

Marcie made her way back to the table clutching a tray with three large lattes on it and three chocolate muffins that hadn't been mentioned. Eve found herself comparing Marcie's mousey-brown hair, loosely fastened in a bun, to Jenkins' severe bright red hair. Even Marcie's floral shift dress was in stark contrast to Jenkins' once signature sharp, black suit, worn with matching glasses frames. Cut-throat and meaning business. Eve missed Jenkins in her own way. They'd never been friends but at least she'd known what she was getting with her.

Marcie put down the tray, shared out the cups and plates and sat. 'Thanks for agreeing to see me.'

Eve sipped at her drink, placed the cup back down. 'It's fair to say you left us no choice after what you said on the phone.'

Marcie smiled as she opened the plastic wrapper of her muffin. Eve was still wary of that smile, questioning whether it was genuine any time they'd met but aware her opinion of the press was shaped by the woman Jenkins had been. A woman who had possessed two smiles – sneaky or smug. Marcie had shown neither and Eve was trying not to judge her by her predecessor. Maybe she genuinely was a nicer, more helpful woman. More interested in reporting the news with facts instead of sensationalism. Maybe.

Marcie took a large bite from the muffin, not waiting to clear her mouth before she spoke, her words mumbled. 'I know you guys are busy so I'll get straight to it.'

She bent beneath the table, rummaging in an oversized bag that lay at her feet, before reappearing with a thick file, paper overspilling its edges. She placed the file on the table, both her hands laid flat upon its battered cover, as if the contents might burst from their confines.

'It appears Jenkins was working on something I believe may be of interest to you, especially with the recent death of Dean Johnstone. I take it you've made the connection between the three boys?'

Eve tried not to show surprise or too much interest in the overstuffed file. 'Give me the short version.'

Marcie leaned in. 'She received a note in the weeks after Andrew Shirriffs's death.' Marcie opened the file, lifted the top sheet from it and passed it across the table.

Eve and Mearns's shoulders touched as they read the note together.

K,

I was there but you have to believe that there's nothing I could've done. I want you to know at least that one truth in all the lies. I think that day changed any hope. That any connection also died. That is something I've had to live with. Call it punishment. But I will make it right.

Eve sat back, not hiding the surprise on her face. The 'K' swirling around in her mind. *Kirk Shirriffs?* She exchanged a look with Mearns. Her colleague was clearly thinking the same thing. If addressed to Kirk, surely this note was a confession of sorts? Enough to support Patricia's comment in the press at the time that she didn't believe her son's death was suicide. But, if the note was to be believed, who was there when Andrew died?

Eve looked across at Marcie. 'Do you know who sent it?'

'There's nothing to say in the file and I've checked through her old computer account. I don't know if she ever did.'

Mearns stared at the note. 'I've never seen g's or s's written like that.'

Eve had to agree. 'Definitely quirky. How far did Jenkins look into this?'

Marcie seemed unsure. 'She spent a lot of time on it but ultimately got nowhere. She had a suspicion it may have been meant for Andrew's father, Kirk.'

Eve wasn't surprised Jenkins had come to the same conclusion.

'Do you know if Jenkins ever spoke to Kirk, or Andrew's mother, Patricia?'

Marcie rubbed a crumb from her bottom lip. 'They refused to talk to the press. They'd lost their son, they were grieving.'

'Fair enough.'

Marcie had more to say. 'No one else would talk either.'

Likely referring to those closest to the couple – Miller and Johnstone. No surprise there. Seemed they made a habit of staying silent.

'Did Jenkins talk to the police?'

'She tried several times to talk with DI Phil Crawford, who led the case. Looks like she got shut down.'

Eve sat back. She didn't particularly like interaction with the press herself, left most of it to the official channels, but there were times in the job where you had no choice. She was struggling to understand why Crawford as lead investigator wouldn't have wanted to look into this. She felt even more suspicious about the missing paper and digital files now.

'And Jenkins left it?'

Marcie coloured, taking Eve by surprise. 'Not exactly. Something came along that caught her attention more.'

It didn't take a genius to figure out Marcie was referring to the murders last year that had ultimately seen Jenkins lose her life.

Eve was wary. 'Why are you giving us this?'

Marcie looked genuine when she answered. 'Because I couldn't sit on this, knowing there may be more to it. You can have the file. I've made copies.'

'What do you want from us?'

'To look into it, but obviously I also have my needs.'

Eve was under no illusion that Marcie not looking as aggressive as Jenkins didn't mean she wouldn't be as ferocious in her search for a story. 'And they are?'

'You give me titbits as your current investigation goes along. I'll help where I can. And, if this comes to anything, you give me the exclusive.'

Eve sat a minute, silence at the table. Marcie was primed, ready to fight her case, but Eve had no argument. If people had been hiding things and were about to be exposed, they deserved to fall. Eve had no problem with that. In fact, she'd happily help trip them up – starting with whoever worked with DI Crawford.

Chapter 38

Monday

DS John Cowan looked like life had shit on him from a great height. With a face as craggy as a Munro, attitude oozed off him and the last thing Eve wanted to be was nice.

She was well aware he was one of the officers who had hung around with Ferguson a year ago. A testosterone overload, most of which had been aimed at Eve and anyone who would listen about what they believed to be her failings. But today she needed something from him. She'd have to play ball.

'What's with the closed door?'

He sat across the desk from Eve and Mearns, one ankle resting on his knee, in a small vacant office they'd managed to nab on his floor of HQ.

Eve had an urge to knock his ankle flying. 'Wanted a little privacy. It's about DI Phil Crawford or, rather, a case he worked on.'

'And you couldn't have called me?'

Eve kept her cool at his tone. 'We have reason to believe it may be a little sensitive.'

Cowan looked between her and Mearns, his fingers picking at the shoelaces on the foot that rested on his knee. 'And it's about?'

'Andrew Shirriffs. The case you worked on about a year ago.'

Cowan curled his upper lip. 'I remember. You don't need to remind me of when.'

Eve gritted her teeth at the attempt to show his professionalism when they both were aware how he'd tried to taint hers. 'The thing is we've been trying to access the case file but haven't had any luck electronically or in hard copy.'

Confusion was clear in Cowan's features; Eve was surprised he'd be so transparent. 'There must be a mistake. I logged that file myself, in both cases, once Crawford signed off on them.'

Eve never took her eyes from Cowan. 'No mistake. We need that file. It may have information that would be pertinent to a case we are working on.'

Cowan didn't ask.

'Do you think there's any way DI Crawford may know what happened to those files?'

Cowan dropped his foot to the floor, glowered as he rested his forearms on his thighs and clasped his hands between his legs. 'What exactly are you getting at?'

'Now, I'm wondering why you would jump to the conclusion I'm getting at something?'

Cowan smirked. 'Let's not bullshit each other. We're both aware of my standpoint on your so-called practices in the past. Do you have a beef to settle?'

Eve didn't falter. 'Files go missing. Maybe Crawford packed the file by accident in a box when he was clearing his office. As I said, I need that file. So don't waste my time with your bullshit.'

Even if Crawford had misplaced the paper copy, that still wouldn't account for the missing electronic file. Someone must have deleted it – whether on purpose or by accident – but without hard evidence she couldn't accuse Cowan of that, much as she would have liked to.

Cowan curled his top lip. 'As ladylike as ever. I doubt he'd have misplaced it. He was pretty thorough, but the poor bastard was pretty keen to get out of here as fast as.'

Mearns was grateful for the opening that one small titbit gave her, instead of getting involved in the disputes between Cowan and Eve. 'More than ready for retirement?'

'Not exactly. Something about being screwed over in retirement payments or something.' He looked at Eve. 'It's hardly fair; he gets shafted for exemplary service and you keep on showing your face every day regardless of your fuck-ups.'

Eve held the retort threatening to burst from her lips. This prick wasn't worth it. Instead she hesitated, doing her job, turning over the facts before she asked her next question – wondering how far someone on the verge of retirement might go if they were desperate, if the plans they'd made had changed due to a financial screw-up. 'And you know nothing about the whereabouts of the file?'

'No. And I don't like what you're insinuating.'

'Jesus, you've got a chip on your shoulder. I'm just trying to find something you or Crawford should've known the whereabouts of.'

'The way you're talking, I'm not convinced you don't suspect Crawford lost those files on purpose.'

Eve heard the loyalty in his voice, all too aware of how pig-headed and blinkered he could be if he thought he was being wronged or someone close to him was. Especially by someone like her. She stayed quiet.

Cowan stood. 'I'll look into it, find out if you've made mistakes in your search.'

Eve didn't react to his belittling. 'Great. As a matter of urgency, please.' And as Cowan left the office, she wondered if Crawford had done wrong or if it was Cowan running scared.

Chapter 39

'FOR GOD'S SAKE, STOP winding them up.'

Cooper froze on the living-room floor, legs raised in the air, the soles of his feet holding his daughter, Hannah, mid-air by the belly, both of them gripping one another's hands. His son, Nathan, who lay beside them, stopped giggling. Cooper looked up at his wife, Louise, surprised at the aggression in her tone, and lowered their daughter to the ground. Nathan began to cry. Hannah, now sitting on Cooper's shins, asked to go high again.

'We're only having fun, Mum. Da—' Hannah stopped when she saw her mother's face.

Cooper gently removed his daughter from his legs, not wanting to annoy his wife any further, feeling like a kid who'd been disciplined. He got to his feet, Hannah standing along with him whilst Nathan grumbled on the floor.

'Can I get you a cuppa?' Cooper tried for brownie points.

'No,' Louise snapped. 'Give me a break.'

Cooper felt as though he'd been slapped. It wasn't like his wife to be so abrupt. With him or the kids. He stepped forward, rubbed the base of her back, something she usually liked, but she moved away, bending to pick up the debris of toys scattered across the floor.

Cooper hesitated before stepping over Nathan and crouched to pick up the toy nearest to him. 'Here, let me do that. You have a seat or read for a while upstairs.'

Louise tutted, forcefully throwing a stretchy Spider-Man figure into the toy box. Hannah looked from her mother to her father and went off to sit in front of the telly, her brother wriggling towards her, *The Never-Ending Story* still playing.

Louise stood looking into the toy box and tucked her hair behind her ear. She looked pale, tired. Nathan was going through sleep regression and Cooper was well aware he hadn't been home enough lately to help. The fact he'd told her he needed to go out tonight, when he'd already worked Saturday, hadn't helped matters. Thank God Mearns had stepped up to the mark the other night by going to Heritage.

'Sorry, Lou. I was trying to give you a break by playing with them.'

'What, by winding them sky-high so they're screaming and then leaving me to deal with them later, when they're overtired and grumpy?'

It would make things worse if he pointed out they hadn't been screaming, just giggling, and that five minutes of play wasn't going to tire them out. Instead he stepped towards her again, took hold of her hand, squeezed. 'Sorry. OK? I know I've been working long hours and you're tired. Shattered, I imagine, but whilst I'm here, let me help.'

For a moment, Louise seemed as if she might relent, but then the moment was gone. She pulled her hand from Cooper's. 'It's things I need to get cleared and organized myself. Preferably before you disappear tonight, again. Sit with the kids, watch the movie, and try and keep it down.'

She stalked out of the room, seconds passing before he heard her banging about in the kitchen. He ambled over to the kids, wondering if there was more to it than his working hours and his wife's tiredness.

Chapter 40

MALONES, TUCKED DOWN SHIPROW off Market Street, was like any other Irish bar – walk into one anywhere in the world and you knew exactly what you were getting.

Eve bumped her shoulders through the Monday-night crowd, surprised it was this busy. She headed for the bar, the smell of the place reminding her of her party days, now part of another life. Cooper was already there, waving to get her attention, a pint of Guinness in his other hand.

'Took the liberty of getting you a Diet Coke.' He pointed towards the drink on the glass-littered bar.

Eve picked it up and turned to face the crowd. She tilted her head sideways, towards Cooper, almost yelling above the music and shouts of others. 'Christ, folk might think we're out on a date.'

'Well, you better look bored, as I'm still wearing my wedding ring.'

Eve grimaced at the joke but caught the underlying tension in Cooper's voice. 'Is everything OK with you and Louise?'

Cooper's mouth twitched. 'Been a bit of friction between us. Nothing a decent night's sleep won't sort out.'

Eve sensed Cooper wanted to leave it there. She checked her watch. 'So much for the devastation Finn's dad spoke about. He's due on in five minutes.'

She craned her neck above the wall-to-wall bodies, many wearing the obligatory tall Guinness-pint fun-hats. A microphone and drum-kit were in the corner, against a grey-brick feature wall and beneath old black and white street signs in Gaelic. The orange, white and green of the Irish flag was reflected in the knick-knacks that hung everywhere.

Cooper raised his voice above the din. 'Do you reckon he'll be any good?'

Eve leaned towards his ear. 'Finn must be half decent to be playing here. He'll think he is anyway.'

'Has Mearns had any luck with getting hold of DI Crawford since Cowan was no help?'

'She's left a message on his home phone. Hopefully we'll hear back quickly.'

The sudden blare of music made further conversation impossible. Going by the cheers that erupted at the same time, Finn's arrival was imminent – that and the swarm of young girls who were pushing their way to the front to be closer to the stage. The atmosphere was charged – the sudden change catching even Eve by surprise.

Nothing compared to her surprise when the guy strutted on to the stage. More of a swagger, stopping centre of the spotlight, his eyes down. The black leather jacket he wore stopped above his hips, an electric guitar slung low and covering the denim at his groin. The room fell silent, a lone wolf-whistle sounding out from somewhere. He raised his head, large intense dark eyes finding their crowd. A lazy smile, but nothing slow about the reaction from the crowd. He ran a hand through his thick floppy black hair, enjoying the attention the move earned him from the screaming young women. And then he strummed the guitar, once and with force. That one note sending the place wild before he stepped up to the mic and let rip.

Cooper shouted, 'Even I'm excited.'

Eve hadn't taken her eyes off Finn once. 'He's definitely got something.'

In those two minutes it was clear how much of a hold this guy would have over anyone.

By the time the lights rose to thunderous applause, Eve had lost the fight to stop her foot from tapping. As loath as she was to admit it, Finn Miller was good. So good she hadn't even clocked the rest of the band. No idea what they looked like or whether they were on a par with Finn's obvious musical talent. Finn stood at the edge of the small stage, sweat running down his forehead, which he wiped with a towel as he signed autographs, eventually passing the soaked towel to one of the girls who had been rooted to the spot staring at him since the set had finished. Eve wrinkled her nose as the girl placed the towel against her cheek, Finn winking at her as he jumped from the stage and made his way to the corner of the bar. A burly, skinheaded guy, who appeared to have lost his neck, stood by him, presumably blocking any unwanted attention.

'Stay there.' Eve pushed her foot off the metal rung which ran the length of the bar, Cooper making a move to say something, his Guinness sloshing in the pint glass, before she placed a hand briefly on his forearm, stopping him. Eve tottered across the floor, not used to the heels, and sidled up to the brick shithouse in the corner guarding Finn. She looked diagonally across the bar; she was still in Cooper's eye line. She laid her Diet Coke on the bar, tucked her fringe behind her ear and licked her lips before making sure she was also visible to Finn.

'Did you like the show?'

That didn't take long.

She turned towards him, saw that lazy smile on his face again. Had to be his go-to gesture, probably practised tirelessly in front of a mirror.

'Not bad. I haven't seen you play before. It seems you have quite the following.'

'I guess you could say it's one of the perks.' He cocked his head. 'Not bad?' His gaze ran down her body and up again, nothing subtle about it. His eyes were surprisingly dark.

Dean Johnstone and Andrew Shirriffs's faces went through her mind, their Jane Doe's too. All of them dead and here was Finn, flirting up a storm as if nothing had happened. She thought of what he – the so-called leader of the Trinity – had done to David Carnegie at school. She had to fight to keep the disgust from her face.

'Yeah.' Eve picked up her drink again, sipped at the Diet Coke. She wanted to say his performance was crap, knock him down a peg or two.

'Vodka?'

'I don't drink.'

'Refreshing.'

'You think?'

'Yeah, a woman in control. Far too often the women I get throwing themselves at me are sozzled. Comes across desperate, you know?'

So does using prostitutes.

She stepped back, maintaining eye contact. 'And do I appear to be throwing myself at you?'

He grinned, clearly enjoying the chase. 'It appears not. Playful too. I like that.'

'You do? I don't have you down as being into older women.'

'You're not all that old.'

Eve smiled, hating herself. 'Smooth. I'm thirty-six.'

'Attraction is attraction.'

The beefhead stepped forward, abruptly blocking their exchange, and whispered something into Finn's ear.

Finn checked his watch. 'Listen, I have to go. What's your name?'

'Amy.' The lie came easily.

'Nice to meet you, Amy. Maybe we could chat again sometime?' He slid a card across the bar.

Eve picked it up. 'Maybe.' She made a show of putting the card in her bag as Finn winked and walked past her.

'Laters,' he whispered in her ear.

Eve held back until Finn had exited the bar, a bevy of girls rushing after him to the door. She looked across at Cooper, who shook his head. She mouthed 'What?', a smile on her lips. She waited as he came over to her.

'Never knew you had it in you.'

'I can surprise from time to time. According to Finn, I'm playful.'

'He should try working with you. What was that he passed across?'

'His calling card. Says we should chat again some-time and then, that immortal classy last line, "Laters."'

Cooper looked towards the door, where the women were slowly filtering in from screaming in the street. 'You know you can't follow that up, don't you?'

'Of course. I wanted to get a feel for him. The real him. Not some act in an interview room.'

'And?'

'And do I believe he's capable of murder?'

Cooper said nothing.

'No way of knowing. One thing's for sure, I bet that guy doesn't love anyone else as much as he loves himself. And I'm definitely not seeing any of the upset and shock at Dean's death that Peter keeps banging on about.'

Chapter 41

Tuesday

Cooper stood at the kitchen window half-dressed. He took a gulp of lukewarm coffee and poured the dregs down the sink, leaving the mug in the basin as he shoved the last piece of now soggy toast into his mouth. He looked at his feet, legs bare, only his boxer shorts and shirt on. His daughter, Hannah, was half sitting on his right foot, her arms and legs wrapped around his lower leg like an over-grown koala bear. He turned from the sink and took laboured steps towards the table, Hannah giggling as he bumped her along.

'OK, Hannah Banana, Daddy's got to get ready.'

Hannah groaned before letting go and bounding from the floor to the kitchen table, beside her mother and her little brother, who sat swinging his chubby legs in a highchair, his face hidden beneath smeared Weetabix which his mother was spooning into his mouth. Cooper bent to kiss Louise.

She didn't turn to meet his lips, offering a cheek instead.

'What's wrong?'

Avoiding the question, she said, 'Don't forget to put on your trousers before you leave.' No humour in her tone. She tutted as Nathan turned his head from side to side, refusing any more breakfast.

Cooper forced a smile, chanced his luck. 'I can remember a time when you used to beg me to take them off.' Said in no more than a whisper, zero chance of the kids understanding the meaning even if they heard it, but the look she gave him made him feel stupid, standing there half-naked. 'Louise. I know the job can be a pain, but have I done something wro—'

Almost in slow motion, Nathan grabbed the Weetabix-covered plastic spoon from his mother's hand and threw it on to the floor in a fit of toddler temper. His sister, Hannah, her elbows on the table, covered her mouth with both hands, stifling her small laugh as brown sludge splatted on to the floor and back up against the leg of her mother's pyjamas.

Louise leaped from the table. 'Great.' She definitely wasn't laughing.

'Here, let me get it for you.' Cooper crouched, stopping midway as Louise nudged against him in an attempt to move away from the table.

He rose again.

'Leave it. I'll get a cloth.' She barged past Cooper to the sink, not looking his way once as she wet the dishcloth and flounced back to where the cereal lay on the floor and wiped.

Cooper stood watching. 'I would've done that.' An edge to his tone now. He'd rather she'd spit it out instead of these out-of-nowhere explosions that seemed out of character for someone who normally took such things in her stride.

Louise straightened. 'What, like everything else you keep meaning to do? Call this a family? How can it be when you're hardly ever here?'

Cooper felt as if he'd been slapped, the hit connecting all the harder with Hannah and Nathan looking between them.

Louise had gone quiet, looking as if she'd shocked herself, that she wished she could take the words back. The look on her face changed his anger to concern. She looked exhausted. He reached out and took hold of her hand. She let him.

They stood like that for a few moments, saying nothing. He'd make an effort to be home earlier tonight, try and make her smile at least. It would be good to give her a break, cook her tea, do the bedtime routine with the kids. Maybe get things back to normal between them.

The ringing of his mobile phone stopped him from telling her that. He tutted, searching her eyes for understanding that he'd have to answer the call. He wasn't sure he saw it before he let go of her hand and turned to the worktop. He lifted the phone jittering across the wooden surface as it vibrated. Eve.

'Yes?'

'Not a good morning?'

Cooper said nothing.

Eve took the hint. 'Where are you?'

He looked at the clock: another hour until he was due in. 'Home.'

Eve went quiet for a moment. 'I was thinking you should take the morning.'

'What?' He turned to Louise and the kids.

'Come in by lunch. I have something to deal with in the meantime – Mearns had a call from Laura Robertson. She's back at the shelter.'

Cooper went to swear, but remembered the kids. They'd all known Laura's violent bastard of a husband would hurt her again, but the reality of the situation was still hard to take.

Cooper looked at Louise and the kids again. 'You don't want me to come?'

'I'm on the way now with Mearns. Better two women and Mearns is a familiar face.'

Cooper knew the hours Mearns put in helping at the shelter. Eve too, but she'd never told him that. 'OK, but there's stuff to be done at the office.'

'Cooper, I'm trying to score you brownie points here. And by the sounds of things, you bloody need them. Be in by twelve.' Eve hung up.

Cooper put his phone on the counter and turned, ready to tell Louise, hoping he'd finally be rewarded with that smile.

Mearns sighed as they pulled up outside the women's shelter. 'I'm surprised it's taken this long.'

The sad truth was neither of them were surprised. Laura would've wanted to believe her husband's promise he wouldn't hit her again. But Colin Robertson had probably knocked her around before the sun had set on her second day home. The burning shame that she had been delusional enough to believe him, and responsible for taking her kids back into that environment, had most likely kept Laura from trying to escape again before now.

Eve studied the two-storey brick building on the quiet Ferryhill street, grey beneath a matching drab sky. She knew to make her way around the back for entry, wading through freshly fallen leaves from the surrounding trees that had all but covered the footpath. The heavy door buzzed open within seconds, the shelter's staff aware Eve and Mearns were coming.

Jean, the woman who seemed to run the place almost single-handedly, greeted them warmly in the entrance hall, knowing they were only ever there to help – at least as much as they were able to, both professionally and in their personal time. The silver-haired woman was wearing the same checked shirt and leggings as the last time they'd been here. She looked fuss-free, as ready to muck in as always.

Jean smiled, deep wrinkles rippling all over her gaunt face, revealing two rows of uneven yellow teeth, a couple missing in the upper row, witness to her own struggles in life. 'Good to see you both. Sorry, too, if you know what I mean.' Her voice was gruff, masking the kindness she showed every day of her life. 'She's through in the day room.' Jean motioned down the hall. 'You know where I am if you need me.'

Eve and Mearns made their way along the corridor, dog-eared posters offering various forms of help littered across the walls. They went for the one open door and the light that spilled out of it.

Laura sat in a worn armchair that formed part of a semi-circle of furniture in the centre of the room, staring at an old telly that wasn't on. The blue and purple battered flesh around her left eye was visible before they even approached. She turned her head towards them, grimacing as she scuffed her cheek against the edge of the cushion behind her.

'Please don't say you told me so.' Laura's voice was a whisper, her large brown eyes looking dead in her face, chalk-white but for the angry bruise.

'That's the last thing we'd do, Laura.' Mearns meant it.

They took a seat either side of her.

'Where are the kids?'

'Through there, painting with one of the staff.'

'Are they OK?'

'As OK as they can be, being dragged away from their home again. At least they were sleeping when this happened.' She raised her hand to her face. 'But they're not stupid. Or the eldest isn't. She saw this the next morning. This and Colin conked out on the sofa with his tinnies.'

'What now?'

'I guess I have to find the strength to do it all over again, follow it through this time. I'm terrified I'll get up there in that stand and they won't put him away.'

It was a possibility, but Eve knew if Laura didn't at least try, she might end up dead.

'We will do everything in our power to make sure that doesn't happ—'

Eve looked round as she heard someone enter the room. The girl standing in the doorway seemed startled. Eve's gaze was drawn to the girl's features: a deep purple splodge travelled over half of her face. But, unlike the purple bruise on Laura's temple, this mark wasn't the cause of the girl's stay here. It was a birth-mark, raised and angry on her skin, but her eyes were beautiful, her lips a perfect pout.

'Sorry.' She sounded foreign, offering nothing else as she tried to back out of the room.

Laura spoke. 'No, come in. I've nothing to hide. Impossible to with this.' She motioned to her eye.

All the women in here were hiding from something, or rather someone. Together, with similar horror stories to tell, they often formed a kinship within these walls.

The girl came further into the room, lifting a slender hand to her stomach, shrouded in a baggy T-shirt and jeans. Eve wondered if the action was down to nerves or something else. The girl motioned towards a pile of magazines on the coffee table, her hand trembling as she bent to pick one up. 'Thank you.' She left the room as quickly as she'd entered it, long hair swishing against her back.

Eve questioned if she would be able to read any of the magazine or if it was merely for the sake of a trip out-side her bedroom, or a need to look at pictures of something, anything, in an attempt to escape.

Laura broke the silence. 'One of the girls said she's been here since last Wednesday. Never speaks. That's probably the most anyone's heard her say.'

Chapter 42

ANDREEA'S BACK PRESSED HARD against the inside of her bedroom door, even though it was now a good five minutes since she'd heard the two women leave.

She'd known as soon as she walked into the day room they were police. The woman talking to them, the one with the black eye – Laura, she'd heard someone call her – had arrived the day before. Her face looked sore, her two cowering children terrified. Laura seemed at ease in the policewomen's presence; it was obvious she'd asked them here. That she believed they might help her.

Andreea's head said the women were gone but her hammering chest was still waiting for the panelled wood behind her to pulse with the thud of their knocks in an attempt to get in to her. The police wouldn't help her. Not a woman who hid in a flat full of prostitutes. Women here illegally, who did what they did. The police wouldn't believe they were made to do what they did against their will. In fear of their lives because of the people who owned them. No, they wouldn't believe that at all and, even if they did, they'd think her the worst of them all. A girl who let what happened to those girls every day happen at all.

Thank God she'd learned long ago never to wear her hair up. To Marius's store, to here. Anywhere. Knowing the tattoo on the back of her neck would draw attention. Attention that could possibly be easily swatted away, but she'd always have the fear someone would know.

Andreea heard Jean whistling further down the hall. She lifted one of her splayed hands from the door, not realizing how hard she'd been pressing against the wood until she felt the need to flex her fingers. She took a deep breath, felt a little light-headed, and dared to step away from the door to sit on the edge of the bed.

She reached for the glass of water on the bedside table and gulped from it before biting into an oatmeal biscuit from the folded napkin she'd taken out of the dining room the night before. Feeding herself, but most importantly feeding the life growing inside her. Andreea looked down, rubbed at her tummy. Her child's life would be different. She would not let anyone harm them. Marius would make it right. All she had to do was hide until they figured something out.

Hide from Bogdi, Vlad and Daria. Give nothing away to the staff who worked here or the girls that lived here.

And stay far away from the police.

Chapter 43

THE BOYS ARE OLDER *than us.*

'So, this is Kid.' El smiles at all three of them as she raises a hand towards me. It's as if I'm being presented to them and I worry they won't be interested in someone like me, that I won't be allowed to be a part of the gang.

I glance at them, feeling like a doll staring out from a shop window. A broken doll maybe, but I know I don't look like a kid any more. My narrow waist is obvious in the denim shorts that are showing off my long legs. I'm proud of them, at least. I pull at the hem of the shorts, feeling awkward. El told me to wear them. I look at my plimsolls, which are muddy, streaks of brown visible on my lower legs. The fear as we ran is forgotten for now.

Two of the boys are staring at me, as if I actually am for sale. I wait for them to say something, knowing I'm far from beautiful. One of them has the darkest eyes I've ever seen, the most serious face for a kid his age. The other one hasn't stopped smiling since I arrived, so different from his friend. And then there's the third boy.

What was the word El had used? Dreamy. His blue eyes twinkle out of a face framed by soft-looking curly hair. His gaze meets mine and I feel the blush creep over my cheeks, spreading everywhere as he asks me in a quiet voice if I'd like to come sit beside him. I'm walking towards him before he finishes asking. Glad I'm not on display any more, proud of myself as I see El's look of surprise.

El goes to sit by the boy with the dark eyes. Eyes I can still feel on me. I'm used to people staring but this feels different. Maybe he's just curious. El's doing everything in her power to get his attention. I would've sworn El would go for the smiling guy. Maybe it's because the one with the smile looks busy with something else. Something that's obvious when the spark of a flame is brought to it.

The smell of weed fills the space between us, the boy's constant smile making sense now as I notice the heavy glaze to his eyes.

He takes a deep drag, takes his time blowing it back out. 'Kid?'

I look to El for reassurance, seeing the boy with the dark eyes still staring at me, a hunger in his eyes that scares me. I move a little closer to the curly-haired boy I'm sitting beside, wondering why when I've not long met him. His eyes perhaps. They're kind.

I look back at the boy with the joint. 'Yeah. They call me Kid and that's fine by me.'

I try to sound grown up, brave like El taught me back in our bunks. I don't feel it. Not even a little. My voice sounds alien. It sounds weird anywhere away from that room. 'So you know my name. What's yours?'

He smiles, takes another drag. 'Names aren't important. Why don't you decide what to call us?'

I look around at the blue-eyed boy, glad I'm beside him and not the others. I smile. 'You can close your mouth, Curly.' I shock myself with my bravery. Even El stares at me, bug-eyed.

The boy shuts his mouth, and as he does so the boy with the joint sniggers.

I want to stay brave. 'Smiler. That's what I'll call you as it's all you do.'

He laughs out loud this time. 'And him?' He motions over to the serious boy with El.

My opinion of something has never mattered; not once have I been asked for it. As if I'm invisible, that I don't count. It feels good being here. I pretend to give it some thought, but those eyes . . . 'Black Eyes. Never seen eyes so dark.'

Smiler howls. 'Well, boys, that's us told, and this, my friends, is your something different.'

I don't know what he means, and I don't want to. So I smile too, the way El taught me, and I take the joint as it's passed my way.

I'm lying on my back, giggling with Curly, feeling safe. Happy. Watching clouds drift across the sky. Talking about hopes for the future. Curly's aiming big. He wants to take after a family member and run his own shop one day. Failing that, maybe something to do with food. I laugh and suggest countless silly shop names – anything to avoid him asking what my hopes are, when I see no future for myself. All I can hope for is escape.

My laughter dies as I realize I have no idea of the time. I bolt upwards, panicked. He sits up alongside me, a gentle hand on my forearm, asking what's wrong.

It takes a moment to make out El in the dimming light, the blur to my vision making it more difficult, and the fact that Black Eyes' lips are stuck to hers.

'El?'

She doesn't hear me at first until I shout a little louder, waking the smiling boy who has fallen asleep.

'Yeah?'

'It's getting dark. We need to go.'

El sounds drowsy. 'Give it another hour.'

I want to be brave, I do, but I can hear that stick, as I often do in my dreams.

'I want to go, El.'

Black Eyes looks at me with that same leer and smirks. 'Go on then. She'll be along soon.'

El giggles. I don't want to go but the fear is too strong. 'Please, El?'

She sighs, surprising me – as if I've annoyed her. That's the last thing I want to do.

'OK,' I say quickly. I'm keen to keep her happy. 'I'll go but please don't be long.'

I walk away, feeling Curly staring after me, and I want to turn around so much, but I don't.

Black Eyes laughs. 'Finally, now the real fun can start.'

El laughs too.

I walk faster, like the worst friend in the world.

Chapter 44

MEARNS PUT THE PHONE on loudspeaker as Eve drove them back to the station. Ferguson's voice filled the car.

'You ready for a busy day?' He sounded pumped, kept busy by tasks with their unexpected call to the shelter and Cooper's absence. 'I've managed to get hold of the Shirriffses. Or the wife, at least. Patricia.'

'And?' Eve was half paying attention, Laura Robertson and the timid foreign girl in the shelter still on her mind. Being somewhere like that made anyone think, but, for Eve, it made her even more determined to help those women – to bring their abusers to justice. She'd already called into the office to get things in motion again for Laura.

Ferguson answered, 'And it was like pulling teeth. She's agreed to meet, as long as her husband can accompany her.'

'It's Kirk I want to see anyway. You get her address?'

'No, they want to meet at their restaurant in the city centre. She says they're there tonight before dinner service.'

'OK, get me a time and text me the details. Can you also find me somewhere to park that won't cost a fortune?'

'You got it. Are you and Mearns on your way back?'

'Yeah. Why?'

'There's someone else I've managed to track down I know you'll want to see before the Shirriffses.'

'Who?'

'DI Phil Crawford's wife.'

'Good work, Ferguson.' No wonder he was pumped. 'What time?'

'Two p.m.'

Eve checked the dashboard. 'Since we're on a roll and you seem to be holding the fort, Mearns and I should pay Robert Johnstone a little visit.'

Eve didn't wait for the groan before she hung up.

Ferguson picked up the yellow polystyrene container with a double napkin, catching the already oozing gravy seeping out of the front.

'Too posh to sit with the rest of us these days?'

Ferguson turned at DS John Cowan's jibe. 'Nah, fancied a fat-bastard moment in private.'

'Let me guess, pie and gravy?'

'Nope. Worse. Chips, cheese and gravy. A mere starter before the inevitable Prezzo takeout later.'

Cowan screwed up his nose. 'Now there's proper comfort food for you. I don't blame you, working for the bitch you do.'

Ferguson bristled, but tried not to show it. Not so long ago he would've joined in wholeheartedly with any verbal beating of Eve. Things had changed, yet he hadn't been man enough to admit as much to Cowan, finding it easy to avoid doing so since they hadn't seen much of each other.

'Do you know she had me in a meeting room yesterday about missing files on a case I worked about a year ago? All up in my face, hinting at dodgy dealings.'

Ferguson didn't comment on Eve being all up in Cowan's face. He also didn't think it was true. 'I'm sure she wasn't hinting at anything untoward, more concerned how both paper and electronic files can go missing on the same case.'

'So, you know about it?'

Ferguson stood clear of the canteen queue, feeling the hot gravy leaking through the napkin on to his hand and hearing his stomach grumble. 'We work on the same team, Cowan.'

'She didn't share everything with you before. Far from it.'

Ferguson had an idea where this was going, and he didn't want to go there. Not any more. 'Listen, mate, I'm sure there's nothing dodgy in it. You'll find those files, no problem.' Ferguson lifted the container in his hand to make his point to Cowan. 'Anyway, I better get going.'

Ferguson stepped away, aware of Cowan staring after him, more than likely pissed off that Ferguson had cut dead the chance to slag off Eve.

Security Sam pulled at the bottom of his navy blazer as he came around the front of the curved reception desk, his brown eyes, magnified by the thick glasses he wore, darting between Eve and Mearns.

'Yes?'

Eve didn't doubt Sam had already seen them walk across the car park via the security camera screens or that he was up and out of his seat before they'd even pulled opened the door.

'We'd like to talk to Mr Johnstone, please.'

Sam shook his head, his hand clutching at the security pass hanging around his neck. The keeper of the keys. 'Mr Johnstone doesn't meet anyone without an appointment.'

'I'm sure, given the circumstances, Mr Johnstone would be willing to bend the rules this once.'

Sam emanated the smugness of a jobsworth under the illusion he held some kind of power. He walked behind the desk, picked up the phone.

Eve wasn't banking on it being that easy.

'I'll ring his secretary, ascertain when his first available appointment will be.'

The security man pressed buttons on the switchboard and turned away as if whatever he was saying needed to be said in private. He swivelled back around, seemingly enjoying the moment.

'He can see you at two p.m. tomorrow.'

Eve walked over and sat on one of the black leather sofas separated by lush green palm fronds. Mearns knew exactly where this was going. She made her way over to sit by Eve's side. They both sat back, making themselves comfortable.

Security Sam fidgeted, phone gripped in his hand. 'Did you not hear me?'

Eve rested her arm on the chair. 'Oh, we heard you fine, but we no longer have time to be fobbed off. We'll

224

sit here until Mr Johnstone shows. Be it to nip out for lunch or to leave for the day. But we will see him today.'

Sam's cheeks coloured as he blustered behind the desk, tutting and sighing, struggling with a response. Instead, he mumbled into the receiver, and slammed down the phone. 'It seems his secretary can spare you five minutes with Mr Johnstone. She's on her way.'

Eve stood. 'Thank you for your help.'

They followed the short, slim, grey-haired woman along the corridor, passing glass-partitioned offices and towering pigpens that emitted muted chatter and were spread throughout an open-plan space. The secretary hadn't uttered a word to them in the lift from reception. Maybe she'd graduated from the same jobsworth school as Security Sam.

The woman stopped abruptly, motioning to the open glass door they stood outside. Robert Johnstone sat behind his desk, studying something on his laptop screen. He didn't look up as they entered or when the secretary walked away.

'Mr Johnstone.' Eve stepped into the office as Mearns closed the door behind them.

His eyes didn't stray from the screen as Eve and Mearns sat in the two seats placed before his desk, not waiting to be invited. It appeared a tea or coffee wouldn't be forthcoming either.

'Do you always treat the friends and family of a dead child with such understanding?' Robert Johnstone's voice was dry with a sharp edge.

'Apologies, Mr Johnstone. It's rare we're faced with such difficulty in talking to people in connection with that child.'

Mr Johnstone sat back in his chair, his gaze looking over their heads and beyond to the pigpens outside. 'Not everyone deals with grief in the same way. My way, I've found, is to lose myself in work and I don't appreciate you turning up here unannounced, or the resulting gossip that will come from it.'

'Why gossip? Surely people will understand we are trying to find the person who murdered your son? Don't you think, if anything, it would be sympathy and understanding they'd be showing?' Even as she said it, she suspected the opposite would be true. The manner of the man certainly didn't bring out the best in her.

Mr Johnstone said nothing.

'Look, Mr Johnstone, I appreciate you're a busy man. Let's get to the point and make this as quick as possible.'

Mr Johnstone grunted.

'Would it be true to say that your . . . let's call it hesitation to talk with us could perhaps be to do with not wanting to talk about your son's personal life leading up to his death?'

Now he did look at Eve. Straight at her. 'Are you insinuating I'm trying to hide something?'

You bet your arse I am.

'Not at all. Perhaps you don't want to talk to us because you don't want Dean's life, and any of its problems, being made public knowledge. I understand your reputation is important to you.'

'Of course it is. I have a company to run, clients to consider.'

'And those things are more important than your son?'

Anger on his face, rage barely contained. 'By no means.'

'Did he have difficulties in the run-up to his death?'

Mr Johnstone looked as if he'd love to cause difficulty for Eve. 'He'd been struggling since the death of his friend last year.'

'Andrew Shirriffs?'

'Yes.'

'Did you try to help?'

'Of course. Dean didn't want the help.'

'What about the original Trinity or the one member left of the most recent Trinity?'

Mr Johnstone turned back to his screen. 'I don't know what you're getting at.'

'It seems that you've all been there for one another since way back. Long-running connections, so to speak.'

'It's called friendship, nothing strange in that.'

'Quite.' Eve voice was clipped. 'Did any of them try to help?'

'We all did. A lot had happened. A lot to deal with.'

'Did Finn in particular try to help him? Being his one close friend left?'

Johnstone straightened in his chair, flattened his tie against his shirt with the palm of his hand. 'You need to ask Finn that.'

'Believe me, we're trying to. We finally met with his father, after various calls and being fobbed off.' Eve had no doubt Johnstone was aware of their recent meeting with Peter Miller. 'As I say, it's proved difficult speaking to anyone from the group.'

'The group? You make it sound as if we have some special power, like we close ranks or something. We're friends, that's it.'

'I guess I do. Funny, because "the Trinity" almost sounds like it could have divine powers. Maybe think it's above others, even the law. Not that I believe that's what's happening here.'

Mr Johnstone licked his lips. 'Ms Hunter . . .'

'Detective Inspector, sir.'

'I'm at a loss as to why you appear to be targeting me or my friends, instead of looking for the person who took my son's life.'

'Not at all. In fact, we may have a development there.' Eve saw him swallow. He'd know from Miller what was coming. Mearns looked at her. 'We believe a woman may have been with your son the night he was killed. We have CCTV footage of her running from the direction of his flat.'

Johnstone flinched. They hadn't shared that little nugget with Miller.

'And how do you know she was there?'

'Her prints were lifted from the ornament used to knock your son out.'

The colour drained from Johnstone's face. Eve was sure he knew more about the night Dean died than he was letting on.

He was struggling to find words. 'She killed my son?'

'Not necessarily. It appears Dean died as a result of suffocation.' In other circumstances she would never have delivered something sensitive so abruptly, but it appeared to be the way Mr Johnstone chose to operate – and a perfect end to their meeting.

'Anyway, Mr Johnstone, we won't keep you, but I would appreciate an answer to one question we have. Were you ever approached by a reporter around the time of Andrew's death?'

His fingers visibly tightened on his chair. 'Not that I recall, other than asking for quotes and offering condolences as they knew our connections.'

'You don't want to take a little longer to think about it?'

'Ms . . . Detective Inspector, I have things to organize before an event two nights from now. Countless meetings to deal with. I have to get going.'

Eve stood to leave; Mearns did the same. 'We'll get out of your hair. This event? Anything exciting?'

Johnstone smiled, not a friendly gesture. 'A monthly fundraiser for local charities at Miller's Hotel.'

'Monthly? Pretty frequent, is it not? Aren't most of these things annual?'

Johnstone's smile stayed plastered on his face. 'We are lucky enough to have the contacts and to move in business circles that consider charity an important priority. We believe in contributing monthly throughout the year and these functions allow us to raise those funds whilst also providing an opportunity to remain abreast of ongoing business ventures through networking.'

And a fantastic opportunity to stoke the ego with great PR and a well-rehearsed spiel. Eve mirrored the smile. 'To be commended. All of you doing your bit for the community.' Eve lifted her hand to the door handle. 'Perhaps you do have special powers after all.'

As Robert Johnstone closed the door she had a feeling he'd already be on speed-dial to Miller.

Chapter 45

THE WOMAN WHO OPENED the door was tanned. Her pale blue eyes were surrounded by deep wrinkles, showing her love of the sun. Her short white hair quite the contrast.

She smiled, wrinkles deepening, and moved back from the door to make way for them. 'Hello. I'm glad you made it.'

Eve and Mearns smiled in return and stepped into the home of DI Crawford, feeling bad they hadn't divulged the true nature of their call. Ferguson had been clear about not mentioning the specific case when he'd tracked Mrs Crawford down, to make sure they actually got time with her husband. The three of them jostled for space in the rectangular vestibule.

'Here, let me take your coats.'

They shrugged themselves free of their jackets, Mrs Crawford hanging them carefully on a peg each before she moved off into the living room. Eve followed her into the small space, where ornaments and knick-knacks filled every possible nook and cranny. No husband to be seen.

Mrs Crawford turned. 'Can I get you anything?'

They both shook their heads.

'In that case, I'll take you through.'

'Through?' Eve assumed she meant the kitchen.

'To his room.' Mrs Crawford's expression seemed to say it should've been obvious.

'Oh.' Eve stepped behind her, Mearns following. Perhaps his room was a study or something, although Eve was surprised there'd be the space.

Mrs Crawford shuffled along the short hallway before opening the only closed door. The scene that lay beyond stopped Eve in her tracks.

A hospital bed swamped the room, sucking out any light coming through the window. Staring at DI Crawford's skeletal frame, Eve was pulled back to another room, another time – one in which her colleague Sanders was still alive. DI Crawford didn't react to their arrival. Maybe asleep. Difficult to tell when both eyes were half-open.

The shock on Eve's face must have been obvious.

'Are you OK?' Mrs Crawford sounded concerned. 'I guess it can be a shock if you haven't seen him in a while. You did know, didn't you?'

Eve shook her head, still struggling to get Sanders out of her mind.

'Oh, I'm sorry. I assumed as you'd worked with him and wanted to visit . . .' She looked over towards her husband.

Why hadn't Cowan told them? 'What happened?'

Mrs Crawford waved them back out of the doorway, closing it softly once they were all clear of it. 'Come through here. I don't like chatting about him in front of him. Never sure how much he hears.'

Eve and Mearns sat next to each other on the sofa, Mrs Crawford in an armchair beside an old-fashioned gas fire, flames flickering behind the black-scorched white panels.

'It was a massive stroke. Five months ago now. He was in hospital for weeks. Such a relief when I finally got him home. It's where he should be.'

Eve heard the love in her words. 'It must be a lot of work for you.'

'I guess it is, but I don't consider it work. Besides, I'm always hopeful he'll improve over time. The biggest stumbling blocks for him are the paralysis down one side of his body and the aphasia.'

Eve rubbed a finger against the raised material of the sofa arm. 'I'm sorry, what's that?'

'Aphasia? It's what they call language difficulties, including talking, listening and understanding. That's all limited with him for now.'

Eve didn't want to ask what his chances were after five months had gone by already.

'The bed makes things easier for me and we have carers coming in to help.'

Regardless of the suspicions she held about Crawford, Eve felt sympathy for the man. 'I'm sorry he only got about six months of retirement before this happened.'

Mrs Crawford smiled half-heartedly. 'Please don't be. The six months we had were fantastic. Did things we never dreamed we'd be able to do. Things we never imagined we'd be able to afford.'

Eve's chest tightened. Mearns froze beside her. Neither of them said a thing.

'We always knew we'd have his pension from the force but to also get that golden handshake too, in recognition for his service. Well, it was something else. I was so proud. That money has also helped greatly with his care since.'

Eve tried to keep her expression neutral, knowing full well what Cowan had told them and that there had been no handshake, and not the pension he'd been expecting. She forced a smile. 'Thank goodness for that, at least. It must have been a substantial sum.'

Mrs Crawford flattened the hair cut short in front of her ear. 'To be honest, I don't know how much it was. I didn't see the need to ask when Phil told me. Not when he said we wouldn't have to worry again and I was to let him spoil me and enjoy it.' Mrs Crawford turned towards the fireplace, sad, perhaps dreaming about what could've been. 'Anyway, excuse my ramblings. If you didn't know, why were you coming to visit?'

Eve was grasping for an answer. It wasn't her place to tell Mrs Crawford where she suspected that money might have come from. For all she knew, that handshake had maybe happened after all. Something she'd be checking for sure. In the meantime, this woman had been kicked enough by life. She wasn't going to be the one to kick her again when she was already down.

Chapter 46

EVE AND MEARNS HAD come back to the office with take-out. The day seemed never-ending and they still had a visit to the Shirriffses to look forward to.

She put down the Prezzo bag in the centre of the desk, Ferguson practically salivating and Cooper looking as if all his birthdays had come at once, since he'd already had the morning off.

Ferguson ripped the bag open, dishing out Eve's and Mearns's with out-of-character good manners before he bit into the calzone they'd ordered for him, tomato sauce and onion dropping to the polystyrene carton on his desk, not bothered he hadn't served Cooper.

Cooper shook his head.

'What? A man's got to eat.'

Eve updated Cooper and Ferguson on their visit to Johnstone first.

'Seems we may have him worried. I'm more interested in that fundraising do at Miller's.'

Ferguson smeared a napkin across his mouth. 'Another late night?'

'Nope, Cooper is with me tonight since he got the morning off. You and Mearns can volunteer for Thursday.'

Ferguson knew better than to object.

Eve moved on to their visit with Crawford's wife, both of them as surprised as she and Mearns had been at Crawford's condition. 'Ferguson, you're buddies with Cowan. Talk to him. Tell him what the wife said about money, hint about the fact something is amiss, ask if he'll consider looking into it further. For you, if not us.'

Ferguson grimaced.

'We need to speak to MacLean. Find out what they may have been trying to hide about Andrew's death.'

Eve dialled, putting the call on loudspeaker.

'Hey, MacLean.'

'Great, the voice I always love to hear.'

'Love you too. I'm calling about the post-mortem report for Andrew Shirriffs.'

'Yeah, suicide last year.'

Eve was not surprised to hear MacLean recalling the case straight away. His mind was like one of those old-fashioned Rolodex files.

'Is there any way it might've been foul play, made to look otherwise?' Eve heard MacLean huffing on the other end of the line.

'Are you questioning my competence?'

Eve didn't hesitate. 'You've questioned mine enough.'

'Touché.' The smile faded from MacLean's voice as he got down to business. 'Everything pointed towards suicide. The way he was tied, the knot done by his own hand. But I suppose someone could've applied the pressure to him leaning forward in the right circumstances.'

Eve remembered the bottle of vodka found on the floor, the cocaine. 'Was that never investigated?'

'Yes, but the officers and forensics at the time ruled out any foul play and, as I say, it all also pointed towards suicide.'

Eve studied her colleagues' faces as they listened to the call. Once again, she wondered how desperate DI Phil Crawford might have been.

Eve waited for Hastings's shout to enter his office this time, not wanting to piss him off before she'd even got going. She pushed open the door, unable to tell what kind of humour he was in.

He motioned to the seat on the other side of the desk from him.

Eve sat. 'Been quite a lot of developments, sir.'

Hastings glared as he pushed back in his chair. 'And you're only coming to me now?'

'It's all happened quite quickly.' They were both aware that the last time Eve had been in here the parting shot had been about her temper. Who'd blame her for staying the hell away?

'OK, tell me.' Hastings placed his elbows on the armrests either side of him, his hands coming together, fingers touching in the familiar triangle as he prepared to concentrate.

'Mearns and I met with Marcie Wade on Saturday. She contacted us about a note Jenkins had received after

Andrew Shirriffs died. We have reason to believe it was written to his father, Kirk.'

Eve filled him in on the contents of the note, that it implied there had been a witness to Andrew's death.

'What are you saying exactly?'

'I'm not convinced about Andrew Shirriffs's death being the suicide it was made out to be.'

The pressure in Hastings's fingertips looked to be in danger of breaking bones. 'Eve, that is a serious accusation.'

Eve leaned forward, eager to get her point across. 'I know, sir, and I wouldn't go there without something to back it up.' She divulged what Wade had told them about Jenkins' attempts to investigate the note, how she'd effectively been shut down wherever she tried to open a door – by DI Crawford specifically.

Hastings parted his hands, dragged one across his forehead. 'You're talking about a fellow colleague. A retired, highly regarded, *gravely ill* fellow colleague.'

'I know, and I wish I'd known he was ill before we went to visit.'

Hastings shot forward in his chair. 'You went to see him?'

'Yes, sir, because I did a little digging and I didn't have to go deep before I uncovered something.'

'Uncovered what?'

'Something that should've been there and wasn't. Missing files. Paper copy and electronic. Everything and anything to do with the examination of the scene, which I have reason to believe might include finger- prints of a woman possibly there that night. The same woman we know was at Dean Johnstone's the night he was killed – our Jane Doe found hanged up at Hazlehead.'

Hastings inhaled sharply. 'And how have you come to that conclusion?'

'Three young men who were best friends. Two dead in their own homes, the third being Finn Miller, which opens a whole other can of worms with what they were into, both recently and historically – their fathers and their connections. The fact our Jane Doe was killed the same weekend as Dean and that Andrew's mother voiced in the press her suspicions surrounding her son's death.'

'So, what's your take on it?'

'We know Dean was murdered. I think Andrew was too.'

'And you suspect it was this woman, your Jane Doe?'

'I can't say it wasn't her, but, if it was, I think she would've disappeared after Andrew's death. I believe Finn is involved – definitely with this girl and I'm not ruling out that involvement including his friends' deaths.'

Hastings had gone pale. 'This is going to cause a shit storm. You need to be sure. To have all the evidence stacked.'

'Which is why I need those files and I think they're in Crawford's home.'

Eve ignored the look of horror on Hastings's face and went on to tell him about what his wife had divulged about the golden handshake and the actual truth of his pension, etc. 'He was desperate. Could've been open to being paid to make those files disappear.'

Hastings sat silent for a moment. 'Who do you think made that payment?'

Eve didn't see the point in beating about the bush. 'At the moment, it's all hearsay, but I'm willing to bet Peter Miller. He had a lot to lose if his son could be placed there – or this girl. I want Ferguson to work on Cowan for me, see if he'll try and get access to those files.'

'Why Ferguson?'

'Him and Cowan have, or at least had, a shared hatred of me. Cowan may do it if he believes it's a favour to Ferguson.'

Hastings looked torn. 'I guess we need to find out either way but, Christ, I hope you're wrong. Crawford was a good officer.'

Eve said nothing; both of them knew officers who had done things out of character in the past. Through circumstances, or loss of morale. Desperation.

'I'm going to see the Shirriffses tonight. I'll ask about that note, find out if they were ever aware of it. Try and probe what they know about their son's death. Also, there's a fundraiser at Miller's on Thursday night. I'm going to put Mearns and Ferguson on it. See if we can find out who exactly these men are running with and so on.'

'Fine. Go easy.'

'I know, I know.' Eve stood, eager to leave before the chat about her sometimes aggressive approach was dredged up again.

She walked towards the door, believing for the briefest of moments she could leave without anything more being said.

'Eve?'

She closed her eyes.

'I got Dr Shetty's report. Seems I'm right to be worried about the temper.'

Eve turned. 'Really? You try eighteen months of having your life picked apart by someone. Of having to tie every emotion, everything you supposedly should be feeling but aren't, or are feeling but not showing, to a key point in the knee-deep crap you've waded through. I bet you'd find it difficult to keep smiling for the doc too. Sir.'

Eve turned back and opened the door to leave, knowing Hastings wouldn't reply. Because he knew as well as she did that he wouldn't last five minutes in Dr Shetty's office.

Chapter 47

'NICE PLACE YOU HAVE HERE.' Eve meant it. The Shirriffses' restaurant was bright and airy, the leafy tree at its centre stretching towards the glass-panelled roof, the roots visible in the large square space of soil that had been left in the flagstoned floor. Wooden tables fanned around and out from the centrepiece. The surroundings were intimate, family run, unlike the characterless chains.

'Thank you.' Kirk Shirriffs was a pale man, deep lines etched around sunken blue eyes that gazed out from beneath a receding hairline. Eve wondered if his pallor came down to hours spent in the kitchen or if the haggardness had set in after the loss of his son.

She smelled strong aftershave intermingling with a floral perfume as she and Cooper were led through the restaurant, away from windows looking out on to Holburn Street and the prying eyes of passing pedestrians and traffic tailed back from the lights at Holburn Junction. She took a seat at the square table for four, Cooper sitting to her right, those hollow blue eyes directly opposite her.

Patricia hovered by the spare seat. 'Can I get you coffee? Tea?'

Eve shook her head, as did Cooper. 'No thanks.'

The woman seemed deflated, as if she'd been desperate to do anything but take the seat next to them. She sat gingerly, fussing at her blouse, glancing between the table top and her husband. Nervous but stunning. Looking a good few years younger than her husband. Tanned, although Eve suspected it was fake, and toned.

Kirk seemed to sense his wife's discomfort. He reached an arm across to her lap and placed his hand there. Her hand stopped fussing. He glanced at his wife, gave a reassuring smile before shifting his gaze to Eve.

Eve noticed Patricia's hand stayed clear of her husband's.

Kirk spoke. 'Apologies, Detective Inspector. As you can imagine, this is difficult for us.'

'I appreciate that. Thank you for agreeing to see us.' Eve looked at Patricia as she said it. It was obvious she was struggling, visibly more so than her husband. Regardless, Kirk appeared to be a breath of fresh air compared to Peter and Robert.

Eve cast a look between them. 'We don't want to cause you any upset. As you know, we're investigating Dean Johnstone's death and it's come to our attention that Dean and Andrew were great friends. Finn Miller as well, we believe. The three of them were pretty tight?'

243

Kirk nodded. Patricia's eyes were now fixed on the table top.

Eve wanted to take this slowly; the pain was clearly still raw. 'Being only a year since you lost Andrew, the news of Dean's death must've come as a real shock.'

'Yes.' Obvious hesitation in Kirk's voice. 'But also, no.'

'Can I ask why?'

'Let's just say Dean didn't handle Andrew's death well. Dean had been used to coming in and out of our home as if it were his own. It was such a big shift for all of us when Andrew died. Like a family splitting up.'

'Did it affect your relationship with the boys' fathers as well?'

Kirk looked surprised.

'In the course of our investigations we found out about the school connection and your long-standing friendship.'

'I see. Yes, I guess it has made things different.'

Patricia turned to her husband.

Kirk didn't look her way. 'Happened without us noticing. In the weeks after the funeral, we invited Dean and his father, Robert, over for a meal. Like the old days – except nothing like those days. How could it be with an empty chair there?'

Patricia's intake of breath was easily heard in the long pause.

Eve hadn't missed the fact there was no mention of Peter and Finn Miller being invited. 'I can't begin to imagine how awful it must've been for all of you. I hope you don't mind me asking, but it came to light recently

244

that a reporter tried to talk to you around the time of Andrew's death. I believe she would've been quite insistent?'

There was clear distaste on Kirk's face. 'Claire Jenkins. The reporter murdered last year.'

Eve wasn't surprised he remembered her name or her demise. Jenkins had possessed a knack for being remembered, usually for all the wrong reasons.

'Yes. Did you ever talk with her?'

Kirk shook his head. 'Not in any great detail. Usually to tell her to piss off until I finally blocked her number.'

Eve could relate to that move. 'Were you ever made aware of a note sent to her?'

'A note?' He sounded confused.

'Someone sent her a note anonymously. One she believed to have been addressed to you.'

Kirk looked at Patricia and back to Eve. 'She might've mentioned something in the few seconds that I gave her airtime. I wasn't in a good place. I assumed anything she had to say would be nothing more than an attempt to get me to listen. To lull me into talking.'

Eve sat back. 'I'm sorry to have had to ask. Jenkins wasn't the most reputable journalist. Perhaps this was a ploy from her, or perhaps some sick prank from someone out there. They certainly do come out in their droves whenever there's a tragedy.'

Eve did her best to sound convincing, all the while looking out of the corner of her eye, watching Patricia. 'Getting back to Robert. What about him and Peter? Or Finn? Do you still see them?'

Patricia flinched.

Kirk, thrown for a second, answered. 'Since Andrew, the time it took for us to function again after, and the hours I put in at the restaurants, we don't see each other the same. I still spend time with both of them, mostly at the monthly fundraiser. That's when I see Finn too.'

Cooper waded in. 'We heard about that. There's one Thursday night?'

'Yes.'

Eve hesitated; then she decided it was worth the chance. 'You seem different from Robert and Peter.'

'How?'

Cooper answered. 'We've had real difficulty getting them to talk with us. Peter has made it particularly hard for us to speak to Finn.'

Eve studied Patricia. She hadn't regained her composure like her husband had.

Kirk didn't look surprised about Peter. 'I guess we've always been different, even as kids. The two of them weren't alike either. But it somehow worked, our friendship. Robert has always been a closed book. Not much emotion there and a need to keep the upper lip stiff. Comes across as a grumpy sonofabitch.'

Eve couldn't disagree.

'Peter was always the party guy, but even he knows that Finn takes it too far. He can be a liability, I guess. He tries to keep him close.'

Eve wanted to know how much of a liability and how far Finn was willing to push the boundaries. Whether it stretched as far as murder. Whether the note was legitimate – if there was a chance Finn had written it. She needed to tread carefully. 'I thought that was maybe the case. We do need to talk with Finn as he seems to be the one who knew most about Dean in the final months and weeks.'

Kirk hesitated, knowing what she was asking. 'If I could help, I would. I don't want to get involved. As I said, things have been different.'

Eve sensed the conversation was going nowhere. Patricia's reaction to the mention of Peter and Finn Miller was playing on her mind.

Eve stood. 'I understand what you're saying, and I know there's not much more you can give us. I'd like to thank you for what you have shared with us and, again, I'm sorry for your loss with Andrew. And now Dean.'

Cooper was probably wondering why she would leave things there, not realizing yet she wasn't. Far from it. Patricia was the one they needed to talk to. Alone. Maybe then she'd say out loud what was going on.

Chapter 48

Wednesday

PATRICIA SHIRRIFFS STEPPED OUT of Nuffield gym in Holburn looking like something out of a sports magazine – toned, glowing and Lycra-clad; a water bottle in hand and a gym bag slung over her shoulder.

'There she goes.' Eve and Cooper sat by the window in the Foundry Bar, a perfect viewpoint for the gym's entrance and exit, and somewhere they'd been sitting for the last half-hour sipping early-morning soft drinks amongst the various breakfasts being served. They stood and left through the side door; Patricia was still in sight as she strolled down Justice Mill Lane.

Eve and Cooper moved fast, catching up with her in minutes.

'Patricia?'

The woman turned, confusion on her face turning to recognition. 'What are you doing here?'

Eve answered. 'We wanted to talk to you.'

'I spoke with you yesterday.'

'You did, but I'm not sure you said everything you wanted to.'

Patricia's eyes flickered to the pavement. 'I don't know what you mean.'

'Do you have time for a quick coffee?' Eve looked above them to the Travelodge sign.

Patricia looked down the street. 'I'm heading to the restaurant to be there for a delivery.'

'Half an hour.'

The woman seemed unsure. 'But Kirk . . .'

'Kirk doesn't need to know.' Eve took advantage of the hesitation, stepped forward and pulled open the door to the Travelodge.

The lounge was pleasant enough, and the coffee good.

'I apologize if I'm overstepping here. I got the impression you might know something your husband wasn't telling us.'

Patricia held the coffee cup with both hands and blew gently on the hot liquid, not making eye contact.

Eve moved closer. 'Patricia, were you expecting Kirk to say more, or would you have – if he hadn't been there?'

Patricia laid the cup down, bit at her bottom lip. 'My husband's a good man.'

Eve didn't hear conviction in the statement. 'I'm sure he is. It's not about that.'

'I'm not even sure what I know myself.'

Cooper pushed at the saucer his coffee cup stood on. 'What do you mean?'

'I've never believed Andrew took his life.'

Eve already knew that. 'The ruling was suicide.'

'Maybe. I don't think so.' She looked down to her lap.

Cooper's voice was gentle. 'If you don't think it was suicide . . .'

Patricia lifted her eyes to Cooper, her bottom lip quivering.

He continued carefully, knowing this was delicate: 'You think Andrew was murdered?'

'I was, *am*, his mum. I knew my son. He wouldn't have killed himself.'

If Eve had a penny for every time she'd heard that statement, or similar, from a parent of a suicide victim. The reality was sometimes there were no signs in advance, no obvious reason, no note left.

Eve trod gently. 'What do you think happened?'

Patricia's voice was abrupt, hard, taking Eve by surprise. 'Believe me, I wish I knew. What I do know is that someone was there when he died.'

Matching Eve's suspicions about the note sent to Jenkins, which appeared to confirm it, and the missing police reports on Andrew's death. Was this what they were trying to cover up?

Cooper spoke whilst Eve tried to gather her thoughts. 'Do you know who?'

'Yeah, a prostitute.'

Eve's heart quickened. Images of their Jane Doe flashed in her head. 'How do you know that? Do you know who she was?'

Patricia shook her head. 'Andrew rented a central, executive flat, an ideal pad for hitting the pubs. The

250

night he died, Finn phoned me in a state. Sounded pretty wasted but that was nothing new. Said he was downtown with Dean as Andrew had wanted to stay in.'

'Did you find that unusual?'

'No, as I knew how heavy their weekends were. As young as they were, there were times I guess he couldn't keep up.'

'What did Finn say?'

'That Andrew had phoned him. Twice, before he saw the missed calls. He said the music in the club they were in was too loud. He'd gone outside for a smoke and phoned Andrew. Said Andrew was slurring, crying, saying he was in a bad way.'

'What did Finn do?'

'He told him to get a grip, that he was having a bad comedown, that he'd send a girl to ride it out until they got home.'

Eve blanched. 'Charming.'

'Partying it out was Finn's answer to everything.'

'And did Andrew calm down?'

'Finn says he did and, after a while, he made a joke about starting on his own.'

'Partying or . . .'

'Sex.' Patricia's cheeks coloured. Probably imagining her baby boy, not the adult he had become.

Eve was confused. 'Why did Finn phone you?'

'After a neighbour called him. A young woman. I think she and Finn had flirted on occasion when he was round at Andrew's. Knowing Finn, he probably played on the whole "rock star" thing. I think his number was given freely, let's say. Anyway, the neighbour heard a woman screaming from within Andrew's flat. By the time the police arrived, she'd vanished.'

'Did you ever get to speak to this girl? Was she not involved in the investigation?'

'The police were never able to trace her. Regardless of fingerprints, they couldn't match them to anyone else.'

Eve's mind was on that missing report again. They needed those prints. 'But Finn org—'

'According to Finn he didn't know anything about her. Fake name, no way of contacting her. A good-time girl who they made arrangements with in person when out and about on the scene.'

Eve didn't miss the subtle twitch of Patricia's hand. 'You don't believe that?'

Patricia stroked her hand. 'I'm not so naive to think Andrew wasn't involved in . . . certain taboo things, but I find it hard to believe he would've done what the report suggested. I've always suspected she was in that room before he died.'

Eve asked her next question softly. 'Do you think Finn or Dean were involved? That they were there?'

Patricia was agitated, as if she'd already said too much. 'Dean and Finn were lost. You know, without their mothers. Andrew was a good kid. I like to think a positive influence on them – kept them from going off the rails, if you like.'

'And you still believe that?'

'Overall, yes. But I think they were strong kids, they had to be with the fathers they had, the way they'd been brought up. I think Andrew was led along from

252

time to time, involved in experimenting alongside them. We all try things when we're young, push boundaries. Perhaps not as extreme as what those boys were involved in.'

Eve's mind wandered to Kirk, his friendship with the boys' fathers.

'Do you think it was a similar dynamic to that of your husband with Robert Johnstone and Peter Miller?'

Patricia's nose wrinkled, her lip curling for the briefest of seconds. Another visible reaction to the mention of the men. 'I don't want to paint Kirk as a weak man.'

'But you feel perhaps he played the same part in the three as your son, Andrew?'

'Yes.'

'Has he told you much about their childhood together?'

'He doesn't have to. I was a part of those years.'

Eve hadn't been expecting that. 'Didn't they go to an all-boys' school?'

'They did. Whereas as I came from the other side of the fence. A children's home.' Patricia looked from Eve to Cooper. 'Don't look so shocked. I've done all right for myself. But back then? I was in awe of the boys, that they even wanted to be my friend.'

Cooper spoke. 'Wow, this must've hit you all much harder than we ever realized.'

Patricia didn't deny it.

'Have you told Kirk what you think about Andrew's death?'

'Of course I have.'

Eve was sure she heard an anger there.

Cooper continued, 'What did he say to it?'

'That I had to face the truth. That Andrew had put the noose around his neck.'

Eve prodded, feeling like Dr bloody Shetty. 'How did that make you feel?'

'Let down. That he wasn't willing to question it. To give his son more credit.'

'Why do you think that was the case?' Cooper, quietly.

'He's scared.'

Eve frowned. 'Scared? Of what?'

'To question it would mean challenging Peter and Robert, asking things about their sons. Opening up things they worked every day to hide.'

'What do you mean *hide*?' A burst of hope that they were finally getting somewhere, that they'd been right.

'All three of them have a reputation to uphold, business relationships, money-making schemes. It doesn't pay to have their offspring bringing bad PR to their door.'

'Don't they have skeletons they'd rather keep hidden?'

Patricia studied the table separating them. 'Everyone has skeletons, DI Hunter. What I do know is that my husband doesn't sleep well at nights.'

'Why? Some kind of guilt?'

'You'd have to ask him that.'

Cooper trod carefully with the next question. 'Have you never questioned his dealings with Peter and Robert?'

Patricia smiled, but there was no joy in the gesture. 'He's a grown-up.'

'What about the monthly meet? Kirk said yesterday it's now the only time he sees his old friends.' Eve hoped she came across as casual.

Patricia licked her top lip. 'Peter has a lot of contacts in the city. He organizes a lot of corporate events, sponsors local companies. The monthly meet is his way of getting everyone together, raising money.'

Well rehearsed.

'Influential figures. It must be quite a do.'

'I've never been. It's a gentlemen's dinner. I remember Kirk being excited to meet Aberdeen Football Club's striker.'

Eve sensed her line of questioning going nowhere – again. 'So, why do you believe your husband doesn't sleep at nights?'

Patricia looked from Eve to Cooper. 'My husband has many struggles, perhaps ones I'm not fully aware of. I do know one thing.' She paused. 'I trust this goes no further?'

Eve didn't let a second pass before answering. 'Of course.'

'The business isn't doing great. Opening three restaurants across the city appeared the way to go and was profitable for a good while.'

'But things are getting worse?'

'It's hard to make up for business lost.'

'Are you looking at closure of any of the restaurants? Are things that bad?'

Patricia picked up her cup, sipped. 'We would've been had it not been for a recent cash injection.'

'From where?'

'The same person who lent us money to get on our feet with the first restaurant all those years ago.'

Eve gawked at Patricia. 'Peter Miller?'

'No.'

'Robert Johnstone?'

'Yes. After Andrew, we were broken and when you experience loss, people, even those closest to you, can sometimes step away. I don't think Robert meant to. I guess he struggled to know what to say or how to be. The extra money was a way of making up for that.'

'I see. Not knowing how to be in these circumstances is common, isn't it? But surprising, what with Robert losing his wife.'

'I was good friends with Dean's mum, Nancy. When she died, I became something of a substitute mother for Dean. Robert was glad of that as he found it difficult being both things for his son.'

'Maybe it brought it all back for Dean when Andrew died?'

Tears filled Patricia's eyes. 'Dean was like his mum. Sensitive. He didn't want to back away like Robert. I did try to be there for him but I was dealing with my own grief. Robert perhaps had a word with Dean. Didn't want us to be burdened because Dean eventually stopped trying to be in contact. With what's happened, I can't help but feel guilty.'

'Had it been some time before his death since you'd last spoken with him?'

Patricia stretched out her neck. 'You asked about a note. If either of them were there that night, it would've been Dean who'd want to confess.'

'What about Finn?'

'We haven't seen Finn since the day of Andrew's funeral.' Patricia set down her cup. 'Doesn't that tell you something?'

Eve leaned in. 'You think Finn had something to do with Andrew's murder, don't you?'

Patricia began to sob. 'I don't know. Perhaps.'

Eve's mind whirred. What if Peter Miller and Robert Johnstone had known their sons were there? Had Dean's death had something to do with that?

She refocused, thinking what to say to Patricia, sensing she wouldn't be pushed any further on whom she suspected was responsible for Andrew's death. 'Do you know if Finn had met with Dean in recent weeks?'

Patricia sat a moment as if weighing up whether to say any more. 'He definitely had.'

'How do you know that?'

'Because Robert blames Finn for Dean's overdose.'

Cooper straightened. This was news to them. 'Dean overdosed? When?'

'About three weeks before his death. Dean had turned up in a nightclub looking for Finn. Dean caused a scene, fell over a table, was escorted out by security.'

Eve wanted more. 'Do you know what the exchange was about?'

'No, I heard the story second-hand from a restaurant customer. But to me it's pretty obvious.'

If Patricia's suspicions were right, Dean must have been carrying so much guilt. Especially if he'd been party to Andrew's death, or in covering up Finn's involvement.

Eve's head spun as she thought of the note again. It was now looking more likely Dean, tortured by his involvement, had written to Kirk to confess. Had Kirk lied when he said he hadn't seen the note? Perhaps he had been the one to send the note to the press, hoping to open a can of worms?

Hard to fathom what reading that note might've done to Kirk. Could it have driven him to kill Dean regardless of his confession, to murder their Jane Doe, knowing about her involvement?

Which only left Finn to be hunted down?

Or did Finn take both Dean and their Jane Doe out, knowing he was disposing of any remaining witnesses and danger to himself?

Chapter 49

FERGUSON STEPPED INTO THE doorway and made his way down the narrow staircase that took him below the city's Broad Street and into the belly of the Illicit Still bar. Mere yards from HQ, it was the perfect meeting place for a beer with Cowan.

He spotted his old friend seated at a booth, two freshly poured pints on the table in front of him, a food menu already in hand. One of the reasons he liked Cowan – his priorities were in order.

Ferguson slid on to the bench opposite him, a twinge of guilt that it had been so long. That he was only here because Eve had put him up to it. 'Cheers for the pint.' He picked up the glass and took a long drink from it. Cowan put down the menu and lifted his pint glass, matching Ferguson's long gulp. 'Ah . . . Been a while. What brought this on?'

Ferguson might've known he'd get straight to the point. Cowan's patience threshold for bullshit was as low as his. 'I need a favour.'

Cowan traced a finger up through the condensation on his ice-cold glass before looking straight at him. 'She wants me to go and see if those files are in Crawford's home, doesn't she?'

Ferguson didn't even consider trying to sugar-coat it. 'Yes. If, that is, you've had no luck in tracing them?'

Cowan didn't confirm or deny it; no need to with what he was about to say. 'Man, he was my boss. A good one. You're asking me to—'

Ferguson butted in. 'I know what I'm asking and I'm sorry to even be going there, but we need those files. We believe they may be the link between three murders.'

'Murders?' The shock genuine.

'Yeah, including Andrew Shirriffs.'

'But Andrew—'

'I know what the findings were. This thing is so much bigger.' Ferguson looked around the bar. 'It's not something I can talk about here.' He lowered his voice to a whisper. 'Crawford may have been paid to make those files go away.'

Cowan didn't hesitate in shaking his head. 'No, no, he wouldn't have . . .' His words trailed off, Ferguson assuming he was giving thought to the way Crawford had left. His animosity at the financial fuck-up.

Ferguson took the chance to strike. 'Listen, I know it's not exactly honourable. You could go to the house, tell Crawford's wife you're working on an old case and you need to check some of his old paperwork.'

Cowan sniffed. 'And you think she'll go for that?'

Ferguson cocked his head. 'She likes you. No need to doubt you. Look at it this way, at least you'll know.'

Cowan took another long drink of his pint, and another, draining what was left of it. He shuffled to the end of the booth bench.

Ferguson shunted forward on the seat. 'Where're you going?'

'I'm off the food.' He stood, hands in jacket pocket, and looked down at Ferguson. 'I'll do it. Only to prove your bitch of a boss wrong.' He turned and stalked away.

Ferguson sent a text to Eve. *He's in*.

Chapter 50

Thursday

'How big is that bloody car park around the back?' Ferguson grumbled as the umpteenth car turned into the hotel, not one of the vehicles more than two years old.

Mearns and Ferguson sat in the car across the street from Miller's Hotel in Albyn, a stone's throw from the main drag of Union Street. They'd purposely chosen the one parking space tonight not beneath a streetlight.

'Elite crowd, for sure.' Mearns pulled her lukewarm takeaway coffee cup from the holder beside the steering wheel. 'Would help if we could see who they are.'

Ferguson checked his watch. 'Let's give it five minutes and we'll go in.'

Mearns looked towards the hotel. 'They can't refuse a couple a drink in the public bar. You never know, they may all be standing there having pre-drinks. A little over twenty mins until the do starts. Although I can't see this clientele mixing with the overnight guests or hobnobbing with the average Joe off the street. They're going to be led into a function suite straight away, doors closed.'

'Maybe.' Ferguson drummed the glove compartment with his fingers. 'If no joy at the bar, we enjoy a quick drink and think up a plan B.'

'Genius.' Sarcasm dripped from Mearns's voice.

'Give me a better idea. Besides, I fancy a nosey at Miller's place. See if they do a good pint, you know, since you're designated driver.'

Mearns rested her head against the window. 'Hey up.' She straightened in her seat, put the cup in the plastic ring. 'There's someone we do know.'

Ferguson craned his neck as he leaned towards Mearns's side. Robert Johnstone's sleek Mercedes slid into the hotel entrance.

'Using a personal reg as a status symbol kind of makes it hard to hide,' said Mearns.

Ferguson tutted. 'Two weeks since Dean died and here's his father already schmoozing.'

Mearns turned to Ferguson. 'What is it they say? The show must go on?'

'In that case, let's get on with it.'

Ferguson jumped out of the car before Mearns could say anything. She beeped the car doors and jogged to catch him up as he crossed the road.

The hotel bar was dead. The guy behind the bar stood polishing a glass, glancing over every now and again to his lone customer, an elderly gent in the corner, and looking as if he wished he was wringing the cloth he held around the man's neck.

'Pint of Tennent's, please.' Ferguson fumbled in his pocket.

'And a fresh orange and lemonade.' Mearns liked to think her colleague was about to order her a drink, but knew better than to give him the benefit of the doubt.

'Sorry, sir, the bar's closed.'

Ferguson was crestfallen. 'Closed? It's twenty past seven.'

'Private function tonight, I'm afraid.'

Mearns tilted her chin towards the old guy in the corner. 'What's his story?'

'That gentleman comes in here most afternoons. He's finishing his drink.'

'Surely the hotel bar doesn't shut because there's a private function?'

'Usually no, but it does for this one. The whole hotel does. Any room bookings are for attendees only.'

'Must be some function.'

'It is. I'm sorry. We would be glad of your custom on another day.'

'Thanks.' Mearns made her way towards the door, half dragging Ferguson with her, keen not to make any kind of scene that would draw attention to them.

Ferguson hissed. 'What are we—'

'Shhh. Follow me.' Mearns walked out front into the dark courtyard. There was a row of tables over to the side lit by fairy lights. She sat at the middle one.

Ferguson stayed standing. 'This is plan B?'

'No. Plan B is currently finishing his drink – and here he comes.'

The elderly gent stepped unsteadily from the hotel entrance, mumbling to himself, clearly not happy with being turfed out.

'Bit of a nightmare as you're getting a taste for it, isn't it?' Ferguson tutted.

'Bloody carry-on.' The man walked over to them and slowed.

'Where's the best place closest to here for a drink?' Mearns's Bolton accent made it easy to act as a clueless tourist.

'I'm heading to the College bar. You're welcome to join me.'

'Well, if you're sure.'

The College was hoatching, apparently popular with the after-work crew, judging by the number of suits milling about. Mearns sat off to the side of the square bar that dominated the centre of the room. She and Ferguson watched Graham, their new drinking buddy, dodging the crowds as he made his way from the bar with their drinks.

'Thanks.' Ferguson smiled. 'I would easily have got them in.'

'Not at all.' Graham looked around. 'Half the regulars from Miller's are in here tonight.'

Mearns lifted her soft drink. 'Is Miller's your local?'

'Yeah. I'm down Holburn. Plenty of pubs around me but full of the young crowd and loud. I like Miller's; it's quiet, there's never any trouble, and you're guaranteed a seat. Got boring in my old age, I guess.'

Ferguson, casual, pretended to watch a guy at the bar. 'You reckon Miller's is boring?'

Their new drinking buddy licked white beer froth from his top lip. 'A lot of them are stuck-up buggers. Comes with the money you need to be able to spend time there, I guess. And of course, there's the crowd you never see. Miller's Millionaires, I like to call them.'

'Miller's Millionaires?' Mearns looked amused.

'Yeah. The crowd in there tonight. Private function.'

Mearns cocked her head, feigning naive interest. 'And they never drink in the bar?'

The old man grunted. 'Are you joking? Peter Miller knows how it all works. He's got his fingers in all the pies. Bars for the young crowd at one end of his port-folio, exclusive hotel at the other, but then there's the elite: that's a personal project of Miller's and I doubt anything to do with his business profile.'

Ferguson lowered his glass to the table, sure he would've got a better pint at Miller's. 'How do you know?'

The man smirked. 'Not hard to suss out when your local closes once a month and the function room remains open.'

Ferguson shook his head, looking disgusted for the guy. 'What's that all about?'

'Your guess is as good as mine. Judging by the cars that arrive and the fact there seems to be a need for pri-vacy, the meal must be pretty Michelin-starred.'

Ferguson whistled low. 'Do you reckon that's all it is?'

'What? A meal? No, I bet there's a little behind-closed-doors entertainment.'

Ferguson shuffled close. 'Like?'

The elderly gent leaned towards him and whispered, 'You heard about that Gentlemen's Club down south, right?'

Mearns pretended to be interested in her phone. Leaving them to their 'man chat'.

Ferguson tapped the side of his nose. 'Yeah, lots of young waitresses brought in wearing next to nothing, countless loaded guys being, let's say, a little inappropriate in their conduct.'

'You got it. I'm not saying there's misconduct as such but there're definitely girls.'

Ferguson pursed his lips. 'As in not the usual staff?'

The man moved closer to Ferguson. 'Oh, these aren't girls they'd have in the main hotel bar and restaurant. Those ones are all white blouses, waistcoats and sensible shoes.'

Ferguson did his best to look excited. 'How did you manage to see these girls?'

'As you probably saw, I make a point of dragging my heels when I'm told to drink up. This one time, they got shirty about me taking my time. Told me to leave abruptly, wouldn't even let me use the toilet. Thought I was being awkward. I was bursting for a piss.'

Ferguson gripped his glass. 'What did you do?'

'Went around the back and sprinkled their plants. I saw a couple of burly guys letting a load of girls out of the back of two big black vans. They weren't wearing the usual waitressing attire. Far from it.'

Ferguson turned his ear closer to Graham. 'How were they dressed?'

'To please, if you know what I mean. Plenty of chat between the two men but the girls were pretty quiet, filing in through the back door yards from where I was pissing. They didn't see me, but I heard quiet chatter between a few of them.'

'Talking about what?'

'I wouldn't have known. They were foreign.'

Mearns lifted her gaze from her phone, fighting to hide her own excitement.

'Where from, do you reckon?' Ferguson didn't have to pretend to be hanging on every word.

'Eastern European, I'd say.'

Ferguson's heart hammered. Was this proof Jane Doe was linked to Peter Miller and his crew?

The man took a gulp of his beer. 'Redefined the term cattle market. Especially when I saw they all had matching tattoos on their necks – a barcode, can you believe it? Like they'd been branded.'

Chapter 51

MEARNS AND FERGUSON SAT in the dark on a plastic sheet they'd found in the car boot, behind one of the few cars that looked as though it didn't belong to any of the Miller's Hotel guests tonight: a ten-year-old Toyota Auris in need of a good wash.

The low muffle of music and group chatter could be heard from the hotel. Ferguson lay back, propping himself up by his elbows. 'We might be here long enough.'

Mearns stretched her legs out. 'True, but it's the only way we're going to see those vans when they come back to pick up the girls.'

After leaving the old man to his pint, Mearns and Ferguson had sneaked back to the car to collect their coats. They couldn't risk being spotted, so had crawled to their current hiding spot via a service entrance into the car park.

Ferguson whispered in the dark. 'If those girls are even in there in the first place.'

'There's nothing to say they're not.'

269

Ferguson tutted. 'And only a drunk guy's story of another night to say they are.'

'What else you got?'

Ferguson grumbled. 'Point taken.'

Mearns sighed. 'You're pissed off I made excuses to leave the College before you'd finished your drink.'

Ferguson snorted. 'Exactly. We could have spent another hour there instead of freezing our arses off here.'

'This is the first potential lead we've had connecting our Jane Doe to the Trinity. Perhaps to that brotherhood tattoo. Do you want to risk missing anything?'

'I guess not but I wish I'd bought a carry-out.'

Mearns went to swat his leg, but stopped as she heard a door open in the distance, music and voices loud for a brief moment before the door closed again. She raised herself up, clutching where the car boot met window and peering through it. A security light came on above the door where a lone guy was lighting a cigarette. She ducked as the door opened again.

'I'm gasping. Thought we'd never get finished.'

The voice was male, well spoken. Mearns was not sure if it was the guy she'd seen speaking or the person who'd joined him. Both she and Ferguson dared to raise their heads to look through the rear window.

The taller of the two men leaned forward, cupping his hand around the light the shorter man offered. Mearns heard him inhale deeply, the orange end of his cigarette glowing before he spoke on the exhale. 'Think it'll take long for them all to clear out?'

'Nah. Once the evening's entertainment's gone, Miller's usually good at getting them out the door.'

Ferguson's elbow dug at her rib, probably hoping, as she was, that they were talking about the girls.

'I better get back in. Last chance to cop an eyeful.' He laughed, the sound higher-pitched than Mearns had been expecting.

'Rather you than me. Makes my stomach turn what goes on in there. If I didn't need the money . . .'

The reply was even more higher-pitched. 'You kidding me? Have you seen those girls? I dream of the day I'm rich enough to get invited. It's like they're up for anything.' He slid something down a side panel to the door and pulled it open, giving Mearns a better look at the one left standing, tutting at his workmate's reply.

He was tall, well built; the top of his arms strained at the white shirt he wore beneath a waistcoat. Mearns was surprised he smoked, as if such a honed physique would shy away from such a thing. His dark hair was undercut both sides, his long fringe quiffed at the front.

'I'll be in once I'm done.'

The shorter guy looked back. 'Aye, make sure that's before I've cleared the bar on my own.'

'If you're lucky.'

Mearns and Ferguson sat back on the verge, not speaking until they heard the door open and close again.

Ferguson spoke first. 'They're finishing up.'

'Yeah, and sounds like the girls are in there.'

They huddled together, towards the centre of the boot, as headlights bounced off the car next to the one they were hiding behind, the vehicle driving in the service entrance and stopping outside the back door where the two men had re-entered the hotel. They heard car doors opening, the bangs heavy and loud as they shut again. Heavy footsteps walked off towards the hotel; Mearns dared to lift her head to look, Ferguson doing the same beside her.

Two men. Gorillas in size and dressed in dark suits that looked in danger of bursting.

Ferguson whispered, 'They're built like brick shithouses.'

'Sshhh.'

Neither of the men appeared to have a neck, their heads seemingly stuck directly on to their wide shoulders. Their shoes shone as the security light clicked on. One of them reached inside his jacket, pulled something out. A pass, obviously; he slid it down the side panel and the door buzzed open, before they both disappeared from view. Mearns looked across the car park, saw the new vehicles that hadn't been there before. Two black Mercedes vans.

'Our Graham wasn't wrong.'

The door opened. One of the burly guys stepped out into the car park. Mearns inhaled involuntarily as a girl stepped out behind him. She held her breath as another followed. And another. Then another. Mearns's breath was still tight as she clocked what the girls were wearing. Short black Lycra tube dresses. Identical to their

272

Jane Doe. The black line snaking behind the man as he made his way across to the vans reminded Mearns of ants. The line of them came to an end as the second of the men stepped out of the door, shoving at the thin girl in front of him.

The first van's side panel was roughly pulled back.

'*Intră.*' The voice was gruff and, although the girls followed obediently, filing into the vehicle, the man still took pleasure in manhandling and shoving them as they entered.

The girls filtered in without a word said between them or to the men, the door sliding shut as abruptly as it had been opened. The same happened with the second van.

Mearns dug in her pocket, took out her phone, risked stretching her arm out past the car in the dark, clicking to take a photo, doubtful if the men would even be in it.

The vans started. Mearns and Ferguson were off and running down the side of the hotel, forcing themselves to slow to a walk as they came out front, desperate to get to their car. They got in and Mearns started the engine, moving away from the kerbside before Ferguson had closed his door. If they were lucky, they'd catch the vans at the next roundabout.

Chapter 52

Eve's legs dangled from the stool next to her workbench. She'd been sitting there for some time, staring. Thinking. The ring of her mobile sounded harsh in the silence, bringing her back. It was Ferguson.

'Hey.' Eve heard a car indicator in the background, and assumed Mearns was driving as Ferguson talked. 'Where are you?'

'Been quite the night. It appears the original Trinity are definitely into the same kind of entertainment as their sons.' Ferguson filled Eve in on the vans and the girls – how they'd come to know they should even look for them.

'Christ. This is much bigger than we thought.'

'Looking like it. The two guys definitely look Eastern European. We managed to get a shot of them on Mearns's mobile. Grainy, dark, but maybe enough to search on.'

'Two guys?' Eve's heart quickened.

'Yup, could've been twins. Seems you might've been right on the brotherhood.'

'Text it through to me so I can get it to Portman, find out if he recognizes them through his trafficking work. If he can confirm it's those Rusu brothers he told us about.'

'Will do. We're following the vans now but thought we better get the go-ahead from you to continue.'

'Without back-up? Ferguson, these guys will mean business.'

'Don't worry, we're keeping a good distance from them. It could lead us to where they're working from.'

Eve wanted to tell them to get the hell out of there, but Ferguson was right. She relented, resigned to it. 'OK, but do not approach them under any circumstances – and keep in touch.'

'We will. There's one other thing.'

Eve doubted anything else could be added to tonight's events. 'What?'

'The guy we spoke to, the one who told us about the girls. He was close enough to see something that confirms our Jane Doe was more than likely working for these guys.'

Eve knew what before Ferguson said it.

'A barcode tattoo. On the back of all of the girls' necks.'

Eve shut her eyes, didn't answer.

'Not only that, their outfits are identical to our Jane Doe.'

This time Eve did answer, no more than a whisper. 'We're going to get these bastards.'

Mearns and Ferguson waited at the traffic lights outside the College bar they'd not long left. It was mainly taxis on the roads at this time, and they were one taxi behind the vans.

The lights turned green. 'Where do you reckon we're going?'

'No idea but we're about to find out.' Ferguson fiddled with his phone, texting the image of the men to Eve as promised.

Fifteen minutes later, the vans were turning off Clifton Road in Woodside into a dead-end street. Mearns didn't follow them in, parking on the main street instead. The only thing down that side street was a multi-storey residential building.

Ferguson turned to Mearns. 'That dead end leads on to a lane out on to Great Northern Road. Nothing suspicious if we take a stroll. We might be residents heading for one of the pubs there.'

Mearns went to pull the handle to open the door but stopped. 'How do you know?'

He winked. 'An old girlfriend used to live around here.'

Mearns and Ferguson made their way down the hilly lane running along the back of the flats. Although they couldn't see the vans parked at the front, they could hear the side panels opening and squeaking on the runners.

Ferguson pointed to a path around the edge of the building. Mearns followed his lead. They stopped short of the view of the car park and listened. Footsteps taken in high heels. The odd yelp or groan, which Mearns took to be the girls being shoved by the men again. The lamp post at the corner of the building was out. Mearns dared to duck forward. Both vans were abandoned in the middle of the car park, the girls filing out one by one, the same as they had entered the vehicles. They didn't talk, pause, or look anywhere but at their feet before they disappeared out of view. Mearns heard a door open, which she took to be the main door of the block; moments passed as she imagined them all walking into the building before she heard the clunk of it closing behind them

'They all live in there?' Ferguson's eyes were wide.

'Looks like it and I doubt they're scattered throughout the building.'

'They can't all be in one flat.'

Mearns looked at Ferguson. 'I bet you they are.'

'What now?'

'They're not going to be leaving their vans like that. Plenty of spaces they didn't take. My guess is Tweedledum and Tweedledee are going somewhere else.' Without saying anything, they turned and made their way back to the car.

The headlights hit the top of the side street before the vans did. Mearns and Ferguson slumped in the car seats, aware they might be spotted if the vans turned left towards them, back the way they'd come. Mearns breathed a sigh of relief as they edged on to Clifton Road and turned right.

The black vans led Mearns and Ferguson through the Aberdeen suburbs of Bucksburn and on to Dyce. When they'd turned off the main road, down on to a narrow country lane, Mearns slowed and drove straight ahead, keen not to make it too obvious the vehicles were being followed. She pulled up at the first available opportunity and waited a few excruciating seconds before she turned the car and indicated right upon spotting the lane.

The road was uneven and Mearns took her time over the bumps and dips as they scanned the fields either side for signs of the vans or property, not wanting to draw attention to themselves. About three-quarters of a mile from the main road, they spotted a wide wooden farm gate. Closed. Nothing fancy, nothing out of the ordinary – apart from the vans parked outside the L-shaped steading that the gate protected. A woman, severe and scary-looking, had come out to the vans briefly, getting whatever she needed before going back in, none the wiser they were there.

Mearns peered after her. 'Doesn't look like one of the girls.'

'Maybe one of the brothers has a girlfriend.' Ferguson shifted in the seat. 'What now?'

'I doubt they'll be moving again tonight.'

They sat in a layby metres past the steading. Headlights and engine off. In the rear-view mirror, Mearns saw light at one of the steading windows. What she wouldn't give to be able to see who and what was going on inside.

She turned to Ferguson in the dark. 'You reckon it's the three of them in there?'

'Who knows. By the looks of things they like their privacy.'

'Seems they also like distance from their girls.'

Ferguson stretched over, stealing a glance in the rear-view mirror. 'Do you reckon the place at Woodside is their only accommodation for these girls?'

'Probably not. But they must be sure of the power they hold over them if they leave them unsupervised.'

'Oh, I doubt they do. Someone must be there keeping watch, or they'll have cameras or some sort of alarm system, I'd reckon. That and maybe the threat of a random visit.'

Mearns looked at the clock on the dashboard. 'Two a.m. I don't want to leave here and miss any action in the morning. Do you?'

Ferguson sighed. 'Fine. But let's find somewhere a little less visible for the car, where we can still have eyes on them. I'd better text Eve, get her say-so for this.'

Mearns smiled. She'd known he'd agree.

Ferguson texted, put his phone in the drinks holder and slumped in the seat as she moved off from the lay-by. 'You're taking the first shift.'

'All right by me.' Right now, Mearns didn't care whether she got any shut-eye at all.

Chapter 53

Friday

EVE PUT THE OFFICE phone between her and Cooper. She stifled a yawn. Eight a.m. and she might as well have not seen her bed. Her leg grumbled, reminding her she hadn't done her morning exercises, that she'd allowed herself to be tired enough for her old injury to be bothering her.

Mearns had called at 6 a.m. to let her know they were still out at the property they'd followed the vans to, hopeful of movement first thing and a better idea of what was going on. Eve had told them to give it until 8.30 a.m. latest; no doubt they'd arrive in a worse state than her. She was yet to hear from Portman. Granted, it had been the middle of the night when she texted through the image of the men.

She looked at Cooper, who appeared to be perpetually tired these days. He'd seemed on edge since arriving. Eve suspected there were ongoing problems between him and Louise.

Eve put the phone between them on loudspeaker and dialled. Lisa Taylor, Dean Johnstone's neighbour, answered on the third ring.

'Taylor Designs.'

Eve had expected something a little fancier for the name of her interior design business, a name that might've taken more than two seconds to come up with. It appeared Lisa felt she was fancy enough as she was.

'Hi, Lisa. Sorry to bother you. It's DI Hunter. We met coming up for a fortnight ago now.'

A pause on the line. 'Yes. Has something else happened?'

'No, no, nothing to worry about. It's something I'm hoping you might be able to answer for me. You mentioned being able to hear women when they were at Dean's apartment. Can I ask if they sounded British?'

After last night's revelation, Eve wanted to take a long shot at whether these girls had perhaps been out on personal loan to Dean Johnstone at home.

Lisa laughed. 'I'm not sure there's much difference in how us British moan to how the foreigners do it.'

Eve tried to join in the joke, keeping her tone light. 'I doubt it either, but did you hear them talk ever?'

'Sure, like I said, he appeared to like role play. I presumed they were playing up to that. You know, the old French maid kind of thing.'

'They spoke French?'

'Thinking about it, no. Maybe Polish.'

'Eastern European, perhaps?'

The line crackled. 'Yeah. I guess. Not that I'm great on accents, mind you.'

'Thanks, Lisa, you've been helpful.' Eve was about to put down the phone when Lisa spoke again.

'Do you think they were prostitutes?'

'We're looking into the possibility.'

Lisa was quiet for a second. 'Christ, he was a good-looking guy. Full of himself. Not shy in coming forward.'

'You don't need to be shy or ugly to use prostitutes.'

'Yeah, I guess I'm stupid thinking that. Some of the stuff I used to hear . . . probably easier for him to pay for that kind of thing.'

After last night, placing the women at the hotel, everything pointing towards the fact the fathers were involved, Eve wasn't so sure Dean had to pay for it at all.

Chapter 54

MEARNS BOLTED UPRIGHT, BANGING her knee on the steering wheel as she pummelled Ferguson's upper arm.

'OK, OK. I'm up,' Ferguson slurred.

'They're on the move.' Mearns pointed to the windscreen as a black Mercedes car in the distance left the steading forecourt and turned left on to the country lane.

Ferguson balled his fists and rubbed at his eyes. 'There's one thing: they're a sound endorsement for Mercedes.'

Mearns yawned. 'One guy in it. The taller of the two. Let's find out where's he's going, shall we?'

The car took Mearns and Ferguson back to the high-rise in Woodside. This time, the man inside didn't leave the vehicle. The car turned around and idled by the kerb nearest to the building's entrance. Mearns and Ferguson sat up on the main road, parked with the smallest of views through a gap in a row of houses and down the hill to the high-rise.

A girl stepped out of the building, too far away to make out in any detail. She teetered on heels that were too high, wobbling as she approached the car and got in.

The car disappeared from view, its nose sticking out of the lane and pulling out on to the main street within seconds. Turning right, the same as last night.

'Surely we're not going to drive back out to where we've come from?' Ferguson groaned.

'Let's see.'

By the time Mearns pulled out of the space, the black Mercedes had gone. She pressed a little harder on the accelerator, tipping over the speed limit, hoping the other car hadn't turned off somewhere.

'There.' Ferguson pointed; a red Fiat Uno separated them and the black Mercedes.

'I'm on it.' She had to admit to enjoying this. The adrenaline rush of getting one up on the bastards.

Ten minutes later they were turning into a housing development of executive serviced apartments in Stoneywood. There was a dedicated M&S store at the residents' disposal.

Ferguson whistled. 'The folk that use these girls certainly like their luxuries.'

Mearns kept a decent distance from the Mercedes, letting it turn into a road on the right before she carried on. She turned the car in the dead end and crept back to the opening where the car had gone.

'There she is. Third block down.'

The woman click-clacked to the door, pressing a button on the intercom for one of the higher flats. Mearns heard music thumping from the block from where they sat. The man in the Mercedes waited, and waited. Eventually the door opened, a resident looking the worse for wear standing there.

Ferguson exhaled sharply.

The man's eyes were glazed. He looked fit, athletic, with a messy mop of hair Mearns knew Ferguson would be itching to fix. The man dipped his chin towards the Mercedes before shuffling the girl inside and closing the door. Perhaps an all-night party that showed no sign of stopping.

Ferguson's reaction hadn't gone unnoticed by Mearns. The Mercedes moved, making its way back to the opening where Mearns and Ferguson sat. They pretended to talk animatedly as the man looked either way before pulling out and away from them.

'What was the sudden puff all about?'

The shock was still visible on his face. 'That was bloody Barry Thompson. Striker for Aberdeen Football Club.'

Chapter 55

ONCE AGAIN EVE FOUND herself in the staff canteen with DI Portman, Cooper alongside her this time. It wasn't that Portman made a habit of hanging out in the canteen, more a case of them taking the opportunity to be fed. Cooper wasn't complaining either. He was polishing off a fry-up that would have filled Eve up for two days.

She pulled the bowl of cereal towards her, pushed it away again. 'I know the photo I sent you last night wasn't great . . .'

Portman took a gulp of his coffee and put the mug down. 'It was enough.'

Eve didn't move. Neither did Cooper.

Portman fidgeted. 'I didn't want to get back to you too early without being sure so I took it to a colleague first thing to confirm what I was already thinking. It is the Rusu brothers.'

Eve forgot about the bowl in front of her, her appetite vanishing in the excitement. 'Have they ever been questioned?'

286

Portman shook his head. 'No, but we've observed them over time. Bogdi and Vlad are their first names. Both of them did a lot of personal travel – both down south and overseas, to Romania mostly. We think young girls travelling separately on the same flights were connected to them.'

'But no proof?' Cooper asked.

Portman took a sip of his water and put the cup on the table, his hand still gripping it. 'No. Look, we work closely with immigration, scrutinizing areas of interest. For example, say we have three Romanian women travelling alone and we obtain intelligence they are not here on holiday, we are presented with an opportunity to interview them.'

'Surely some of the time these women are coming here for work?' Eve wanted to know everything.

Portman nodded. 'Yes, but a lot of the rich, established businessmen who are targeting these women masquerade as legit businesses.'

'OK. Such as?'

'Nail bars, for example. In recent years it's quickly became apparent there are links to the Central Belt and the north-east.'

'How?' They were firing questions at him, both buoyed to be getting somewhere.

'Follow-the-money-type scenario. A paper trail, if you want. They like to shuffle these people about, capitalize on untapped areas by expanding business.'

Eve paused. 'Do they always bring these girls in via the airports?'

'No. The Dover crossing is a popular method. South coast of England and the Channel Tunnel.'

'Why not act on these paper trails, as you call them?'

Eve was aware she was making it sound as if Portman was under investigation.

'Because, as I say, they're hidden behind legit businesses most of the time. Most of their illegitimate business – these girls, for example – is done online. Internet. Social media. Adult websites. Many of these internet sites are utilized by businessmen with enterprises down south.'

Eve remembered what Rosie had said. 'Businessmen who come up here for the Oil Exhibition, for example?'

'Yes, that's one of the biggest draws of the year. And, of course, a lot of these dealings are easily orchestrated and near impossible to trace.'

'Why impossible?' Cooper asked.

Portman didn't seem fazed. 'Media disappears. Look at Snapchat.'

Eve had never used Snapchat, but she'd heard about uploading pictures or messages that lasted minutes before automatically deleting. Something like that. 'Do these men have contacts in the places they expand to?'

'In some cases, I expect they do. For the majority, I think they like to keep themselves to themselves. To be in control of their own business, as it were.'

Eve asked Portman if he knew anything about what went on at Miller's.

'It's not something I've been party to but I'd believe it if some of the big hitters were involved somewhere, at least from time to time. Having people of that calibre on their side is probably a big factor in why the Rusu brothers fell off our radar about a year ago.'

Eve didn't doubt the truth of that. The question was whether it was a partnership or if Miller had found himself a pawn in Bogdi and Vlad's overall game, with the end prize being to control his business as well as their own.

Chapter 56

'FERGUSON, CAN YOU GET the door?'

Eve looked towards the rest of the team. Cooper yawned in time with her assessment that, as expected, Mearns and Ferguson were looking pretty rough after their night sleeping in a car.

She pulled her shoulders back, stretched. 'What've we got?'

Mearns pocketed her phone as she spoke. 'Turns out it was worth keeping an eye on the men from Miller's. We followed one of them from their place out the road to a flat this morning in Stoneywood. One girl got out. She knew which door.'

Eve wasn't sure she wanted to hear who was behind that door. Someone else prominent in the city involved in the sleaze.

Ferguson took the glory. 'Barry Thompson's flat.'

Eve rubbed her chin. 'Why do I know the name?'

'Striker for Aberdeen Football Club. Half decent as well.' Ferguson sounded surprised, as if that was unusual for the Dons.

Cooper raised his eyebrows. 'That's not someone I'd imagine would be short of female attention.'

Ferguson turned to Cooper. 'He's not. At least his girlfriend of two years probably doesn't think he is. She's a looker as well. I wouldn't be straying elsewhere with her in my bed at nights.'

Mearns groaned. 'Shame for the girlfriend but maybe he likes to dabble in things it's easier to pay for.'

Eve was reminded of her earlier call with Lisa. Almost word for word what she'd said about Dean.

Cooper agreed. 'Or with someone who's not likely to sell a story to the press. These girls aren't your average kiss and tell.'

Eve straightened. 'Are we sure it's this Barry Thompson?'

'Yeah, recognized him straight away. Even though he looked like shit. Obviously been partying in some way or another all night.'

Eve didn't want to think about what might have gone on at that party. 'Good work. These men are operating a high-end, confidential service. Even without the events at Miller's last night and since, Barry Thompson would've confirmed it for me.'

Ferguson looked at her. 'Why?'

'When we were talking to Patricia about the monthly meet at Miller's she mentioned him, said her husband Kirk had been excited to meet him.'

Mearns tucked a stray hair behind her ear as she read something on her phone. 'Holy shit.'

Eve looked at her. 'What?'

'Companies House couldn't have timed it better.'

'Timed what?'

Mearns's eyes were scanning her mobile phone screen, fast. 'They've finally come back with the info I requested about Miller's properties.'

Eve shifted from one foot to another. 'And?'

Mearns continued to read rapidly. 'It's fair to say Peter Miller could be acting as a way in for the folks that run these girls.'

Eve was short on patience. 'Mearns, spit it out.'

'There's a long list of Peter Miller's legit businesses, the ones we all know him for. But there are a whole raft of other businesses you wouldn't expect. Nail bars, massage places, Airbnb lets.'

'And these are all owned by Miller?'

Mearns pointed at the screen. 'Umbrella company going by the name of Trinity Properties.'

Eve gasped. 'You're kidding me?'

'Wide open for everyone to see but set up anonymously. And guess where else comes under that umbrella?'

Eve saw where this was going. 'Shirriffs's restaurants?'

'The very same.'

Eve hesitated. 'But Patricia said Robert gave them the money to start up. Bailed them out recently too.'

'Maybe so, but Peter registered the company.'

Eve shook her head. 'This gets muddier by the day.'

'You're not joking, because, according to this, he has a few private, supposedly non-business rentals beneath the Trinity umbrella too.'

Eve let out the breath she was holding. 'Woodside?'

'Yup. Same block. That right there is a direct link to those men.'

'Miller has fingers in pies all over Aberdeen. No wonder no one wants to talk. There must be a lot of the city's elite losing sleep over this. Especially now we've found one of the girls hanging up at Hazlehead Golf Club.'

Ferguson was bursting. 'Same tattoo, same outfit as the girls at the hotel.'

'We need that missing file from Andrew Shirriffs's death.'

'I'm sure Cowan will deliver the goods if they're there to be delivered.'

Eve hoped so. In the meantime, now they had clear confirmation of where the girls were being held, she had someone she wanted to revisit.

Time to give their Jane Doe a name.

Chapter 57

THE BELL ABOVE THE door announced their arrival, no chance of sneaking in unheard. Eve's nose wrinkled; the smell of spiced meat was stronger this time. Within seconds, Marius appeared from around the side aisle, the smile plastered on his still badly bruised face slipping away as he recognized them.

'Hello.' His greeting didn't sound welcoming.

'Hi. Sorry to drop in unannounced. Are you free to talk?'

Marius looked around the store, as if hoping customers would materialize and give him a reason to say no.

Eve stepped forward. 'We won't take up much of your time.' That would only be the case if he played ball.

'OK.' He turned and walked to the back of the shop. They followed his lead until he went behind the counter, putting a divide between them.

'Could I show you that picture again?' Eve placed it on top of the counter.

Marius didn't look at it, concentrating on Eve. 'I told you, I don't know her.'

'Fine. But perhaps you know these guys.' Eve slapped down the picture of the men from the vans.

This time Marius's eyes did flicker.

'Please, take a look.'

Marius stepped back. Eve didn't have to ask whether he recognized them. The fear was clear on his face. 'I'm sorry. I can't help.'

Marius took another step. Eve was not sure if he was trying to get away from looking at the picture or whether he wanted to flee.

'You can. And I think you do know who the girl is.'

'I don't. I—'

'I understand you're scared but we know they have accommodation close to here. We know what they're doing to those girls. Did they do that to your face?'

'No, I told you. Shoplifters.'

'I know what you told us. I don't believe you.' Eve fought to find a reason why this young man might have been targeted by the thugs. 'Did you do something wrong?'

'No.' He shook his head. 'Nothing wrong.'

The penny dropped. 'Marius, are you trying to protect someone?'

Marius's face crumpled, the tears taking them by surprise. He moved forward, grasped the edge of the counter. 'Please. They can't know.'

'Know what?'

'About my girlfriend.'

Eve looked at Cooper as he leaned forward and placed a hand over the young man's, comforting, not patronizing. 'I'm going to turn the sign to closed. Let's go through to the back, get you a cup of something and we can have a chat.'

'My uncle . . .'

'Half an hour. We need to talk without any interruptions.'

Marius didn't stop them as they made their way round to the same side of the counter as him.

Cooper and Marius sat on upturned crates at the back of the shop, both of them hugging mugs of coffee. Eve sat on the one chair, a gentlemanly offer from Marius which Eve hadn't wanted to refuse. She sipped at her coffee and looked at Marius.

'Tell us about your girlfriend.'

Marius seemed less wary, relaxed even, as if a weight had been shifted. 'Her name is Andreea. She's one of the girls who lives in the accommodation you spoke of. She's pregnant.'

'She's pregnant?' Eve didn't hide her shock.

'Yes.'

'I'm sorry to have to ask this . . . It's yours?'

Marius looked hurt the question needed to be asked.

Eve rushed to explain. 'With her job. What the girls are being made to do.'

Marius's expression relaxed. 'No, you don't understand. Andreea wasn't like the other girls. She kept house.'

Eve didn't want to keep interrupting his flow. She'd find out why later.

'I've wanted for so long to get her out of there. When we found out about the baby, I wanted to talk to my uncle. I wish I already had. He can be . . . difficult. I worried what his answer would be. I was weak. Besides, Andreea would not be talked into leaving the other girls behind.'

Cooper answered. 'Not weak. That would be scary for anyone.'

Eve nodded. 'When did you get finally talk Andreea into it?'

Marius's face fell. 'When she told me Elena was missing. The girl in your picture.'

Eve thought of the woman laid out on MacLean's table. Elena. She had a name.

'Andreea was three months gone – still not showing but not far off – when she said Elena had found a way to get them out of there.'

'But you already had a plan for getting her out?'

'I know but she said Elena's way would mean all of the girls would be free, like she wanted.'

'Why? Did Elena know someone?'

'More a case of *what* she knew. Elena had been involved in something bad. She planned to approach one of the people wrapped up in it all and talk him into telling someone what they knew.'

Eve's eyes flashed with hope. Is this why Elena had been at Dean's flat, to persuade him to tell the truth about Andrew's death? 'What did she know?'

Marius looked at the floor.

'Do you know what Elena was hiding?'

'Yes, but I'm scared to say. Scared what it will mean for Andreea.'

Eve thought for a moment. 'Marius, why was Andreea different from the other girls? It sounds as if Elena's disappearance would've been much more dangerous for Andreea.'

His eyes rose slowly towards hers again. 'Andreea has a birthmark. On her face. She's beautiful. I've always thought so. But those men, they're not interested in her, so the brothers made her keep house. Shopping, cleaning, reporting on anything out of the ordinary. For her to have known about Elena and not reported it, or even if she had, would've had devastating consequences for Andreea.'

Eve immediately thought of the timid foreign girl with the birthmark on her face back at the shelter where she'd gone to visit Laura Robertson with Mearns. No doubt in her mind she'd already met this Andreea. Now she understood the fear coming off the girl in waves, how much she needed to be in hiding. Eve had to find a way to make Marius talk. 'What did Andreea do when Elena failed to come home?'

Marius looked up again. 'She was devastated but also terrified. She came here as soon as she could. Wednesday as always. She told me Elena had disappeared. I had to get her out of there. Too dangerous for her to go back.'

'What did you do?'

'I put her in a taxi to a women's refuge.'

'And then what?'

'They came looking. They knew this was the last place she'd been. The only place she ever went. I gave them nothing.'

Eve now knew for sure who had caused his injuries. 'Marius, what if we talk to you and Andreea together? Reassure you both we can keep you safe. That you can tell us everything you know?'

She didn't want to tell him she might have already met Andreea. It was important for him to be the one to engineer the way forward for them as a couple. To feel he was in control.

Marius said nothing, hands squeezing at his thighs as if needing something, anything, to concentrate on. To think.

Eve tried again. 'Marius, please. We want Elena's killers brought to justice, and Andreea can help us with that. We need to speak to her. Can you arrange that for us?'

Chapter 58

MEARNS AND FERGUSON WALKED into the public bar at Miller's. Mearns's heart leapt as she scanned the staff and saw the barman they wanted there. The undercut to his hair was fresh, those upper arm muscles still straining against the shirt he wore – definitely the same guy they'd overheard when smoking outside Miller's party.

'Good afternoon. What can I get you?'

'Pint of Tennent's and a fresh orange, please.' Ferguson fished in his pocket for money. 'Long night?'

'Not too bad. I get off in an hour.'

'Nice.' Ferguson handed over the exact change, lifted the drinks from the bar, and moved away, Mearns following his lead.

They took a seat off to the side, one of the only tables left, the place busy with suits – ties loosened and ready for the weekend. Mearns was glad she couldn't see their drinking buddy, Graham, from last night.

'At least we don't have too long to wait.' Mearns slid the fresh orange on the table towards her as her mobile pinged in her jacket. She pulled out the phone. A text from Eve.

'What?' Ferguson paused and took a long gulp of his Tennent's.

'They've made progress with the guy at the shop. We have a name for our Jane Doe.' Mearns looked up at Ferguson. 'Elena.'

'Makes it all the more real, doesn't it? This case has been intense. Wish I could sit here tonight and get hammered.'

'I don't. You're bad enough sober.'

Mearns was surprised when Ferguson's smile disappeared. A fleeting moment before it was plastered back on his face. She felt an unexpected stab of guilt. 'You're growing on me though.' She wanted to take back what she'd said, realizing for the first time that maybe Ferguson's bravado didn't run as deep as she'd thought. Their banter was a big part of their working relationship, but the reality was she didn't know much about him outside it.

Ferguson grinned, the gesture looking forced, and reached for a menu in the centre of the table. 'I guess we could eat. You know, since we're here.'

Mearns watched as he skimmed the menu. 'You won't get a calzone here and I doubt they'll have those protein drinks you insist on drinking.'

Ferguson lowered the menu. 'I do eat other stuff, you know.'

'I'm sure you do, but you definitely have your go-tos, your routines.'

'Are you trying to say I'm predictable?'

Mearns feigned shock. 'I wouldn't dare. But doesn't it get boring?'

'What?'

'All the shakes, and the muscle building. The perfect hairdo every day.'

Ferguson's eye twitched, the frown covering his face. 'What is this? You trying to pull my chain?'

'No. I'm honestly curious.'

Ferguson lifted the menu again. 'Nothing wrong with looking after yourself.'

'I guess not. So, was your dad into fitness big time, is that where you get it? Or maybe your mum?' Mearns realized she'd never heard Ferguson talk about his family.

Ferguson didn't look up, eyes locked on the menu, but Mearns didn't miss the deep swallow he took. 'I didn't have folks.'

Mearns studied him over the rim of the laminated card in front of him. 'What? What do you mean?'

'I was brought up – or rather dragged up – in a children's home.'

'Ferguson, sorry, I never—'

'Yeah, well, it's all in the past, let's not spoil my appetite.'

She wanted to say and ask much more, but it was time to change the subject.

Mearns put her fork down, beaten by the mammoth-sized portion of macaroni cheese, and clocked the barman looking ready to leave. She kicked Ferguson's foot under the table. 'You'll have to leave the rest of that, sunshine.'

Ferguson groaned, moving quickly to engineer their exit at the same time the barman came off the bar.

'After you.' The barman smiled and held the door open for them. They stepped out into the courtyard, fussing with coat zips, waiting to see where the barman went. He stopped by the same table where they'd waited on their drinking buddy the night before, clearly desperate for that end-of-shift smoke.

Fairy lights swayed above the barman's head in the gentle breeze as Ferguson spoke. 'You'll be glad to be done for the night. Hectic in there.'

The barman smiled again. 'Always the same on a Friday.'

'I'll bet. Different animal from the private functions.'

'Totally different. Once the door closes and a function starts, you know that's the amount of folk you're dealing with for the night.'

'Do you work a lot of the functions?'

Hesitation showed on the barman's face. 'Yeah, most of us do.'

'If it's a regular crowd, you'd remember some faces?'

'Yeah.' The response slow, the barman wary.

'Could I show you a picture of someone, and you tell us if you recognize them?'

The barman looked between them. 'What is this? You police?'

Ferguson was direct. 'Yes. I'm not going to stand here and lie to you. We're trying to identify a woman and believe she may have been involved with this hotel.'

The barman glanced towards the door. 'Listen, I need this job. I—'

'I appreciate that. You won't get into any trouble. Your boss won't even know you did this.'

'You don't understand. It's—'

'Believe me, we do understand. We're aware what's going on at these functions but we're not here about that. We want to identify this woman.'

The barman's eyes flickered to the hotel door again before resting on Ferguson. 'I don't agree with what goes on here.'

'I'm sure you don't, and I understand, to you, it's a job. But if you don't agree, please help us.'

'If I do this, and what goes down here is exposed, I'll lose my job.'

'We're not here to bring the place down but, whether you do this or not, we already know enough to get the place shut.'

The barman crushed his fag beneath his feet and rubbed at the back of his neck, weighing up his next move.

'Can we go somewhere else?'

Ferguson turned. 'We're parked across the road, down from here. Do you want to take a quick look at the photo before you decide?'

The barman lifted a hand. Ferguson passed the photo to him.

The young guy peered at the photo, held it against the fairy lights to see it more clearly. Recognition spread across his features. 'She's dead?'

'I'm afraid so.'

'I recognize her.'

Ferguson took the photo back from him. 'Let's go get in the car.'

The barman slipped into the back.

'Please, we need to move somewhere else.' He turned his head this way and that, clearly nervous, even in the dark.

Ferguson had already started the car engine, having a much better idea of the trouble they could get the young guy into.

Ferguson looked in the rear-view mirror. Part of the guy's face was visible in the darkness as they passed by streetlights. 'What's your name, anyway?'

'Brett.'

Mearns turned in her seat. 'That your real name?'

The barman shifted the zip of his leather jacket to one side. 'Says so on my badge.'

Ferguson stopped the car down a dead-end back lane in Albyn and turned sideways to better look at Brett through the gap in the seats. Mearns did the same.

Ferguson smiled. 'Busy night?'

Brett looked from Ferguson to Mearns. 'Yeah, not bad. Few good tips.'

'Do you get good tips at this . . . monthly gentlemen's club, let's call it, or do they save that for the ladies?'

Brett looked a little taken aback at the sudden dive into the subject of why they were here. 'I don't know much about it. The girls must be paid for in advance.

I've never seen money exchanging hands, and definitely no tips.'

'But you must take money. At the bar, I mean?'

Brett shook his head. 'Miller runs it as a free bar every month.'

'What, these guys don't even tip the bar staff?'

'They do, but it's done as one large payment at the end of the night, which is added to our wages.'

'A good earner for you?'

Brett looked as though he wasn't going to comment at first. 'I don't like what goes on there. And I know you're going to ask why I don't leave.'

'Brett, it's none of our business what your reasons are for staying.'

'No, I want you to know. I have a girlfriend, and a kid. He's eighteen months old.'

'What's his name?' Mearns wanted the guy to relax, to feel he could speak.

'Josh.' Brett fumbled in his jacket pocket, pulled out a wallet and passed a photo to Mearns. She peered at the image under the streetlight.

'Cute.'

'He's awesome. Me and Nikki met working in the same pub a couple of years back. We hadn't planned on kids, not so early anyway. Shit happens.' Brett paused. 'You know what I mean. Neither of us has much in the way of family. We struggled to get a flat, to keep ourselves afloat, especially once Josh arrived. When this job came up, I couldn't say no.'

'How did you get the job? I'm assuming Miller has a pretty lengthy interview process?'

'His son, Finn, used to come into the bar where I worked. Didn't know him as such but we'd chew the fat, I'd tell him about the latest beers and cocktails. He came in one day saying his father was hiring and I'd be good for the job. He liked my work ethic.'

'You went for an interview?'

'Yeah, and it wasn't like any interview I'd been at before. Extremely personal questions, in-depth checks, and we had to sign paperwork saying we wouldn't talk about anything that went on in the premises.'

'I can understand why you're wary of talking to us. Thank you for doing this.'

'It's OK. I hate what they do to those girls. Every time I see them filing in, staring at the floor, looking shattered and unhappy. Then the lights go up, the smiles go on and the guys get their fun.'

'What goes on at the meets?'

'The girls dance for them, accompany them at tables.'

'Does anything physical go on?'

Brett fingered the picture of Josh in his hand. 'Not in the function room. Maybe the odd grope under the table, but Miller likes to keep it clean.'

'You surprise me.' The bitterness in Mearns's tone at the mention of Miller was evident.

'Only in the function room. He doesn't care how dirty it gets out of there.'

'Out of there? You mean they take the girls to their rooms?'

'Yeah, that's why the hotel effectively shuts for the night. Rooms are only available to attendees. Miller can afford to take the hit.'

Mearns was willing to bet any hit he took to the hotel was more than covered.

Brett ran his finger across the image of his son. 'It makes me mad. When I think of Nikki at home. My son. What I'm watching happen. What I'm allowing to happen. So we can keep a roof over our heads. Sometimes I worry it makes me as bad as them.'

Mearns looked at him. 'Not in any way. You're doing what's best for your family. You're not condoning it and you're doing the right thing for them all by talking to us.'

Brett mumbled, 'What happened to the girl in the photo?'

'Elena?'

'I never knew her name.'

Mearns's face was sad. 'We found her hanging up at Hazlehead Golf Club.'

'That was her?'

'Yeah.'

'We know Miller and his cronies were involved with her, and that's now confirmed largely thanks to you IDing her. Can you tell us anything about her?'

'She was one of the popular ones. Loads of guys wanted her at their table. Wanted her for the rooms.'

'Who would you say was most interested in Elena?'

'The younger crowd. The sons, especially. Finn and his two friends, Andrew and Dean.'

'What about other folk when the young guns weren't around her?'

Brett thought for a moment. 'Kirk Shirriffs spoke with her once for a while. I never saw him leave the room with a girl, figured he had more respect for his wife.'

'Never?'

'Never. Not until the night he took Elena.'

Chapter 59

ANDREEA SAT IN THE front office of the women's shelter, the space vacated by Jean and the other staff to provide a little privacy, and to allow Marius and Cooper to be there.

Eve knew Cooper being here was right. He'd been the one who'd been speaking with Marius all this time and Andreea would be able to see her boyfriend trusted him. That and the fact Mearns was busy with Ferguson.

The couple sat side by side, their single chairs pulled as closely together as the wooden armrests would allow. It still didn't look close enough for Andreea, her pale face and shaking hands making Eve determined to be gentle.

'Thank you for agreeing to see us.' Eve wasn't sure Andreea had exactly agreed, more that it had to be done. 'We're glad you're safe here, Andreea. What you've done is brave and I need you to be brave for a little longer.'

Andreea looked up from where she'd been staring at Marius's and her joined hands – her face softer, less panicked than when she'd first come into the room. Perhaps relieved Eve came across as approachable.

'We know you're scared. Especially after what happened to Elena.'

Andreea's sharp intake of breath was audible, tears forming at the corners of her eyes.

'We need you to tell us what happened that night.'

'Did she kill herself?'

Eve wanted to hug the girl. 'No, Andreea, she didn't. Someone tried to make it look as if she had.'

Andreea shook her head. 'She was good.'

Eve kept her voice quiet. 'I'm sure she was a good friend to you.'

Andreea's gaze fixed on Eve. 'I don't know much. It was big. If they know I've told—'

Cooper leaned forward. 'Andreea, we will protect you, as much as the women here have. Telling us what you know will help us to find the people who did this to Elena.'

Andreea turned to Marius. He squeezed her hand. 'Elena knew things. Things people didn't want others to know. I worried for her. That they would find a way to silence her.'

'Bogdi and Vlad?'

The shock on Andreea's face was clear.

'We know about them, about the flat in Woodside. You don't have to worry. Concentrate on Elena.'

The girl continued: 'No, not Bogdi and Vlad. The other men involved.'

'Why do you think the brothers didn't silence her?'

'Because she was one of their most popular girls. Lots of people wanted Elena. They trusted her to remain loyal.'

Eve trod carefully. 'OK, tell us what you know. Please.'

Andreea closed her eyes, sat there as if trying to work out where to begin. Eve gave her the time, surprised at the focus when she opened her eyes again.

'Elena had been taken to men. Men who liked to do certain things. Dangerous things. Things that one time went too far.'

Eve's heart thumped. Those fingerprints at Andrew's flat. Patricia Shirriffs's belief he didn't kill himself. 'Do you know what happened?'

'A game. One of the men pulling too tightly on what was around the other man's neck.'

'Are you sure?'

'Elena said she tried to stop him, the other man there did too, but he was easily convinced it was all a game, that what was happening was OK.'

'The man, the one with the thing around his neck, died?'

Andreea started crying, nodding as she wiped at her face. 'The men told Elena to go. Told her they would fix it. She didn't know he was dead. Until later.'

'Do you know how many men there were?'

'Elena said there were three. She didn't tell me their names, but I know she had been with them before. I heard her crying in bed on those nights. They were too rough. She had bruises.'

Eve looked at Cooper, adrenaline pumping through her as she listened to Andreea. Dean and Finn had been

there. They'd lied. About the phone calls, about sending the girl.

'What did Elena plan to do?'

'She didn't sleep much after. For a long time. She
wanted people to know. What made it worse was they
still sent her to the other two men. Lots of times.'

Eve thought about Lisa Taylor, Dean's neighbour,
about how she had heard two men regularly with one
woman. Dean and Finn.

'Why did she wait a year before trying to tell
someone?'

'She said one of the men was not well. Struggling
with guilt.'

Dean.

'She saw a way of telling the truth. It would set us all
free, she said.'

'What did she do, Andreea?'

'She knew a night was planned when it was only
going to be one of the men. The man who had tried to
stop the other one and what had happened. She decided
she'd get him to help her.'

Eve was silent. Elena had gone to Dean Johnstone's
wanting him to expose Finn and what had happened to
Andrew. But it had gone wrong. Something had happened to make Elena hit Dean over the head, knocking
him out.

Bogdi and Vlad had known she was there.

'Do you know if Bogdi and Vlad went to the man's
flat to look for her?'

Andreea's tears were flowing freely. 'I know they
would've. The girls were always dropped off and picked

313

up. But when I told Daria that Elena was missing, she appeared to know nothing about it.'

Daria? Eve remembered Ferguson's description of a woman out at the steading where they'd followed the Rusu brothers to. 'Who's Daria, Andreea?'

Andreea sought reassurance from Marius again. He gave a slight nod, still gripping her hand.

'Daria finds the girls for Bogdi and Vlad. She tricked me and Elena, made us ready for what Bogdi and Vlad wanted. She keeps an eye on everything we do – depends on me to tell her about anything happening that shouldn't be.'

'Do you think she knew about Elena when you told her?'

'Maybe. Maybe Bogdi and Vlad got word of Elena's plan. Perhaps they killed that man fearing, with her persuasion, he would talk.'

Eve remembered the schoolkids and what they had seen. Could it have been one of the brothers and Daria in that car? Elena in the boot?

'Andreea, do you think Bogdi and Vlad could've killed Elena, made it look as if she took her own life?'

The girl sobbed harder. Eve gave her space.

'I don't know. People say the brothers make things disappear. Make people disappear. It doesn't sound like something they would do.'

'What do you think happened?'

Andreea wiped at her eyes with her one free hand. 'I don't know. All I know is she didn't come home.'

Chapter 60

I SMILE AT THE three boys; there's a funny feeling in my chest as Curly smiles back and looks happy to see me.

I wasn't going to come but I wanted to see those blue eyes again. The decision made easier by the fact El had returned over an hour later than me last time and it had gone unnoticed.

The three boys are sitting around a bottle of vodka and a stack of plastic cups. Placed in the centre untouched, the message clear they've been waiting for our arrival. El goes to sit between Black Eyes and Smiler. I crouch by Curly, a new excitement as my thigh brushes his.

El reaches forward, not waiting to be asked, and uncaps the bottle, pouring a large slug into a cup. She passes it to Black Eyes, who does nothing to hide the fact he's staring at me. Then he surprises me, looking goofy at El's attention. But he never stops staring. Surely he can't be trying to make me jealous. Not when he has El.

El leans forward again and pours herself one.

I'm shocked when she gulps it back quickly. Worried too.

Smiler laughs. *'Well, there's enough to go around.'*

And as Black Eyes pulls out a joint, I wonder, as I did after his parting comment when I left last time, whether it's only the joints and the drink he's talking about.

'Something's wrong with her.'

Black Eyes, no longer goofy or staring at me, isn't lying as he slurs the words. El's on her back in the grass, chalk-white and still. Spew cakes her lips and smears her cheeks, trickling into her hair.

'What happened?' I'm on my knees, slapping El around the face as if it's going to help. My heart's racing and I'm sobbing, slapping harder in my panic.

Smiler kneels beside her but he's not smiling now. He'd tried to crouch, but had been too unsteady. I look up at Curly who is staring at El, a look of horror on his face.

Black Eyes' breathing has gone funny. 'We were sitting talking, having a laugh.'

'Well, she's not laughing now.' The shout and venom in my voice take me by surprise. 'She's not breathing.'

'Sssh, someone will hear you.' Abrupt coming from Curly, but I stop talking.

Black Eyes is shaking his head as if the action will make all this go away. 'I went for a piss. She was giggling, drunk, as I went away into the bushes. Then she stopped. I thought she was just being quiet, waiting for me to get back, or I was too far away to hear her.'

'You didn't hear her puking?' My upper lip is quivering, the reality of what's happening hitting me.

Black Eyes growls. 'No. Do you not think I would've come running?' He looks desperate for me to believe him. I don't know why. The same as I've never known why he looks at me all the time even when he has El.

I glare at him. 'What do we do now?'

Curly steps forward. 'Turn her on her side.'

'What?' I pull at El's shoulder; Smiler tugs at her hip to push her on to her side.

'Maybe she conked out, didn't wake when she puked.'

Black Eyes cradles his head in his hands. 'Shit, man. Shit. Shit.'

'Check her mouth.' Curly, trying to make out he knows what they are supposed to do.

I'm sobbing harder now. Curly bends to pull me up by my waist, making eye contact with me and hugging me as I stand.

Black Eyes glares at him, hands twitching by his sides.

Smiler leans forward on his knees. His hand hesitates beside El's mouth and then he places a forefinger and thumb on her lips and prises them apart. Thick brown liquid oozes from her mouth.

'Fuck. It stinks. What now? It's not doing anything.' His eyes are wide, voice panicked, staring at Curly, who holds me, as if he has the answers.

'I don't know.' His shoulder is saturated with my tears. Even in the panic, he holds me tight.

We all stand there helpless, waiting for anything to happen. Nothing does. Nothing except from El's face changing colour and not for the better.

'We're too late.' My cries fill the clearing. Feral. No one tries to shut me up. No one moves. And no one mentions the underpants rolled halfway down El's legs.

Chapter 61

'MEETING IN THE BOGS? Honestly?'

Cowan unlocked the middle cubicle and stepped out towards the washbasins, a thick A4 plastic wallet in his hand. He'd phoned Ferguson's mobile as he and Mearns were making their way back to the office from Miller's.

Cowan glared at Ferguson. 'Let's say I'm not in the mood for a pint with you right now and I sure as hell don't want anyone seeing me with this.' He almost threw the file at Ferguson as if holding it would leave burn marks.

'You could've come upstairs to the office.'

'What, and give Eve bloody Hunter the satisfaction of me being there when she's proved right? No thanks.'

Ferguson's heart lifted a little; no need to ask what Cowan had found or what was in the folder. 'I'm sorry, Cowan.'

Cowan made a show of washing his hands, never looking up from the basin. 'You make sure you deal with those bastards and you get that link you're looking for. Don't let what I did come to nothing.'

'Sure. I promise.'

'I don't need your promise for that. After all, it'll be the bitch's goal. I want you to promise you won't go after Crawford. He's had enough and so has his wife.'

Cowan didn't wait for an answer, barging past Ferguson to the door without drying his hands. Ferguson was glad, not sure he could promise anything.

Eve packed the mouthful of spaghetti into her mouth as Ferguson walked in.

'Please tell me you're not eating Prezzo takeout?'

Cooper grinned through calzone-full cheeks. 'OK. We won't. We also won't tell you we're reading the paper. Guess who's playing Malones again tonight?'

Ferguson groaned. Eve wasn't sure if it was for missing Prezzo or disbelief Finn was playing again.

Eve wiped at her mouth, set down her fork. 'Get your mind off the grub, Ferguson. Mearns here told us what you had to eat at Miller's.' Eve looked at the folder in Ferguson's hand. 'Cowan?'

Ferguson's grip tightened on the folder. 'He's pretty upset. Asked me to promise we wouldn't go after Crawford.'

Eve couldn't promise. 'Let's get what we need out of those files first – send the prints through to forensics as a matter of urgency, see if we can get a match.'

Ferguson opened the file, finding both the missing paper copies and a memory stick. 'There's a lot of other stuff in here. I'll get the prints sent along now and then I'll go through it all. Mearns can update you on the rest.' Ferguson disappeared out of the office before Eve could answer – not sure if it was the need to do something with the file or the thought of having to watch others eat Prezzo.

Mearns tutted. 'That's me told. An update. As I said before Ferguson flounced in, we've had positive ID on Elena from the barman.'

Mearns went on to fill them in, right down to the detail of Kirk taking Elena off on her own.

Eve tried to piece it all together. 'OK, in light of that, let's say the note was sent to Kirk. Or Dean did speak to him. Told him he was there when Andrew died, that he knew what happened.'

Mearns screwed up her face. 'Wouldn't Kirk have told the police? Or gone to Miller and Johnstone?'

'There's nothing to say he didn't go to them. Maybe that's why the two of them have been cagey. But I don't think he did.'

'Why?'

'Perhaps Kirk feared the repercussions. What about if they wanted to silence him, or Patricia? Not just Robert and Peter, but also these men running the girls, the Rusu brothers. Think of what Kirk could've exposed about everyone, not only the Trinity, their sons, the Romanians – but all the high-flyers involved throughout the city. Would certainly spoil the little monthly charity fundraiser at Miller's, and, let's face it, it wouldn't merit a memorial for the boys out at Heritage this Saturday.'

Mearns swung in her chair. 'Yeah. I get it. Far-reaching, devastating. But enough to not vilify those responsible for the loss of your son?'

Eve thought about it. 'Some would say no. But on a personal level, Kirk stood to lose more than his son by exposing the truth. A long-running complicated friendship, yes, but also his livelihood.'

Cooper understood what Eve was referring to. 'Of course, Miller and Johnstone are wrapped up in Shirriffs as a business.'

'Exactly. Exposing them would have meant the loss of Kirk's income, his home, his lifestyle.'

Cooper asked what they were all thinking. 'What do you reckon he did instead?'

Eve was on a roll. 'Maybe he used Elena to do it for him. Told her to get Dean onside, knowing the hell he was going through with his guilt, with his hurt Finn had all but deserted him.'

Mearns whispered, 'It went wrong and she phoned Kirk?'

'I think she may have. And that he told her his home was a safe place to go.'

Cooper hung on every word. 'And then what?'

'And then someone went to Dean's home and killed him whilst someone else got to Elena, tried to make it look like a suicide.'

'You think it was one of the Rusu brothers at the golf club with Elena?' Cooper asked. 'What about Finn?'

Eve's head spun. 'Maybe he was only involved with Andrew's death. The couple at the golf club could have been one of the Rusu brothers and that woman Andreea told us about, Daria. Or maybe Finn and Elena. Either way, I find those much better options than the alternative.'

Mearns's voice was high. 'The alternative?'

'That Kirk did actually have the balls to seek revenge. That the couple in that car were Kirk and Patricia trying to get rid of the body.'

Chapter 62

IT WAS LATE. ONE by one his colleagues had left the office. Cooper had begun to wonder whether Eve would ever leave. She'd finally left two minutes ago, making him promise he'd do the same – making him feel worse when he promised her he would – aware what he was about to do.

Cooper tapped on Hastings's door, feeling like a traitor before he was called to enter.

'Come in.'

Cooper opened the door, closing it behind him quickly. He didn't want anyone else to find him here. He stood in front of the desk, a cold sweat coming over him.

'You asked to see me, sir?'

Hastings pointed to the chair.

He took the seat grudgingly, unwilling even to try to make himself comfortable whilst being expected to screw Eve over.

Hastings straightened, put down the paperwork he'd been reading. 'I haven't heard from you.'

'About?'

Hastings's eyes narrowed.

'Eve? Yeah, there's been nothing to say.'

'Nothing? There's never a week goes by when there's nothing to say about Eve.'

Cooper smiled, hoping the gesture reached his eyes. 'Nothing out of the ordinary, I should've said.'

'She's OK?'

'Yes.' Cooper's thumb curled into the palm of his hand, digging into the skin there, hating himself for being here.

Hastings didn't look convinced by Cooper's answer.

'Sir, with the greatest respect, could we leave it that if there's anything amiss, you know I'll come to you with it?'

Hastings didn't argue. 'Fair enough, but make sure you do come to me. I know you're loyal to Eve, but remember – I'm your boss here.'

Cooper stood and made his way to the door, relief flooding him.

'Cooper?'

He stopped short of the door, closed his eyes for a second, and turned to his boss. 'Sir?'

'She's lucky to have you.'

Cooper dipped his chin and turned to the door, assuming he had to say something to at least sound as if he was open to snitching to the boss, even when he never would. 'Sure. And I'm aware she can be a hot-headed pain in the arse. I promise, I've got my eye on her.'

He stepped out into the corridor, looked sideways and came face to face with Eve.

Eve's face was crumpled with anger. Cooper edged towards her, as if the further away from Hastings's door he got, the less guilty he'd look.

Eve didn't move. 'I forgot my car keys.' She looked beyond Cooper's shoulder towards Hastings's office. 'What were you doing?'

'Nothing.' Cooper silently cursed the break in his voice.

'Nothing? Same as last time I saw you sneaking out of there, but I said nothing. You know – since you didn't feel the need to.'

Cooper gulped, stunned by the realization she'd seen him.

'So, what was nothing about both times?'

Cooper struggled for an answer that wouldn't sound like the lie it would be.

Eve looked wounded. He felt it keenly in his chest.

'These walls aren't soundproof. Especially as you're walking out of a door.'

Cooper's heart lurched, remembering his final comment to Hastings. 'Eve, I—'

'Save it. I hope you managed to gather enough shit on me to report back.' She moved towards him.

His whole body clenched, his mind wondering what was about to happen, surprised when she carried on past him and darted into the incident room. When she thundered back out into the corridor, she didn't look his way or say a word, just kept walking, her car keys gripped vice-like in one hand.

He stood there, unable to move, already worrying how he could ever make this right; the same upset and fear he'd been feeling all too lately with his wife.

Eve barged into her work shed and slammed the door behind her, shouting into the darkness before she turned on the light. 'How dare he.'

She wasn't totally sure at whom her anger was directed most, Cooper or Hastings, knowing they both deserved it in equal measures. She paced the shed, chest thumping, temples pulsing. She needed to find somewhere or something to get her temper out.

She stood at the window, hands grasping the edge of the sink, seeing her reflection framed against the darkness outside as she tried to breathe, to calm herself.

They'd been meeting secretly. Hastings had doubted her. Cooper had agreed to be his mole.

She stopped trying to breathe deeply. Who was she trying to kid? It was some bullshit she'd read somewhere that supposedly worked. It didn't. She turned from the window. The rectangular Hobbycraft boxes were still lying where she'd left them, untouched, unable to get herself into the zone in order to escape into a project. She punched at one of the boxes, shoving it across the workbench before it clattered to the floor. No release when her fist didn't hit something stationary, something solid. She flew around the edge of the bench, stamped the box into the ground, kept stamping until the box flattened and spread out across the floor. She pulled another box from the bench and did the same. And again. And again. Picturing the faces of the people who were making this case difficult, rather than the two she'd came in here angry at.

None of it helping.

Robert Johnstone. Peter Miller. Finn.

Finn's face provided extra stamping power at the thought of what he might be responsible for, how his privileged position might have let him get away with murder. They still hadn't been able to question him. She stopped, mid-stamp, something creeping into her mind. He'd given her his card at Malones that night. His mobile number.

She kicked at the wrecked cardboard at her feet, fighting to let go of the idea. An idea she shouldn't even entertain. Something stupid, dangerous to her job.

She lifted her mobile, knowing what she was about to do was crazy. Not caring. The way she never cared when her temper took over.

Fuck them. If Hastings reckons I can't be trusted, that Cooper needs to spy on me, I might as well give them something to talk about.

Even as she typed the text, stabbing at the buttons with her fingers, she knew she should stop. But now the idea had been planted, there was no way of getting rid of it.

Cooper sat at the kitchen table, his hand still holding his mobile phone after the call he'd received, buoyed at the news Elena's prints had also been matched to the scene of Andrew Shirriffs's death. But not as buoyed as he would've been had he not been stressing over his fall-out with Eve.

He sat; the house was silent, as it had been when he'd got home. Louise had taken the opportunity to get an early night, going down the same time as the kids and leaving a note on the fridge telling him so, no mention of anything for his tea.

He wanted to call Eve, to go over there, hoping she might be in her workshop trying to block out what had happened at the office. But he knew when something hit close, unbearably close, Eve's temper couldn't be blocked out. That worried him more than anything. He picked up his mobile, hit her number on speed-dial and listened to it as it clicked straight through to her voice-mail. Same as what happened when the office had tried to get hold of her first with confirmation of the prints.

He understood her ignoring him, but it wasn't like her to miss a call from work. Cooper lifted his head, crumbs of the kids' fish fingers scattered across the table catching his eye, a trail of them leading to today's paper, which he'd always meant to cancel the delivery for, since he saw the whole raft of them daily in the office. Louise didn't care to read them, said she never got the chance. He'd already seen the paper today in the office. Something flashed in his memory. Remembering the *What's On* guide, he jumped to his feet and snatched his car keys from the kitchen worktop, hoping to hell Eve wouldn't be that stupid.

Chapter 63

'NICE TO SEE YOU again, Amy.'

Eve jumped as Finn's warm breath tickled her ear, instantly wishing she hadn't tucked her hair behind it.

'Sorry, didn't mean to scare you.'

She heard the smile in his voice as he spoke. She turned, hating that in one movement he'd stretched his arm upwards and placed it against the pillar to the side of them, effectively pinning her to the bar.

'I like the music here.' She looked at the ground, going for seductive, knowing she didn't have a bloody clue about these things.

'The music?' He tilted her chin with his free fore-finger and thumb, grinned.

'A lady never tells.' She ducked from beneath his arm, needing to get away from the closeness, hoping she looked playful.

'Hey, where're you going?'

She shouted over her shoulder, fighting against the din of stereo speakers and the gathering crowd's chatter. 'Ladies room before the real music starts.'

She was betting on his surprise at her having the balls to walk away from him.

Eve stood staring at herself in the mirror, wondering what the hell she was doing here. Was she expecting him to give anything away? How would she even get him talking about any of it in the first place? And, even if she did manage, the way in which she was going about it – under false pretences, *entrapment* – would be inadmissible. Enough to lose her her job.

She closed her eyes and tilted her face towards the ceiling, gripping the edge of the washbasin, sighing out loud. What she was doing was exactly what Hastings had probably wanted to hear about from Cooper, except worse than anything he'd imagined her getting herself wrapped up in.

She opened her eyes as the door swung open and a girl, unsteady on her feet, swayed in. The girl banged against the doorframe as she disappeared into a cubicle.

She should leave. Get out of this mess without going anywhere near Finn. But the temper burning in her chest at what she'd found at the office was still there. Staying a little longer on the off chance wouldn't make any difference. No one would know.

She turned on the tap, splashed water against her cheeks, pulling a towel from the dispenser to dry herself off. No one would know. And as she balled the paper and threw it in the bin, she questioned how dangerous that was if this guy had killed his one remaining best friend to cover up the murder of another one.

Chapter 64

'I'D LIKE TO GET a chance to talk with you in private.' Finn was breathless and sweating after his performance. He lifted his drink from the bar, gulped.

'To talk to me?' Eve let out a giggle, cringing at herself. 'Like I believe that.'

'Come on. I want to get to know you a little better, Amy.' His voice was slightly slurred, his pupils black holes. 'I have a room. Nothing special, where we get changed and hang before a show.'

'In here?'

'Yeah, round back. About the size of a cupboard but quieter. A seat and a drink?'

Doubt crept in but Eve pictured Cooper's guilty face as he'd left Hastings's office and her resolve hardened. 'Sure, why not?'

Eve sat on a fold-away metal chair clasping her hands on her lap, not sure what to do with them otherwise. Finn took a bottle of vodka from a rucksack on the floor, his hands shaking a little, and poured two healthy shots into plastic cups. A vision of her mother flashed before Eve's eyes. Her mother with a drunk man. Alone. No one to come running when she needed them. Nobody even aware she was in danger.

Eve glanced at the door as he passed a cup to her. She smiled as he tapped his one against hers. 'Cheers.' He necked the drink in one go and poured another.

'Cheers.' The word almost stuck in her throat. She pretended it was the fumes as she put the cup to her mouth, sipped, then gulped, wondering what the hell she was doing.

Keep him talking.

He spoke before she needed to try. 'So, tell me about yourself.' His slur was pronounced, his eyes glazed. Not from drink. Eve suspected he'd taken something before the show.

Her clammy hands cupped the drink. 'What is it you want to know?'

'I don't know. What do you do?'

Eve laughed, hoping it didn't sound forced. 'What, apart from hang out with rock stars in dressing rooms?'

Finn smiled lazily, downed the second drink. 'You like to play, Amy, don't you? So do I.' He walked over and offered his hand.

'What, you want to dance?'

'No, I want to see you up close.'

Eve's stomach lurched. Ill at the prospect of any part of her being up close to Finn. She ignored his hand and cleared her throat. 'Why don't you tell me something about you?'

He brushed a stray hair off her face. 'Not much to tell.'

'Oh, I'm sure there's plenty. How did you get into doing gigs?'

Finn leaned against the wall. 'Always loved music. Only thing I was any good at. Helped that my father pulled strings to get me on a stage in the first place.'

'Your father?'

'Oh, I'm sure you've heard of him. Peter Miller.'

'Wow. You don't look like him.'

'Lucky me.'

He offered his hand again, not taking no for an answer this time.

Eve took it, at a loss as to what else to do. She let herself be pulled up, heart thudding as she stood eye to eye with him. She smelled the vodka on his breath. He pulled her to him, began to sway. She stiffened at the contact. It wasn't clear whether he was attempting to dance with her or suffering the effects of whatever he'd taken. He held her hand against his chest, no space between their bodies. Eve closed her eyes, wanting, *needing* to be out of there. Wondering again what the hell she thought she was going to get from him.

She swayed alongside him, hating the feel of his body, the smell of his skin, thinking about the women he'd used. She studied the door, desperate to leave, to say something to get out. Anything.

'It's locked.'

Eve's heart froze. She pulled back from him, hoping he was joking.

He smirked. 'It's you and me babe, all alone.'

Eve wriggled her hand free of his. 'I thought you wanted to talk?'

He brought his face close to hers, gripping her.

Eve pulled herself free, dived for the door, Finn's arm clutching at her top, pulling her back, his arm circling her waist from behind.

She kicked back with her foot, connecting with what she took to be his shin. 'Get off me, you sonofabitch.'

He laughed, not letting go. 'Shit, lady, you're a feisty one; we will have fun.'

An image of her mother, what might've been said to her that night down the lane, the night that would change everything, grew bright in Eve's mind. Fuelling her to fight for freedom.

He pulled at her again, managing to get her all the way back against his body before he turned, taking her with him, pinning her against the wall, her cheek rammed against the cold plaster. He grasped at her trousers. Panic within her began to rise, tears threatening at the thought of how her fate could be set to intertwine with that of her mother. How she could've allowed herself to be in this situation when she'd spent her whole life avoiding any kind of physical interaction with anyone.

And then the sound of banging. Finn's grip loosening but not letting her go, both of them looking towards the door. The lock rattling with every blow, the fifth and most ferocious dunt to the woodwork busting the door open.

'Get your fucking hands off her.'

Finn didn't need asking twice when he saw the look on Cooper's face, and heard the venom in his voice.

Cooper rushed towards her, pulling her into his arms, Eve letting herself be held for the briefest of moments before the sound of Finn's laughter made Cooper let her go.

'You never mentioned a boyfriend.' That fucking smile again – disappearing as Cooper spun towards him and lifted a fist.

'Cooper, no.' Eve's shout surprised them all.

She went to her colleague. 'Come on, let's get out of here.'

They made their way to the doorway, the beefhead security guy reaching it the same time they did. He stood a moment, blocking the door, until Finn lifted a hand and the guard stepped to the side. His face was like thunder, matching Cooper's.

They sat in the dark down by the beach. Cooper had driven them here, needing to say his piece, and Eve had let him – rather that than both taking their anger home.

'At least now you have something solid to take to Hastings.'

Cooper shook his head. 'Not even remotely funny. What were you thinking?'

Eve had listened to various forms of Cooper saying the same thing for the last fifteen minutes. He wasn't going to be letting her off the hook easily. She deserved that.

'Like I said, I clearly wasn't thinking.' She looked at her lap, feeling stupid, like a scolded kid. But most of all vulnerable, something she hated. 'Are you going to tell Hastings?'

Cooper whipped his head round as if he'd heard the most stupid thing ever. 'Do you believe I'd do that to you?'

Eve turned; the outline of his profile was visible against the little light there was. 'I didn't think you'd ever be in that office behind my back once, never mind twice.'

Cooper turned to face her. 'I never said a thing against you. In fact, I'd told Hastings to stop asking me to keep an eye on you. Everything I said to him was only ever in support of you. What you heard was a token to convince him I'd be willing to share if need be. I never would.'

'What you said was right. Confirmed tonight. I'm a hot-headed pain in the arse.'

'Yeah, but you're my pain in the arse.'

Eve, glad Cooper couldn't see her, swallowed the lump in her throat, feeling even worse that she'd ever doubted him.

'What now?'

Eve jumped on the chance to change the subject. 'We're going to get the truth. From Finn. From his father. Johnstone and Shirriffs too.'

'How?'

'We're going to take them by surprise. Knock them off kilter. In a place where they can't refuse to see us or ask us to leave without causing a scene. A place with a guaranteed audience.'

'And how do you propose we do that?'

'By crashing a party. You with me?'

Chapter 65

Saturday

THE LINE OF GUESTS snaked from the top of Heritage's stone steps on to the gravel driveway, slow moving due to everyone being greeted by the original Trinity at the pillared entrance.

Eve stood on the third step from the top, alongside Cooper, feeling as if she'd been wrapped in tinfoil like a stuffed turkey and left to roast.

'At least try and look elegant.' Cooper smirked.

Eve smiled as she pulled at the stomach of the black glittery number Mearns had lent her last minute. Nothing would dampen her enjoyment at the thought of how their arrival was about to go down.

She looked back down the steps, saw Mearns and Ferguson standing with David Carnegie, the social worker who had been bullied by Finn and his friends, who was chatting to them as if he'd known them for years. A willing participant tonight. She stood patiently, hearing condolences being offered to the men in front.

They edged further up the line, finally reaching the front.

Peter Miller visibly flinched, but the smile was quickly pasted back on. Unnatural. 'Ah, DI Hunter, DS Cooper. We weren't expecting you this evening.'

Eve smiled. 'I hope there's enough punch to go around.'

Robert Johnstone, standing alongside Miller with Kirk Shirriffs, glowered. Kirk merely looked from Miller to Eve, wondering what was going on. He dipped his head in acknowledgement. Miller, aware of the attention and whispers from the guests behind them waiting to enter, stepped forward and grasped Eve's shoulders, air-kissing either cheek. The grand show.

Teeth gritted, she allowed it to happen and kept smiling as Cooper shook hands.

Miller lifted his arm, motioned to the warmth inside. 'Delighted you came. Please get yourselves a drink.'

Eve and Cooper stood by the stage of the grand hall, on the edge of the crowd and with a good view of the room. Patricia Shirriffs moved through the throng, exchanging pleasantries, looking nervous every time her eyes flickered towards them. Guilt, or perhaps fear that she'd spoken behind her husband's back, was evident on her face.

At the sound of metal clinking against glass, Eve and Cooper turned towards the stage.

Mr Henderson, the head teacher, stood decked out in a dinner suit and waited for the attention of his guests as the chatter died. A large blank screen hung behind him, images flickering to life on it as he began to speak.

'Ladies and gentlemen, thank you for joining us tonight. As you know we are here tonight to celebrate the lives of Andrew Shirriffs and Dean Johnstone.'

School shots of the boys on the screen showed the innocence they'd once supposedly embodied. Murmurs rippled throughout the crowd.

Mr Henderson paused a moment before continuing. 'Two boys who graced the corridors of Heritage and grew into remarkable young men . . .'

Eve switched off from the speech, using the time to steal glances in every direction. All guests welcomed, the Trinity were now working the room, but they couldn't be further apart from each other if they tried. Perhaps the cracks Eve had hoped for between them were showing after all.

She craned her neck, looking throughout and over the crowd. Countless well-known faces here, ones she recognized from the gossip magazines. Mearns was in the corner, looking at her. Eve dipped her chin and turned back to the stage, the screen now showing a picture of flower bouquets and cards.

'We have received phenomenal donations in memory of both Dean and Andrew. Donations that will ensure Heritage continues to be the pillar of education and community investment it has always striven to be.'

Eve scanned the screen: a close-up photo of handwritten cards pinned on a wall, open and overlapping one another. A few clear to read, some illegible.

Her gaze caught on one of the cards, heart jumping as she peered at it. Mr Henderson was still droning on.

'The support and love we have received for these boys has been quite emotional. We have cornered off a space along the main corridor with some of the cards and tributes we have received. Please feel welcome to read them . . .'

Eve was aware of the piece of paper in her jacket pocket, a photocopy of the note Marcie Wade had given them. Not sure why she had chosen to carry it with her here tonight but goose bumps travelled the back of her neck and into her hair as she realized what she was looking at.

'Cooper.' She nudged him. 'Cooper.'

He turned from the stage, whispered, 'What?'

'Bottom left of the screen. You seeing what I am?'

Cooper took a moment to realize what Eve meant. 'Holy shit.'

The handwriting unmistakeable, the curve of the G, the slant of the S. The uniqueness of the handwriting they'd all commented on after reading the note Marcie Wade had given them. Unless Dean had found a way in death to write his own condolence card, it was clear someone else had written that note to Kirk Shirriffs.

'Close your mouth, Cooper. Find that card.'

Cooper went for the hall door. Eve calmed herself, nodded at the guests around her, and moved off amongst the crowd. She spotted Peter, smarming all over an immaculately dressed couple, the woman's jewellery glinting in the overhead chandeliers.

'Good evening.'

Eve turned at the familiar voice, coming face to face with Kirk Shirriffs. 'Hi.'

'You sure know how to ruffle a feather or two. Can I get you a drink?'

'No thanks, Cooper is off sorting that.' Eve marvelled at the brass neck of Kirk approaching her but remembered how affable he had been that night at the restaurant. She couldn't fault his acting skills. 'It must be difficult for you tonight.'

'Yes and no. It's nice for Andrew to be remembered fondly by everyone, for him to be celebrated.'

The emotion was raw in his voice. Had he been driven to kill?

'Is Patricia here?' Eve already knew she was but said it for want of conversation.

'Yes.' He turned. 'There she is. I'll call her over.'

Eve went to stop him – too late as he waved his wife towards him.

Patricia looked dazed as she approached; those nerves had nowhere to hide as she rubbed at her hands.

Eve smiled, not wanting the woman to worry; she would keep her promise that Kirk would never know that Patricia had spoken to them. 'Your dress is lovely.'

Patricia gave a half-hearted smile. 'Thank you.' Her gaze danced anywhere but towards Eve and froze.

Eve turned subtly, following Patricia's eye line. Robert Johnstone stood across the room; a short woman was talking animatedly at him, oblivious to the fact he wasn't listening as he was too busy staring their way with a look of disdain.

Eve didn't try to hide her own disdain in return. 'I better go find Cooper. He appears to have got lost with that drink.'

Kirk smiled. 'Enjoy.'

Eve walked away, leaving Patricia clinging to her husband.

Eve found Cooper in the corridor trying to edge through the swarm of bodies in front of the wall of cards and flowers. It appeared everyone wanted to read the tributes.

He turned and saw her, his face looking as if his patience was waning. She waved one hand forward, encouraging him to push in as she helped herself to a flute of orange juice from the waiter's tray as he passed her by. She raised the glass to her lips and stood there – not planning on moving until she knew who'd written that card.

Ferguson pretended to be in deep conversation with Mearns and Carnegie as he tried not to miss a thing going on around him. Cooper and Eve had left the hall and he was at a loss as to what was going on. Kirk and Patricia were still standing on the spot where Eve had left them.

He saw Kirk whisper in his wife's ear before moving off into the crowd. Across the room, Robert wasted no time in getting over to Patricia.

Mearns bristled next to Ferguson, watching things unfold alongside him. 'Look at that.'

Ferguson was surprised as Robert took hold of Patricia's elbow, subtly yet forcefully guiding her out of the hall, not realizing he was being watched now Eve and Cooper had left the room. Ferguson said something about nothing to Carnegie as the two passed by in silence, Patricia looking panicked, Johnstone looking fierce.

Ferguson turned to Mearns. 'I suddenly need the loo.'

'Keep in touch.'

Ferguson patted his pocket, his mobile fully charged.

Eve was one sip away from finishing her drink by the time Cooper broke through to the front of the crowd gathered by the wall. Her heart thumped as he scanned the countless cards on display – and she saw the shock in his features as he spotted what he was looking for.

The seconds waiting whilst he looked for the signature dragged – the expression on his face as he turned in her direction telling her whatever he'd read was about to change everything.

Ferguson knew they were standing by the main office even though they were out of view, the curve in the office's glass front allowing him to move closer.

'What do you mean you spoke to them?' Johnstone hissed.

'I didn't plan to. They came to me.' Patricia's voice trembled.

Ferguson assumed they were talking about Eve and Cooper.

'You're a bag of nerves tonight. Obviously so.'

'I can't help it.'

'Clearly, but it's the last thing you need to be.' Johnstone's tone appeared to soften.

'I want to go home. For all this to be done,' Patricia croaked, as if she was crying.

'We should get out of here. Get some air.'

'But Kirk . . .'

'Is busy entertaining, as is Peter. I doubt we'll even be missed.'

'And go where?'

'I want to talk to you. What better place than where this all began?'

Ferguson didn't hear the reply; he was walking away down the corridor as he heard them move. He turned to see Johnstone and Patricia leave via the main entrance, Johnstone's hand still clutching her elbow.

Cooper's shock was obvious as he walked towards Eve.

So many scenarios. Was it Finn? Had she been wrong about it all?

Cooper's mouth opened. 'Robert Johnstone.'

The words slapped her in the face; her mind tried to compute what that meant. '*Robert Johnstone* wrote the note to Kirk?' Eve jumped as her mobile phone vibrated in her bag. She lifted the phone out, looked at the display. Ferguson.

'What's up?' Eve could hear nothing but silence in the background of the call, which didn't match the noise where Ferguson had last been. 'Where are you?'

He answered in a whisper. 'Outside. Johnstone led Patricia out of the building. I heard some of their chat before they left. Something's not right.'

'Where are they going?'

'Don't know. Out back, into woodland. I'm following at a distance.'

'I'll text Mearns, let her know what's happening. We're coming out, Ferguson.' Eve ended the call and texted Mearns, updating Cooper as she typed and pressed send. She shut up as Kirk approached.

'Hi. I don't suppose you've seen Patricia? I can't find her inside – and she's not in the toilets. I got someone to check.' Kirk looked worried, clearly used to his wife's nerves and being her protector.

Eve decided to take a gamble. 'Robert left with her.'

Kirk looked towards the door. 'What? Why?'

Too far in now . . . 'We're here because we believe your son's death may be connected to Dean's. We know there was a woman with them both on the night of their deaths. Something Robert and Peter appear to have tried to cover up.'

Eve pulled out the note and handed it to Kirk.

Kirk began to read, his frown deepening, his expression turning to horror as his hands trembled. He looked up at Eve, still clutching the note in both hands, fighting to regain his composure. 'If this is what I think it is, this goes way back. Years before anything. I know where they might've gone.'

Chapter 66

I HAVE NO IDEA how long we've been here. Barely a word said between the four of us as we try and fail to grasp the scale of what's happened.

Darkness fell a long time ago. I can no longer feel my fingers and toes but, in this moment, I know I can't allow myself to feel anything. Not the fear we haven't made it back to that bunk bed. And definitely not the terror that El never will.

Black Eyes breaks the silence. 'We can make this go away.'

I'm on my feet and in his face before I know what I'm doing. 'Make this go away? What, like she never existed? That this never happened? She was like a sister to me.' I'm crying again, struggling to breathe.

Black Eyes actually looks hurt, as if I've attacked him with my words, and I'm wondering if it really was El he wanted.

'Take it easy, Kid.'

Anger and sadness well inside me as I spit on him, shocking and disgusting myself as he flinches. 'You don't get to call me that. Only her. My name is Patricia and it's about time names mattered.'

Black Eyes doesn't hesitate, as if he wants my approval. 'Robert. My name is Robert Johnstone.'

I turn to Curly, who, until I'd lunged for Robert, had never stopped holding me.

'Kirk Shirriffs.'

I nod and look at Smiler, his face sombre, voice cracking as he speaks. 'Peter Miller.'

And in that moment – against everything I believe I stand for and all I owe El – I become that coward again. Scared my already worthless life will be made worse. No parents. In care already. Only to wind up in jail. It's not what El would've wanted for me.

Curly's hold on me tightens before he speaks. 'Now we are all part of this. Together. And I promise I won't ever leave you. I'll protect you.'

I look up into his eyes and I know, even if this horrible thing hadn't happened, the look in his eyes is something I've only dreamed of having, something I'm not willing to lose.

I nod once.

A secret pact made in a single second that will keep us linked to one another for ever.

Standing there in the moonlight as we take it in turns to scrape at the earth, to dig a space deep enough to make it all go away, we have no idea how big an impact that link will have on our future.

Chapter 67

KIRK HAD LED THEM deep into the forest. They'd found Ferguson first, hidden in bushes, watching Johnstone and Patricia in a clearing, visible beneath the full moon. It had taken Eve a lot of whispered persuasion on the way here to get Kirk to stay with them until they knew what was happening. All eyes were on Robert as he let go of Patricia's arm and looked at the ground. There was more emotion on his face than Eve had ever seen.

'This is where it all started.' His voice was a monotone.

Patricia glowered at the top of his bowed head. 'No. This is where it all ended. The Kid never made it out of here. None of us did. Not as the children we were.'

Robert lifted his hand, a sad smile on his lips. 'Kid. I haven't heard anyone call you that in years. If I could change what happened, I would. I've wanted to talk to you many times over the years, have written countless letters. I had the courage to send one of them. I still believe if that day hadn't happened, things might've been different for you and me.'

Eve's mind whirred, conscious of Kirk beside her, trying to catch up, wondering what this meant about the note they now knew was written by Robert. Not to Kirk. To *Kid*.

Patricia shook her head. 'That day didn't change anything for us. I've always been Kirk's.'

Now it was Robert shaking his head. 'That's not true. The way you used to look at me . . .'

'I don't know what you're talking about. I used to catch you staring at me, but it wasn't returned.'

'But over the years, how much you helped me with Dean when I was on my own. Taking both of us under your wing.'

'You were my friend, Robert. Though sometimes I doubt if that's even true. If any of us are friends. If we aren't all just bound by the lie we chose to live with.'

'That's what I mean. If it weren't for that lie, things would've been different. If we could've changed what happened.'

Patricia's face hardened, surprising Eve. 'The only thing that changed for me that day was that I realized what a dangerous bastard you were.'

Robert stepped back, reeling. 'What are you saying? She choked. You saw it.'

'No. We assumed she choked. Over the years I've often wondered how long she'd been lying there before we came running. What you'd been doing to her before she died.'

'What do you mean?'

'Her underwear, Robert. No one ever mentioned it. That doesn't mean we didn't see it.'

Robert stepped forward, shock on his face. 'Don't be stupid,' he faltered, 'she'd gone to the toilet, same as I had before I found her lying there.'

'She was my friend, a rare thing in the life I'd had until then.' Patricia didn't look at Robert as she spoke. 'A friend – and I've left her here all these years, alone, no one to even notice she'd gone.'

Eve wasn't breathing. Someone had died here and no one had noticed. Like Elena. How long it had taken them to find someone who might've missed her.

'And then I lost my son. My wonderful, bright, brilliant son. And I knew Dean and Finn were there. That one of those girls was there. But you covered it up. Again. To cover your arses. If you got away with it once . . . Believing all these years you were invincible, but it was my fucking son and, back in the beginning, the closest thing I had to a sister. Do you realize what you've done to me? What you've all done to me?'

Patricia was sobbing. 'I was glad of that note you sent to me after El died. I kept it, knowing there would come a day when I would use it. It was twisted karma that it so easily lent itself to my son's death. I sent it to the press.'

Johnstone seemed shocked, quickly followed by looking as though he might explode. 'You did what?'

'I wanted it all to end. I wanted them to believe K was Kirk, to have them investigate whether something else had happened that night, that my son didn't kill himself. But, as I should've known, it went nowhere, shut down by the power of the Trinity as per usual.'

'Why would you do that? Think what it would have done to all of us!'

Patricia glared at him. 'I should've done it after what happened to El. We should've all taken whatever they dished out to us. Maybe life might've been different then. Maybe I'd still have a son. You too.'

Johnstone stood silent.

Patricia dragged a forearm across her tears. 'Too late for all that. We all had to live with the guilt. I've spent my life sleeping with one eye open, fearing the truth would come out. And, if that wasn't enough, you had to come telling me about my husband. The one thing I had left. What the fuck was it? You'd lost your wife, and your son was more or less lost to you by then too, so you wanted me to lose Kirk as well?'

Kirk straightened, went to move, held back only by Cooper and Ferguson's grip.

Robert tried to take hold of her hand, but it was snatched away. He looked crushed. 'If I had been your husband, I never would've done that to you.'

Patricia was shouting now. 'You could've kept me in the dark. I wouldn't have been so hurt, so angry. I wouldn't have done what I did.'

Kirk gasped. Eve's gaze darted towards Robert and Patricia. The fear that the two had heard was palpable in the bush where they all hid.

Robert went to reach for her again. Stopped, dropping his arms to his sides. 'I panicked. You suspected what happened to Andrew wasn't the truth. That little slut Elena wanted to tell you. Dean called me. Told me she was coming around. That they were going to tell you everything.'

'And what did you do?' The disgust on Patricia's face was clear.

Johnstone looked at the floor. 'I told him if he let that happen, I'd kill him.'

Eve was stacking all the facts, realizing now that Dean had tried to stop Elena after the call to his father. Maybe that was why she'd hit him. Maybe he'd got too rough with her. But who had smothered him once she ran?

Johnstone was talking again. 'That slut would've taken us all down.'

The hatred in Patricia's voice was clear through the sobs. 'You believe that? That you and Miller, your sons, hadn't already set that in motion? That poor girl was trying to do the right thing. You set me up.'

Robert looked stunned. 'I . . . I—'

Patricia was screaming. 'What did you expect me to do, Robert? You called me. I had minutes to process the fact you were telling me she'd killed my son. To realize my husband had been sleeping with prostitutes. Sleeping with *her*.'

This time Kirk stood; no grip strong enough to hold him. Eve toppled from her crouching position as he barged past, bursting through the bush and into the clearing.

Robert froze. Patricia looked as if she was going to be sick.

'What did you do, Trish?' Kirk's voice was strained, scared.

Patricia was sobbing. 'You had gone to bed already. She called your mobile. I texted her our address, saying it wasn't possible to speak on the phone. I hit her. I wanted to hurt her for what she'd done to our son, what she'd done to our marriage.' She whimpered, stepped towards Kirk. 'What you'd done to our marriage.'

Kirk didn't move. 'He lied about that too.'

Patricia's head whipped towards Robert, her eyes wide.

Kirk's voice cracked as he spoke. 'I never slept with anyone but you. I spoke to Elena alone, once. I guessed she would've known Andrew. I was trying to find a connection to him, Trish. Everyone was scared to talk about him. I needed to talk. To remember. Dean and Finn sure as hell weren't any more. We chatted. She said she'd known him but she seemed scared in what little she said. I offered help if she ever needed it, gave her my number.'

Patricia stiffened, tears rolling down her cheeks.

Kirk stepped a little closer to her. 'I wanted to tell you, but Andrew's death had already broken you. Changed you. I wanted to find a way, to offer Elena a way to make this right if she knew anything.'

'No, no . . .' Patricia was shaking her head over and over, staring now at Robert through her tears. 'Tell me you didn't do this, Robert. Please. Tell me you didn't lie to me about Kirk. That you didn't know she was coming to my home and what I'd do . . .'

Johnstone looked at Kirk, the hatred for his rival clear. He turned to Patricia. 'I hoped we could start again. Now there was no Andrew, no Kirk.'

Kirk lunged at Robert, knocking him to the ground. Eve and her team were up, bursting into the clearing within seconds, their arrival barely making an impact as Patricia stood in a state of shock as her husband and Robert locked together and rolled on the ground.

Kirk was shouting: 'You bastard. You set that girl up. You set my fucking wife up. Over what? Some fucking delusion that Patricia loved you?'

Eve saw Patricia pass the two men. Zoned out. Zombie-like. She walked over to the base of a tree, fell to her knees, oblivious to anything going on around her. Rocking, crying uncontrollably.

Eve stood in the clearing wide-eyed with Ferguson and Cooper, all three of them knowing they should break up the fight but strangely hypnotized by what Patricia was doing. They turned at the snap of twigs. Mearns and Miller.

'What the hell is going on?' Miller's voice boomed in the darkness, crashing into the clearing, the sound of his voice stopping Kirk and Robert's fight in its tracks where Eve and her team hadn't. The men now aware of them for the first time too. But nothing was stopping Patricia, who scraped at the muddy ground, her sobs the only sound in the clearing.

'Stop.' Kirk let go of Johnstone and got to his feet, running towards his wife.

Patricia carried on clawing, faster.

Kirk banged to his knees beside her, grabbed at her wrists.

Her eyes were fixed on the ground and she was struggling to breathe. 'She deserves a proper burial. We should've told the truth; we should've got help.'

Robert pulled himself from the ground, glancing at Eve and her team but seeming not to care they were there before he turned and shouted towards Patricia: 'I dreamed we'd have a life.'

Miller moved further into the clearing. All four of them there now, as Eve imagined they had once been here as kids.

Miller spoke. 'We didn't have a life. Not the one we should've had. Money, business, success. Doesn't mean jack-shit when we've become the people we have. When our sons became who they were. Two of them dead.'

Eve heard the disappointment and regret in Miller's voice, and questioned how much it was to do with how Finn had turned out. If he knew what his son had done.

Miller wasn't stopping. 'You're right, Robert, it should've been different, we should have handed your arse over to the police.'

Johnstone's steely eyes fixed on Miller. 'I didn't kill El.' He turned to Patricia, who was being held in her husband's embrace. 'Don't believe him, Kid.' He moved towards her, crouched to her level. 'You know me.' He held out a hand towards her. 'Please, you know me.'

Patricia turned into her husband's chest, but fell backwards as Kirk leaped to his feet, knocking Robert over. He lifted Robert by the neck of his shirt, spittle flying as he shouted through clenched teeth: 'Stay away from my fucking wife.' He punched him, square in the face, knocking Robert out. Kirk turned back to Patricia, took her in his arms and gripped her tight.

The clearing was silent.

Eve and her team knew what was left to be done.

355

Chapter 68

Sunday

'Thanks, Portman.' Eve put down the phone and looked at her team grouped around the table. 'Twenty girls taken out of that flat overnight.'

Ferguson gasped. 'All from one flat?'

'Yup. No sign of the Rusu brothers, or Daria. There or at the steading. Place has been cleared out. Seems they got wind and disappeared.'

'They get away with it?' Mearns as pissed off as they all were at the thought.

Eve said the only thing they could hope for. 'For now. Further down the line . . .'

Cooper put his mobile phone down, his attention only half on the conversation until now. 'What about Patricia and the Trinity?'

'Not sure what will happen with Patricia. She may not have killed Elena, but she hit her and knocked her unconscious before Johnstone strangled her. To think Kirk was asleep upstairs. Johnstone's staying silent but she's admitted everything. Robert strangled Elena and

356

persuaded Patricia that hanging her up at the golf club, making it look like a suicide, was their only option. Peter Miller's got some hotshot lawyer but we've got the evidence now that he bribed Crawford to make the files disappear, to cover up the fact Finn was involved in Andrew's death, so we've got him on that at least. And Finn will be investigated for his part in Andrew's death.'

'What a mess. And that poor girl's death all those years ago being covered up too.' Cooper shook his head.

Mearns swung on her chair. 'What about Dean? We still don't know who smothered him after Elena left.'

Eve's eyes lit up. 'We do.'

Eve paused as all three of her colleagues turned their attention to her. 'According to Portman, one of the girls taken out of the flat admitted to hearing the brothers talking up front in the car the day after Elena went missing, about how they'd been unable to find her but at least the man had been dealt with, and there was no way of knowing they'd ever been there.'

'Jesus.' Mearns rubbed at her eyes.

Eve tried to sound positive. 'There's two good things to come out of all this.'

Ferguson waited, impatient. 'What're they?'

'Andreea leaves the shelter this week to move in with Marius and his uncle.'

Ferguson smiled. 'Have you seen Marcie Wade's exclusive in the *Aberdeen Enquirer* today?'

Eve nodded. 'Yeah, I spent a good while on the phone to her last night. That's the second good thing. I'd like to believe keeping our promise to her will keep the press off our backs for a while but . . .'

Eve looked at Cooper, who had said nothing. She saw him lift his mobile phone to type again. 'Cooper, what is it with you today?'

Cooper coloured. 'Sorry, it's Louise.'

Eve wondered if things were still as strained at home. She decided to bite the bullet and ask. 'Everything OK?'

Cooper lowered the phone. 'I don't know. Been a bit of a nightmare lately, like I've said. Don't suppose it helped being at Heritage last night or in here today. The whole weekend, basically, but, saying that, I can't do anything right anyway. She's seems in a good mood today though. I'm making the most of it.'

'Why the good mood?'

Cooper shrugged. 'Don't know. I'm trying to get her to tell me.'

Cooper's phone pinged again. He opened the text, eyes moving side to side as he read. A huge smile spread across his face.

Eve found herself smiling in response. 'What?'

'I can stop worrying whether she's about to leave me. It all makes sense now.' He turned the phone towards them: a photo of a pregnancy test and two blue horizontal lines dark against the white background.

Eve winked. 'Make that three good things.'

Acknowledgements

WELL, AFTER A SEVERE case of the second-book terrors and worrying whether I actually *could* write another one, it seems I got there in the end. But, as with most things, I certainly wasn't alone in that.

Huge thanks as always to the AM Heath team, especially my fabulous agent, Oli Munson, for always being there and managing to calm my fevered brow.

I'm indebted to the Transworld UK team – particularly my wonderful editor, Tash Barsby, for all she does to knock my writing into the story she knows it can be.

On the research front, I'd like to thank Detective Superintendent Alex Dowall of Police Scotland's North East Special Crime Division, for giving me an insight into human trafficking and then answering all of my rookie questions. Any mistakes are my own.

I'd also like to thank Aberdeen Airport Duty Manager Robert Horsburgh, for explaining what would happen if a passenger had to be intercepted at Departures and interviewed on the premises.

I am eternally grateful to my fab family and friends. My previous acknowledgements were rather lengthy, and many folks were mentioned, but I thank them all again – as well as anyone I missed (as I know I did!). I hope you all know how important you are to me every day.

Finally, and importantly, endless thanks to everyone who read, reviewed and shouted about my debut *Hold Your Tongue*, to those who have come back for more by reading this one, and those who are finding DI Eve Hunter and her team for the first time. You have all made the little girl inside me, who always dreamed of writing a real book, a very happy grown-up.

I hope you enjoy this one as much as the last.

dead good

Looking for more gripping must-reads?

Head over to Dead Good –
the home of killer crime books,
TV and film.

Whether you're on the hunt for an intriguing
mystery, an action-packed thriller
or a creepy psychological drama,
we're here to keep you in the loop.

Get recommendations and reviews from
crime fans, grab discounted books at bargain
prices and enter exclusive giveaways
for the chance to read brand-new releases
before they hit the shelves.

Sign up for the free newsletter:
www.deadgoodbooks.co.uk/newsletter